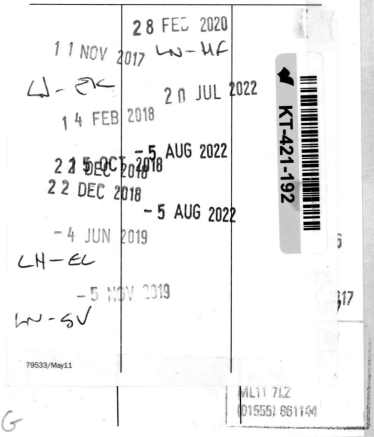

Sealed with a Kiss

After moving around the world from
the Highlands of Scotland to Australia and back,
Rachael Lucas has settled by the seaside in the
north west of England with her partner, their
blended family of six children, a very hairy dog
and two-and-a-half cats. She likes listening to
BBC Radio 4 and thinking about writing.

Find out more about Rachael at her
website rachaellucas.com, say hello on
Twitter @karamina or visit her on Facebook
at facebook.com/RachaelLucasWriter

Sealed
with a
Kiss

RACHAEL LUCAS

A CIP catalogue record for this book is available from the British Library.

Typeset by Ellipsis Digital Limited, Glasgow
Printed and bound by CPI Group (UK) Ltd, Croydon, CR0 4YY

PAN BOOKS

First published in the UK 2013 by Rachael Lucas

This edition published 2014 by Pan Books
an imprint of Pan Macmillan, a division of Macmillan Publishers Limited
Pan Macmillan, 20 New Wharf Road, London N1 9RR
Basingstoke and Oxford
Associated companies throughout the world
www.panmacmillan.com

ISBN 978-1-4472-6702-7

The right of Rachael Lucas to be identified as the
author of this work has been asserted by her in accordance
with the Copyright, Designs and Patents Act 1988.

The author would like to thank Graham Cowley
for his winning bid to the Authors for the Philippines appeal
(AuthorsForPhilippines.Wordpress.com), which led to his daughter,
Sian Cowley, being named as a character in this book.

Visit www.panmacmillan.com to read more about all our books
and to buy them. You will also find features, author interviews and
news of any author events, and you can sign up for e-newsletters
so that you're always first to hear about our new releases.

To Ross, with love always

Acknowledgements

Lots of people have helped me along the way to publication, and I'd like to say a huge thank you.

To my friends Elise and Wendy, who were there when I wrote my first novel every night in my nanny's kitchen and couldn't come out to play.

To Polly, because she knew one day I'd do it. To Sarah, for the angels. To Nicola, for hooting. To Diane, for being there. To Melanie, for inspiration and eels. To Holly, for giggling. And to my girls Elana, Katie, Rhiannon and Victoria: love.

Dan Bramall and Michael Everson did sterling art and editing work on the first edition – thank you. Thanks to Richard Saunders, DZooMed MRCVS, Veterinary Advisor to the British Divers Marine Life Rescue, who checked all the seal rescue parts for accuracy.

To my fab agent Amanda Preston and my editor Caroline Hogg – I can't quite believe I've fallen on my feet with you two. Here's to many more girly lunches with a little bit of work on the side. Thanks also to everyone at Pan Mac who have made me so welcome and made the publishing process such fun.

I've been lucky to have friendship and support along the way from some of my favourite writers. Enormous thanks to S. C. Ransom, Julia Williams, Katie Fforde, and Christina Jones, all of whom took the time to read, give advice and cheer me on. Thank you all, so much. And a huge thank you to everyone on Twitter who helped out with emergency queries ('Can someone please shove a photo in their AGA and see what happens?').

To Ross, and our children, Verity, Archie, Jude, Rory, Rosie and Charlie, with all my love.

To my mum, Anne, and my sister, Zoe – love you.

And thank *you*, too, for reading.

When angels fell, some fell on the land,
some on the sea.
The former are the faeries and the latter were
often said to be the seals.

ORCADIAN MYTH

1

Kate's Escape

'If you're waiting for me to get down on one knee, I wouldn't hold your breath.' Ian swigged his beer, wiped his mouth and nodded towards the dance floor.

Kate took a deep breath. If they carried on much longer, she wouldn't even *like* Ian, let alone love him. Why on earth couldn't she pluck up the courage to say it out loud?

'Come on, you two, you can't sit there all night!' Emma swirled across to their table, glorious in a Grace Kelly-style wedding dress. She looked beautiful. Her décolletage was covered – the dress was buttoned to the neck – and her arms were sheathed in lace, but the demure dress was having quite an effect on her new husband Sam. Arms wrapped around her, he whispered into Emma's hair and she giggled, raising her eyebrows in shock.

Ian stood up and pulled Kate into an awkward embrace. Shuffling round the floor, watching the other couples dance, Kate winced, thinking about the squabble they'd had that morning as they got ready for the wedding. Ian had been furious at Kate's untidiness, insisting on cleaning the entire kitchen before they left, just to make a point. The never-ending bickering was so exhausting. They'd driven to the church in silence and had barely spoken to each other during the service, or the wedding meal. There was something about a wedding that brought out the worst in both of them. It wasn't helped by the well-meaning comments from winking friends that it must be their turn soon, or the questions cheekily asking what was stopping them from making their way up the aisle? Kate shuddered at the thought.

Ian leaned closer, his mouth on her ear. 'I think it's over, don't you?'

Kate stiffened, but carried on dancing, plastering a fake smile on her face.

'What d'you mean, over?' Her primary feeling was irritation that he'd decided to bring this up now, of all times. She swallowed away a wave of panic, imagining waking up alone. Emma caught her eye and mouthed 'You okay?'

Kate nodded at her friend, giving a tight smile. Faced with the prospect of singlehood, she suddenly felt quite small and abandoned. She squeezed Ian's arm, trying to placate him. 'We're fine, aren't we? Have I done something wrong?'

'Come on, Kate,' Ian ran his hand across her back, looking at her with a gentle expression. 'You deserve better than this.'

She caught his eye. Lovely, sweet, ever so slightly dull Ian, who'd been her best friend and lover for the last five years. But what was the alternative?

'I can't be on my own.'

'Look, it's for the best. Believe me.'

Tears were stinging her eyes now and she tried to pull away. He held her closer, whispering into her hair.

'There's nothing left, Kate. You know it as well as I do. All we ever do is fight.'

'That's because you moan at me for leaving crumbs in the bed, and coffee cups on the bedside table,' said Kate, looking at him and remembering the first disagreement they'd had that morning.

'And you moan at me for being boring and predictable. It's as I said before. There's nothing left, Kate. One of us needs to be brave and say it.'

'It's Emma's wedding day, for God's sake. Why now?'

'There's never a good time to say something like this, is there?' Ian looked at her and shrugged, his mouth a resigned line.

Kate's face in the mirror looked exactly the same as it had that morning. But the dark-brown hair, which had been blow-dried straight, had waved in the heat; her black eyeliner was smudged beneath grey eyes in a freckled face; and her strapless top had slipped down so that she was showing far too much cleavage. She wriggled it back up and ran her hands under the cold tap. Everything looked just the same from the outside, but inside everything was upside down and very wrong. She grimaced at her own reflection.

'Darling, what's happened?'

Just what she needed. Her mother's concerned face appeared in the adjoining mirror. Emma and Kate had been friends since primary school, and her mother's pride at seeing Kate's best friend married off was equalled by her concern that Kate herself was still unattached.

'If he's not made wedding noises after five years, darling, he's not going to.' Kate had heard this with increasing regularity over the last few months. 'You'll be thirty and unmarried at this rate, darling.'

As usual, hours after Kate had started to look scruffy, her mother's blonde hair was still immaculate, her bosom safely encased in a blouse from Jaeger, and her concerned eyes scanning Kate's reflection for signs of – what? Could she actually tell? Was it so obvious?

'I think Ian and I might have split up. No, scratch that. We *have* split up.'

Kate's mum stopped halfway through applying her lipstick, her mouth a startled O, and looked at her daughter in the mirror. Her eyebrows raised, she opened her mouth to speak.

'I'm okay.' Kate held up her hands in a gesture of protest. 'In fact, I'm more than okay. Don't say anything. It's Emma's day.'

'Me? Say anything? Of course I wouldn't. Now give me a cuddle.' Elizabeth squeezed her daughter's shoulder, not wanting to crumple her outfit. 'And wipe

4

those eyes. All that crying has made your eyeliner run. We'll talk about this later.'

She popped her lipstick back into her bag, taking a deep breath and giving a decisive 'That's enough for now' nod. Kate scrubbed at her eyes with a piece of loo roll. Never mind that her eyeliner was always smudged. Easier to smile and agree. She took a deep breath and returned to the bar.

Ian was holding forth about something in a corner, with a collection of their male friends. He looked at Kate, a questioning eyebrow raised, still concerned for her well-being. She knew he was right. They'd been treading water for the last year, clinging to the wreckage of their relationship. His sudden announcement was the lifebuoy they'd both desperately needed.

'We'll talk later,' she mouthed at him. He raised his head in a half-nod of agreement. Kate turned to the bar and was swallowed up by the crowd. Five minutes later she emerged, wobbling on her unfamiliar heels, carrying a tray of gin and tonics. Checking that no one was looking, she ducked behind a pillar, knocked back a couple and returned – her smile superglued on – to the dance floor.

They made it upstairs at 2 a.m. Kate took off her make-up. Ian brushed his teeth beside her, avoiding her eye in the mirror. They didn't talk, but wove in and out of each other's way with the familiarity of routine. He folded his suit, neatly. She dumped her dress on the

5

chair, topped with the tangled mess of her tights, complete with knickers caught up inside. They climbed into bed naked, out of habit. He looked down at their bodies and pulled a wry face. Together they pulled up the covers.

Ian was asleep in seconds. Kate lay awake, the room spinning slightly. The trouble was, she thought, that habit had characterized their relationship for so long they'd forgotten to notice that nothing was left. Ian rolled over in his sleep, draping his arm across her waist. She picked it up to move it, thought better of it and curled into him for the last time.

'No, Mum, I don't want to move back home.' Kate shifted the phone from one ear to the other and rolled her eyes. She was standing in the garden, contemplating her half-dead herb bed. Not much point in salvaging any of it. In fact it was a rather unfortunate metaphor for the state of her relationship. 'I have no idea where I'm going. Emma and Sam have said I can stay in their spare room.'

Kate lifted up a snail shell to see if anyone was living in it. Empty. Perhaps she could move in there.

'And what would it look like? "Hello, have you met my daughter, Kate? She's twenty-six and lives at home with us. Oh, and she doesn't have a job, or any prospects." I'd feel like something out of a Jane Austen novel. And I'd end up with you trying to marry me off to a vicar.'

No room for a dog in a snail shell, Kate reminded herself, and after all this time spent living with Ian, who was allergic to anything small, cute and fluffy, she was determined that a dog was part of her future. Who needed men? A dog and some cats would do. And maybe some sensible shoes and a tweed skirt.

She placed the shell back in the flowerpot, realizing that she hadn't a clue what her mother had said.

'Mum, listen. It's not Ian's fault – it's not anyone's fault. We should have split up after university, instead of taking the easy option. He's taking over the lease, and we've sorted all the money – it's fine. I need to pack. Call you later. Love you.' Kate made a kissing noise down the phone and cut her mother off in mid-flap.

'You off somewhere nice, love?'

Alan-from-next-door looked up from his begonias as Kate hauled her suitcase out of the garage.

'Visiting friends.' She couldn't face explaining.

'Ooh, lovely. Have a nice time, duck.' Alan looked happy enough with the reply.

Standing on the front path, she looked up at the house as if for the first time. A red-brick semi on an executive estate, the house was perfectly pleasant and inoffensive. 'Usefully situated on the outskirts of Cambridge, with easy access to public transport and motorways,' the letting agent had told them – but after four years it still didn't feel like home, and she wasn't sad to leave. The house was soulless and sterile; or perhaps, thought Kate, looking at Alan and Barbara's sweet cottage-style garden next door, it just echoed her feelings. Turning around

7

the little cul-de-sac, she saw happy piles of colourful welly boots and ride-on toy cars outside the door of no. 23. Veronica-from-across-the-road had obviously returned from the stables, because her little 4x4 was parked in the driveway and the lights from the kitchen window were glowing.

She shook herself and headed back inside. Looking at the now-empty kitchen worktops and the spotless steel appliances, she felt a rush of relief. No more battles between his desire for minimalism and her never-ending piles of clutter. When they'd first met, he'd found her untidiness as endearing as she'd found his order. 'Opposites attract,' they used to say, smiling at each other. But that was five years back, in their final year of university, when Kate, desperate to create a sense of home, had moved into a tiny little basement flat with Ian. It made her feel safe and secure, being part of a couple. KateandIan. IanandKate. When the occasional doubts about their brother-and-sister-style relationship popped up, or she wanted to eat crisps in bed just to annoy him, Kate put them to one side. Nobody had a perfect relationship, did they?

When the subject of buying the house came up, though, Kate couldn't shake off the sense that things really *weren't* right. She couldn't bring herself to sign a mortgage and tie herself to the house for the next twenty-five years. Surprisingly, Ian didn't seem that concerned – maybe he, too, had realized that their relationship was more a convenience than a grand passion?

She placed her much-loved Dualit toaster, bought with her first pay packet, into the packing box, showering crumbs everywhere. Then she stuffed her cookery books down the sides along with an assortment of sharp knives, a box of scented tea-lights, some photo frames and a wonky, completely useless, leaky clay vase.

She taped up the final box and surveyed her work. Ten packing crates weren't much to show for a five-year relationship. Funny, she thought, at twenty-six she'd still never lived alone. She'd gone from home to halls of residence at Edinburgh University, and finally, when she and Ian graduated, they'd moved in together, more from force of habit than from any great desire. Now she would be lodging with friends, like a student again.

Rather than try and divide up the furniture, the ever-practical Ian had suggested that he give her a lump sum of money. It was sitting in an envelope on the kitchen worktop, with her name and a smiley face (oh, how that drove her mad!) written across the seal.

Kate slipped the envelope into her pocket, and left the key in its place. Sam would collect the boxes later. She left the house with only a small suitcase and an overnight bag – looking, she thought, as if she was popping off for a weekend away with friends, instead of walking out of one life and into another.

2

The Road to Duntarvie

'You can't just go and live on an island.' Emma was chopping onions so furiously that she was in danger of ending up with half a finger in the chilli con carne. 'They could be mass-murdering fiends. They might chop you up and put you in the freezer.'

She swiped the onions from the chopping board and into the saucepan as if to illustrate her point. Olive oil hissed, filling the kitchen with a delicious smell.

Kate turned away, smiling to herself. Emma wasn't exactly a stranger to impetuous decisions herself. She'd met her husband Sam when he'd rung her IT company looking for help with a computer that had crashed, with all his files on the hard drive. He was a widower, father to twin girls of three, and had been on his own for eighteen months. While fixing his laptop, Emma somehow sneaked into his heart, and into those of Katharine and Jennifer. Then another broken computer just happened to need fixing, and Emma just happened to stay for dinner (spaghetti hoops on toast, with fromage frais for pudding and chocolate milk – 'That's a special treat for visitors,' Jennifer had told her, solemnly).

In a ridiculously short space of time they were living together as a family, which horrified Sam's ex-in-laws, until they realized how happy it had made Sam, and their precious granddaughters. Emma and Sam would have carried on as they were indefinitely, had it not been for the girls, now six and deeply entrenched in the pink-and-princesses stage. They were desperate to see Daddy and Emma doing Proper Dancing, and Emma wearing a lovely dress.

Kate had loved arranging Sam's secret dancing lessons, finding ways to distract Emma while he disappeared twice a week to a studio in the centre of Cambridge. Booking a babysitter for the girls ('It's the least I can do, seeing as I'm your honorary best-woman'), Kate had taken Emma on a mission to relive their teenage years, when they'd escaped from Saffron Walden to admire the big shops and bright lights of Cambridge. They'd hung out in cafes, reminiscing over their teenage dating disasters, and watched fourteen-year-olds as they hovered hopefully round the make-up counters in John Lewis, desperate for free samples. She smiled to herself now, remembering.

'Pass us some tomatoes, Kate.'

'Sorry, I was dreaming.' Kate reached up to the cupboard. The room was comfortably untidy, strewn with school books and egg-carton dinosaurs. One end of the long table was covered in laptops, wires and mysterious pieces of computer, which Kate, who was resolutely untechnical, chose to ignore. Emma still ran her IT company, bringing tired laptops back to life and recovering data that had been magicked away, quite often by the fingers of small helpers. She had a constant stream of repairs coming in, and did the occasional small office upgrade, but now it was a kitchen industry in every sense of the word. She had slipped into the role of stepmother to Jennifer and Katharine easily, probably because, as one of six herself, she was used to the muddle of family life. Kate had loved spending time at Emma's house as a teenager – the place was busy, and full of love and noise. The guilt she'd feel at leaving her grieving mother alone would disappear as she'd slip, unnoticed, into the hot fug of the kitchen. Emma's mum was always baking something delicious and shouting about homework, or lost shoes, and didn't have time to obsess about her daughter's every movement.

'Kate! She stole the red!'

Jennifer's shriek of indignation coincided with the slam of the front door. Kate threw the tin of tomatoes to Emma.

'Can't you two share? Look,' said Kate, leaning across the table and passing the furious Jennifer a scarlet biro, 'you can have my pen.'

'That's not FAIR!' Katharine looked up from her picture, thunderous with the injustice of it all.

'My darling girls.' Pulling Kate's ponytail with affection, then curling his arms around Emma's waist and turning her away from the cooker for a kiss, Sam was home from the office. Kate was reminded once again why her friend had fallen instantly for him. He was kind, and loving, and sweet. She watched the two of them as they leaned over the girls, now peaceful and colouring in their pictures at the kitchen table. It was time to go. Two months of pottering around, living rent-free and taking the occasional temp job, had been just what she needed, but she wasn't part of this family, despite their protestations to the contrary. And coming home from their honeymoon to a lodger wasn't exactly romantic, by anyone's standards.

Kate zipped up the final holdall, adding it to the pile of cases in the hall. Emma had insisted they should leave the next morning at five, on what was going to be the journey from hell. She clambered into bed, lying back and trying not to think about what she was letting herself in for, or why she was running so far away from home.

She had barely unpacked a bag at Emma and Sam's place before her mother had come to visit, bringing cake, flowers and a copy of *The Lady* magazine, folded over to the Appointments page, with several suitable vacancies circled.

'Not that you're looking, but you could meet someone very nice through that kind of job, darling. Ellen Lewis at my yoga class told me her daughter went to work as a PA and married her boss. She lives in Barbados now. Gorgeous villa by the beach.'

Kate had rolled her eyes.

'Mum, you said yourself there was no rush, and that the last thing I needed to do was end up in a relationship again. I don't want to end up being the trophy wife to some divorced millionaire who's decided to marry the hired help.'

'Yes, I *know*, darling, but there's no harm in keeping half an eye out, is there? Time passes very fast, you know, and you'll be thirty before you know it. And – well, you know what happens then . . .'

'No, Mum, I have no idea. Am I going to have a little sign above my head saying "Past sell-by date"?'

'Don't be silly, darling. Just take a look.'

'It's been a matter of weeks since Ian and I split up. I hardly think I'm on the shelf just yet.'

Muttering under her breath, she'd taken a cursory glance and had snorted at the thought of herself as 'Personal Assistant for Family: Regular Travel to Dubai required'. Her organizational skills were pretty hopeless, for one thing. She'd managed to wing it through her temp jobs with a large helping of 'Oops, I think I just redirected that call to Peru' jokes, never staying long enough for her lack of confidence to become a real issue, but the truth was that she didn't have much faith in her own ability. A job that involved keeping a rich family organized as they flew back and forth across the world didn't really appeal, although the lying-around reading books on the beach sounded quite nice. Kate suspected, though, that the job would bore her to tears. She'd been

stuck in offices since leaving university, bored to tears
doing admin work (badly). Arts graduates were ten a
penny, and despite pressure from her mother to 'Do the
right thing, darling, and take a postgraduate teaching
course', she'd resisted.

Kate had promised to look at the magazine, just to
keep her mother quiet. The following night she was
reading it in the bath with a large glass of wine. As she
smiled to herself at her mother's kind, but as ever slightly
smothering, attempts to get her settled in a suitable position – preferably one with a suitable relationship attached
– an advert caught her eye:

Serviced cottage available, free of charge, in exchange
for Man or Girl Friday (3 working days per week)
on country estate on Scottish island.
Write: Box No. 2314.

There was something about the old-fashioned nature
of the advert that had amused Kate. Did anyone write
using Box Numbers any more? More to the point, Kate
wasn't quite sure what a Girl Friday would do in this
day and age, but it had to be better than another position as Admin Assistant (read: glorified office slave) or
any more temping jobs (read: lots of hanging-up on
important people while flicking through a magazine).

She had slopped out of the bath, wrapped herself in
a towel and curled up on her bed to write a response,
explaining that she had lived in Scotland while at

university, and exaggerating her organizational skills quite a bit. She'd put down Sam, and another old boss (who had had a soft spot for Kate because he'd worked with her father), as references. At least Girl Friday sounded interesting; it implied a bit of everything, she thought, but hopefully wouldn't result in her having to work in an office. Any more filing and phone-answering and she would go insane.

The reply, which had arrived by post a few days later, was printed on the most delightful engraved notepaper. She opened it, expecting to discover that she'd been let down gently. But no: the cottage and the position were hers, subject to references, and would be available immediately.

Suspecting that her family and friends would consider her to be irresponsible at best, and taking her life into her own hands at worst, she'd lied about a telephone interview and had satisfied them with fuzzy images of the Auchenmor estate on Google Maps. Kate had decided that, if nothing else, it would be a chance to escape reality for a few months, assuming that her employers didn't kill and eat her. And even then, she supposed, she'd be escaping another tedious office job or the prospect of her mother trying to marry her off to one of her friends' nephews.

Leaning across and peering at the screen of Emma's huge computer, Elizabeth had tutted. 'But there's nothing *there*, darling,' she'd pointed out, looking at the images of the island.

'Yes, there is, Mum, there's plenty there. There are beaches, and an ice-cream parlour, and . . .' She paused, trying to rack her brains. There wasn't really much else, actually. Emma had spent a morning on Google, with Kate sitting beside her drinking tea. They'd established that the island hadn't really embraced modern life and was a bit behind the times, in comparison with the tourist-savvy islands like Mull and Arran, with their visitor websites, downloadable walking maps, lists of hotels and restaurants. 'Anyway, I don't want shops. I want stamping along the beach in the rain, and taking my dog for a walk on a frosty morning. I want lying in bed reading a book all day and doing all the things I couldn't do because Ian thought they were lazy, or untidy, or pointless. I might even take up painting. Or write a book.'

Her mother had raised her eyebrows. 'Maybe a bit of time away from reality will be a good thing. But I'll be checking up on you, you do realize that? No running away and wallowing in self-pity. And if you're not happy, I'll be coming to rescue you.'

'It's the west coast of Scotland, not the North Pole,' Kate had laughed, handing Emma yet another tissue. 'Stop crying, silly. You should be glad to get me out of your hair – you're the only newly-weds I've ever known who've been stuck with a lodger to cramp your style.'

'The girls do a good enough job of that, anyway.' Emma blew her nose and took a deep breath. 'But you can't call round for a cup of coffee when you live a six-hour car journey away, not to mention an hour-long ferry crossing, too.' Kate squeezed her friend's shoulder. 'On the plus side, maybe I can sneak off for girly weekends.'

'You can. We can hit the town. I hear there's a monthly ceilidh at the village hall – just don't forget your sporran.'

Kate did a little Highland jig, making Katharine look up from her Barbie dolls and giggle.

'Seriously, though, what exactly *are* you going to do? I mean, apart from build a house for Robinson Crusoe, or whatever Girl Fridays are supposed to do?'

'I have absolutely no idea. And believe me, after five years of living with a man who had a spreadsheet to manage everything, that feels pretty amazing.'

'Not *everything*, surely?' Emma's eyebrows rose in horror.

'Not *that*, no. But he was the one who'd tell me when my period was due. I suspect that was more because he was terrified I might get pregnant. That'd be just my luck.'

Emma flinched, almost imperceptibly. Kate watched as her friend reached for the pile of washing on the table and started refolding it, automatically.

'Sorry. You know I don't mean it like that.'

'I know. But it's . . . hard. I feel like it's never going to happen.'

Nearly two years ago Emma and Sam had decided – helped along by a lot of nagging from the girls – that

18

they'd like to have a baby. So Emma had come off the pill and had waited. And waited.

She'd searched every website, read every book, visited specialists first at the hospital in Cambridge, then down in London, taking the train with her heart full of hope, convinced each time that they'd find the answer. But, Emma explained to Kate sadly, unexplained infertility is exactly that: every month they hoped, and every month their hopes were crushed. She loved the girls with all her heart, but they desperately wanted a little brother or sister, and so did she. Having to explain over and over again that babies don't come to order was excruciating. Emma found herself staring at photographs of the girls' mother in their bedroom, wondering how it had felt to carry not one, but two little lives. Sam didn't really understand: he was so full of love for Emma, and happy to have found love again when he'd least expected it, that for him another baby would be an added blessing. For Emma it was a desperate, primal longing.

'It will happen. I promise you.' Kate gave her friend a kiss on the cheek. 'And it'll be a lot easier to make it happen without me lurking around the house all the time, getting in the way.'

She had planned to sneak off to the island alone, but her mother and Emma had other ideas. Emma drove them to Scotland, all five females together, in a hopefully never-to-be-repeated six-hour journey in their people carrier. Jennifer had been sick after three miles.

She had spent the journey pale green and silent on the front seat next to her mother, holding a plastic bag in her hands. Katharine had played a computer game that appeared to have no volume control. Kate's mother, as usual, tried to second-guess every situation that Kate might encounter on the island and plan how she should deal with it.

'If you get there and you don't like the cottage, call me and I'll fly up and get you. Or if the job isn't right . . . you know, I've never heard of anyone taking a job with such a vague title. Do you even know what you'll be doing? You don't, do you? It could be anything. I hope you don't mind, darling, but I took the number and gave Mrs Lennox a call myself, just to see how the land lies. She's meeting you off the ferry.'

Kate caught Emma's eye in the rear-view mirror. Emma's pop-eyed expression of horror made Kate snort with laughter. 'I know. She told me on the phone. And then she presumably told you the same thing. She's probably expecting me to arrive wearing a luggage tag, like Paddington Bear.'

'I only wanted to make sure you were going to be all right, darling. Mrs Lennox completely understood. She said she has a daughter herself. You know, you take these notions and disappear to the other end of the country and, even if you're twenty-six, you're still my child.'

'I know, Mum, it'll be fine.'

Poor Emma, thought Kate. At least I get a reprieve

when I get to the ferry. Emma's got an overnight stay with friends in Edinburgh, then another six hours in the car with Mum again tomorrow.

Kate smiled, remembering the look on her mother's face. She felt a knot of fear in her stomach as she climbed the narrow stairs that took her up onto the deck of the ferry. What kind of lunatic gets on a boat, to live in a house on an island they've never visited, four hundred miles from home? she thought, with sudden panic.

The urge to get off the boat and go back to everything safe and familiar was sudden and overwhelming. She grabbed her suitcase and her holdall and ran forward onto the slippery metal deck. This whole idea was insane. Faced with another boring temp position and another pile of rejections for decent jobs, she'd grabbed this chance on a whim. But she didn't do things like this. She'd always taken the safe option, avoided risk. This was madness! She'd tell them she was coming back – tell them it was a mistake. She would start afresh back home. Moving in with her mother wouldn't be that bad, would it?

But then she thought of Ian, and of moving in with him because it made her feel safe. And of being twenty-six and living with her mum and getting excited about an *EastEnders* special, and having Aunty Linda round for tea. Life in Saffron Walden with her mother breathing down her neck wasn't an option – it couldn't be. The thought of her dad's photograph in the hall popped into her head suddenly. She could hear his voice in the hall the last day she'd seen him, big shoulders shrugging into his raincoat, picking up his battered briefcase. 'When your time's up, my darling, your time's up.'

He'd been talking about their favourite writer, who had died that morning from cancer. The words had stuck in Kate's head, spinning round and round on a perpetual loop for what felt like months. He'd never come home, hit by a motorbike and killed as he dodged the Cambridge traffic on his way to the office.

'You only get one chance.' Kate echoed her dad's words aloud, reassuring herself.

The ferry shuddered and she grabbed the railing in front of her. *'Welcome aboard the 3 p.m. Caledonian MacBrayne sailing to Kilmannan. Please listen carefully to the following safety announcement . . . '*

One chance. She looked down at the shoreline. Her mum was wiping her eyes and passing Emma a tissue, which was received with a rather damp smile. Katharine and Jennifer ran into sight, squawking like the seagulls above, arms out and hair flying in the sea breeze, brave and bold and beautiful. And her mother, her best friend and her two best girls looked up at her and smiled their biggest, bravest smiles.

'Love you, darling. Be careful and have fun!'

'Call me when you get there. No – before!'

'Send us a postcard, Aunty Kate; send us lots and lots!'

The engines were growling into life, and the boat was

turning around with unexpected speed and grace, leaving the mainland behind. The crisp salt air was so clean it almost hurt to breathe. It was fear catching at the back of her throat – fear of the unknown, of stepping outside the narrow circle of her comfort zone. There was a knot in her stomach, but Kate told herself it was to be expected. She closed her eyes against the tears and swallowed hard.

'You'll be Kate Jarvis, then.'

It was a statement, not a question. She hadn't heard the woman approaching. Kate had stood in the wind and the sea spray for long minutes, watching as the people she loved grew smaller and smaller, becoming tiny dots on the shore and then disappearing. She'd been so lost in thought that she hadn't even noticed the beautiful scenery, but on looking up, she realized that while the mainland was nearly out of sight, there was a cloudless blue sky, and in the distance were the purple shapes of distant island hills.

'Come away inside and we'll get you a cup of tea. That's a long way you've been travelling.'

The woman was tall and straight-backed. Her dark-grey hair was firmly sprayed into a short, bouffant helmet. Kate suppressed a nervous giggle. That hair had probably been the height of fashion in 1982. The island was even more behind the times than she'd realized.

'Sit yourself down there. I'll bring a tray over.'

Kate looked around, taking in her surroundings for

the first time. The ferry lounge was surprisingly modern. The boat hummed soothingly, and she found herself closing her eyes for half a second, only to be woken by the clatter of teacups and spoons.

'You'll be needing your bed tonight.'

'I will. The rest of my things should be arriving tomorrow. I spoke to Mrs Lennox, who works on the Duntarvie estate. She said she'd made up my bed, which was kind of her.'

'She has done indeed. And she's baked you some shortbread and set the fire, and made you a pot of soup as well.'

Kate looked at the woman, puzzled. Everyone had told her about the hospitable nature of the islanders, and that everyone knew everyone else's business, but this amount of detail was unnerving. Maybe everyone on the island knew she was coming?

The woman's grave face allowed a small smile. 'Jean Lennox,' she said, holding out her hand and starting to laugh. 'Very good to meet you at last. I don't mind admitting we were all a wee bit worried you'd be a mad axe-murderer.'

Kate realized she'd been staring, open-mouthed. 'Sorry, I think I left my brain back in Cambridge. You must think I'm a bit vague.'

Jean shook her hand and then poured out strong, dark tea, adding milk and handing the cup and saucer across the table. 'Not vague, no, but you've got to be a wee bit unusual. There's not many people these days would travel four hundred miles to the Western Isles to take a job and a cottage, on the strength of a couple of letters and a phone call. That's not to say we're not glad that you have. Roderick doesn't like to see the houses sitting empty, and there's hardly any young people staying on the island these days. They all head off down south as soon as they're eighteen.'

'And here I am, coming in the opposite direction. But don't worry – I don't have my axe today. It's arriving with the rest of my stuff.'

They both laughed, Kate thinking that Jean seemed as relieved as she was to discover that she was reasonably normal. Jean took a sip of tea and looked Kate up and down. 'Those boots will no last long, with the mud on our estate,' she said, inclining her head towards Kate's pale suede fur-lined footwear. 'Up here there's mud from September until May. In fact, we've a saying on the island: if you don't like the weather, wait an hour.'

'I heard the same when I visited the island of Arran when I was at university. It was a bit unpredictable then, too,' Kate smiled. 'My mum brought me this waterproof coat. I think she's worried I won't be able to look after myself, so far away from home. She forgets I'm twenty-six, not six.'

'Aye, she called and spoke to me yesterday.'

Oh God! Kate had temporarily forgotten about that phone call. What exactly had her mother said?

'We had a nice long chat. She was telling me how she thinks a little break will do you the world of good.'

'Is that all?'

'Indeed. I told her a wee bit of fresh island air and some hard work would do you good. You'll forget all about that Ian, before you know it. Oh, and she warned me I was to stop you from falling into the arms of the first man you meet.'

'That makes a change, for her. She's probably worried I'll end up living here permanently, and she'll not be able to keep tabs on me.' Cringing with embarrassment, Kate looked at Jean. 'Did she give you my whole life story?'

'I think she's a wee bitty worried about you.'

'Mmm.' Kate hid her irritation with a smile. Thank the Lord there were no flights onto the island, so at least if her mother was planning to swoop down and start smothering her with well-meaning advice, she might have a few hours' notice. Kate leaned her head against the window, eyes drooping for a second. She nodded, lulled by the restful hum of the boat's engine. Mustn't fall asleep, she thought.

'You must be worn out. We're nearly there now, dear – time to go down to the car.'

Kate jolted awake with a sickening lurch. She hadn't slept on the long journey up, having found herself sandwiched between her mother, who was listing all the things she should watch out for (killer eagles, ravening wolves, gamekeepers with evil intentions), and Katharine, who was intent on teaching her how to play a video game that had made no sense.

She followed Jean down the stairs into the car deck, where a dark-blue Land Rover was waiting. A craggy-faced man in a green van nodded and smiled at her, then wound down the window.

'You'll be the lassie come to join us at Duntarvie? Mind Jean doesn't work you too hard. She's a right taskmaster, that one.' He winked at Jean over Kate's shoulder.

'Enough from you, Billy. It'll be a fright you're giving her and she'll be back off on the next boat, and us with nobody to polish His Lordship's boots.'

Boot-polishing? Oh God, thought Kate. She'd been thinking more along the lines of floating around the estate, perhaps supervising the odd lambing or – well, actually, she suddenly realized she still had absolutely no idea what a Girl Friday was supposed to do. Maybe boot-polishing was the thin end of the wedge, and three days a week she'd be wiping down cows' udders, or something equally hideous.

The Land Rover footwell was filthy and covered in dog hair. Jean removed a mud-smeared woollen blanket from the passenger seat and motioned for Kate to get in.

'Sorry, this is Roderick's car. He never goes anywhere without his two dogs, and he will not put them in the back.'

'It's fine. I love dogs – in fact, I'm hoping to get one,

now I'm here.' Kate smiled to herself at the thought, and was already lost in a daydream when she realized they were moving forward. The ramp was down and a handful of cars, vans and a horsebox rolled off the ferry and onto the island of Auchenmor.

'Och well, we should be able to do something about that. No shortage of animals on this island. We're outnumbered.'

Jean drove the Land Rover down the ramp and off the ferry. She pulled the car over to the side of the road, stopping to send a text. Kate watched the ferry workers quickly load up the boat and send it back on its last journey of the day.

She felt a tingle of excitement as she looked down the main street of Kilmannan, the principal town and heart of the small island of Auchenmor. It was no longer a picture in a guidebook or a fuzzy outline on a computer screen. It was real, and she was here. She suddenly felt very far removed from reality. Sea and the distant islands were all she could see: the last ferry had gone. She was trapped now.

'We'll take a wee run round the island first, if you like,' offered Jean. 'It's not big, so it'll not take long, and I can give you the low-down on everyone who lives here.'

Jean winked at Kate and cackled with surprising laughter. 'Don't look so shocked. You'll learn soon enough there are no secrets in this place. Sneeze over your breakfast and by lunchtime the whole island will know you've got a cold.'

Oh, help! Kate had envisioned a remote island paradise, albeit with pine trees instead of palms, where she could go to ground, wander around without bumping into anyone she knew, and work out what to do with the rest of her life. Instead it looked as if she was going to be the talk of the town, just by virtue of having arrived here.

'I'll drive up the High Street first; that way you can have a wee look at the shops.' Jean switched on the engine and started to drive at a pace slightly faster than a jog. Kate looked around anxiously for an irate driver with road rage. 'My niece Ellen says the shops here are terrible. She gets on the ferry on a Saturday morning at 6.30 a.m. to go down to Glasgow. I couldn't be bothered myself. There's our supermarket – it's lovely and new.' Jean pointed at the squat, modern supermarket, which stood apart from the splendid Victorian buildings of the High Street. Kate thought it was hideous, a bright scar amongst the tattered and faded shops with their peeling paint and sea-rusted signs.

There was a fishmonger, a butcher and an old-fashioned greengrocer. The clothes shop had a window display that didn't look as if it had altered since 1972. The windows were covered on the inside with a thick, yellow-tinted transparent plastic, which curled at the edges. Behind it Kate could see faded boxes, and mannequins with thickly plastic wigs, wearing aprons and polyester slacks. Terrifying, thought Kate, who had always thought she was pretty much impervious to fashion. Perhaps I'm going to be the height of sophistication here.

And then they were out of the town of Kilmannan, and the road curved upwards through the rocky, heather-covered countryside. Sheep grazed along the roadside, pausing to chew the cud and stare as the Land Rover trundled past, still travelling at about fifteen miles per hour. Kate felt her eyes prickle with sudden, unexpected tears. It was so wild and beautiful, and completely empty of people or cars. They swept through the moorland, with Jean pointing out the occasional long, low white house: the old crofts.

'It's mainly incomers that live in them now, of course. Artists, and there's a writer up there on the hill. Keeps herself to herself, mind you. There's not many islanders stay on here now. It's a real shame.' Jean shook her head. 'Thank goodness Roderick is trying to make a go of the estate since his father died.'

Kate allowed herself a little smile at the prospect of Roderick. He was clearly the apple of Jean's eye, and she could just imagine him. Single, bedecked from head to toe in a hairy tweed suit and green wellies, probably a bit podgy and balding. His car smelled of wet dog, and Jean had shifted a couple of magazines out of the way before she sat down. Kate glanced at the back seat to see what they were: *The Scottish Farmer* and *The Field*. Not much chance of discussing the latest goings-on in *EastEnders* over a cup of tea with her new boss then.

The car rose out of a dip in the road and crested a hill.

'Oh my God!'

Jean stopped the car in the middle of the road. She switched off the engine, turning to her left and facing Kate.

'I'm so sorry!' Kate had blurted out the words without thinking. She had read somewhere that many of the islanders were fervently religious. Wondering if she was about to be ejected from the car for blasphemy, she sat frozen for a second.

'Now, you can't beat that, can you?' smiled Jean.

The scene was breathtaking. The low, setting sun was burnt across the sky, light reflecting off the sea and tinting the white sand of the deserted beach orange. Waves lapped at the shoreline and, as Kate watched, a kestrel hovered overhead, pausing before shooting down towards its prey. On either side the hills rose, framing the picture.

'We don't have much in the way of shops and social life, but we have this to make up for it. And you can't put a price on that.'

They shared a smile. Kate watched Jean as they drove along the moor road. Her features had softened as she had relaxed on returning to her beloved island. She no longer looked stern and forbidding. And was that even a twinkle in her eye? Her time at Edinburgh University had taught Kate that the Scottish sense of humour was often so dry as to be imperceptible.

At the top of the next hill the countryside changed. The heather-covered, rock-strewn moorland, surrounded by forests of pine trees, was replaced with rolling pastureland. Cows grazed on rich grass that reached down towards another deserted bay, this one surrounded by rocky outcrops.

Then they reached the southernmost tip of the island. The rough grass was dotted with rocks, and gorse bushes huddled together, fighting against the strong winds. In the distance Kate could see the sleeping giant of Eilean Mòr, the uninhabited island situated five miles to the south.

'That's pretty much it, Kate,' said Jean, 'that's our wee island. What do you think?'

'It's perfect.' Kate was desperate to explore every inch of the island, but was suddenly overcome with tiredness. Her legs felt leaden, her eyes were drooping, and she needed to be at home: wherever home was. She had no idea what her new house would look like, or where it was. For all she knew, she could be right in the middle of nowhere, like those crofts Jean had showed her. That would be 'taking time alone' to a ridiculous degree. Plus she was fairly certain that if she lived in the middle of nowhere she'd make precisely no effort to get to know her fellow islanders.

They drove down past a loch, which Jean informed her was home to the fishery and part of the Duntarvie estate. 'One of the parts that actually makes us some money,' she added with a wry smile. They swung left and through stone gateposts, upon which two pock-marked, lichen-covered lions were resting.

'Duntarvie House,' read Kate, marvelling at the faded grandeur, 'I'm here at last. It doesn't seem quite real.'

The Land Rover rattled over a cattle grid, shaking her back to reality. No sooner had she recovered from that than her head thumped the roof of the car.

'Ouch!'

'Sorry, the potholes on this driveway are an absolute menace.' Swerving to avoid another huge hole in the road, Jean slowed even more. 'Every winter the snow breaks down the driveway a wee bit more, but it's such an expensive job and Roderick keeps putting it off. At this rate we'll be soon be better off driving on the grass verge.'

Kate gazed out of the window. The driveway was narrow, with rhododendron bushes gathered in huge clumps on either side. They passed over a stone bridge and the driveway rose up a hill. Looking ahead, Kate could see a square white building, with windows and doors painted a dark burgundy. As they approached, she saw there was a stone archway and caught a glimpse of a stable yard through it, with doors painted to match the house. In front of the house, a field stretched down to the drive and was full of fat, hairy Highland ponies that raised their heads to watch their progress – ears pricked, dragon-breath clouding from their nostrils.

'That's Morag and Ted in there,' said Jean. 'He has a mail-order business, and she breeds the Highlands.'

The road arced round, revealing a row of long, low cottages, again with the same rich, dark, red woodwork, and beautifully kept gardens behind manicured beech hedges, still holding their russet leaves. 'Susan and Tom, Helen and George, Mr Jamieson.' Jean pointed out each house, one by one. 'You'll be meeting them soon enough – they're your new neighbours. Everyone likes to keep an eye out for each other around here.'

Kate suspected that keeping an eye on people had as much to do with keeping up with village gossip as it did with kindness. But it was comforting to know she wasn't going to be left squashed under a wardrobe for weeks on end, if the resident gossips had anything to do with it. Looking out of the window, she couldn't disguise the huge, face-splitting yawn that took her by surprise.

'Och, you're exhausted. I'll show you the big house in the morning. It's no going anywhere.'

Jean turned left off the main driveway and down a stony track. Nestled by itself, surrounded on three sides by trees, was a white cottage. Smoke curled from the chimney, and in the gathering dusk a warm light glowed from the windows. Kate jumped out of the car almost before Jean had turned off the engine.

'Don't get yourself too excited – it's needing a wee bit of work,' Jean said, but more to herself than to Kate, who was crunching across the gravel path to the front door.

It was unlocked. The same burgundy paint covered

the windows and door here, too, bubbling in places to reveal patches of hot-pink undercoat. The cottage smelled of wood smoke and, faintly, of damp. In the hall the woodchip-papered walls were painted a terrifying orange. The carpet appeared to have been modelled on giraffe skins, but Kate didn't care. After years of living with Ian's love of neutral decor, even the hideous colours seemed warm and comforting. The house felt welcoming, thanks to the wood fire burning in the sitting room. A long passageway ran parallel to the front wall of the house, with doors on the right opening into each room. After the sitting room came the kitchen. Kate laughed aloud at the ancient Formica worktops and metal-edged 1960s cupboards. It was all so completely contrary to the modern box that she'd spent the last three years living in – and she loved it.

'As I said, it's needing some work, but maybe you'll enjoy that?' Jean led Kate up the steep staircase to the bedroom. The iron bedstead was huge, filling the room. 'We thought you'd be tired, so I made you up a bed this morning. Roderick was off the island yesterday just to get you a new mattress, and there are more blankets, if you need them, in the bottom of the cupboard here.'

Kate walked forward into the room. The low, sloping roof gave it a cosy feeling, and flames were flickering merrily around a fresh pile of logs. Someone had obviously been in and banked up the fire just before she arrived.

It was heavenly. She was impatient for Jean to leave

so that she could run a bath and get into bed and sleep for a week.

Reading her mind, Jean turned around, touching Kate on the hand with a look of concern.

'You look exhausted, my dear. Get some sleep, and I'll pop in tomorrow before I go to the supermarket. Don't forget I've left you some food in the kitchen.'

Kate could have squealed for joy at the prospect of being left alone at long last, but instead she thanked Jean very properly.

When she'd closed the door, and the Land Rover had scrunched up the path out of sight, she let out an almighty whoop of joy and leapt onto the sofa. It was the first time in her life that she'd lived completely on her own, and she was certain she was going to love it.

Returning to the kitchen, she found a saucepan of vegetable soup waiting on the gas hob. In the fridge were a bottle of milk, some cheese and, rather more excitingly, a bottle of champagne with a Post-it note attached: *Welcome to Duntarvie. Hope you'll enjoy living and working here. R.*

The famous Roderick. Kate had noticed that Jean talked about him with a motherly pride. She had built up a pretty detailed picture of her new employer: living on a country estate that he'd inherited, complete with his own staff. He definitely wore a waxed jacket, and spent his time shooting things; and, to top it all, he probably read the *Daily Telegraph*. Still, he'd supplied her with a bottle of champagne, and that was a good start. Kate popped the cork.

'Here's to me. And to living alone, and to crumbs in bed.' She poured the champagne into a mug, having failed to find a glass. Clearly Roderick hadn't investigated the contents of his estate cottages that closely. 'Cheers.'

The bathroom was freezing cold. It had black-and-white tiles on the floor, and a huge cast-iron bath. The walls were a nauseating pink. Kate pulled the string hanging down from the wall heater, then quickly turned it off again when it smelled as if it was about to burst into flames. She was desperate for a hot bath. She turned the taps on full. They clanked alarmingly and, after a couple of false starts, water came pouring out, filling the room with steam.

Refilling her champagne mug, Kate grabbed her phone and quickly texted her mother and Emma to let them know she had arrived:

Hi Mum, cottage is gorgeous. This is the sitting room.
Jean looking after me. Love you lots, K Xxx

She snapped a quick photograph of the battered brocade armchair and the smouldering log fire. She batted away the tiny moment of panic at being miles away from everyone and everything. This is an adventure, she told herself. I can go home in six months and

I'll have proved my point, and I'll be able to put 'Girl Friday' on my CV and confound potential employers. I can do this.

> Hi darling, house is heavenly. Look, free champagne from His Lordship. Hooray! No axe-murderers yet. Whole island seems to know I am here already. Big kiss to you all. Xxxx

Emma's message was sent with a photo of the champagne and the mug. She'd fill her in on what the house was like later, but it was time to sink into the bath, which was now full to the brim and invitingly bubbly.

Kate rapidly removed her foot from the water. It was freezing cold. The water heater hadn't been on long enough to heat the whole tank. A huge swimming-pool bath wasn't so appealing when it was cold.

She washed her face in icy-cold water, climbed into the pyjamas she'd packed in her holdall and pulled back the old-fashioned counterpane.

Proper blankets.

Huge, heavy, hairy blankets, and starched linen sheets.

She squeezed herself into the tightly made bed and was asleep in seconds.

3

Sir Roderick of Posh

Kate woke up shivering. In place of the roaring fire there was a heap of grey ash. She extricated herself from the blankets and shuffled down to the kitchen.

Eight o'clock. She'd had fourteen hours of dreamless sleep. Since she'd left Ian she'd struggled to get five hours in a row and had often found herself flicking mindlessly through TV channels at 3 a.m. Perhaps it was the sea air or the interminable journey that had tired her out, but she felt she could sleep as long again and still be exhausted.

Taking a cup of coffee through to the sitting room, she was relieved to discover a central-heating thermostat. Log fires were all very romantic, but not first thing in the morning. The house was just as pretty by daylight, but the silence was deafening. Mission one would be to find the much-longed-for dog. Or cat. Or even both, thought Kate, smiling to herself at having nobody else to please.

After a short shower – she wasn't taking any risks with the hot water this time – she decided to explore the grounds of the estate.

'Kate?'

She spun round, surprised to hear her name at all, let alone at this time of the morning. She hadn't got very far, having left the cottage and made her way gingerly up the muddy drive in her fluffy suede boots.

'Morag Banks.'

The woman in front of her had short, close-cropped hair and strong, handsome features untouched by make-up. She was carrying a horse's head-collar, and wiped her hand on muddy jodhpurs before holding it out.

'How d'you do? Used to ponies?' She was brisk, but smiling. 'Come and give me a hand, and then I'll make you a cup of tea. Must be a bit strange for you, waking up so far from home.'

Kate wasn't sure if it was an instruction or an invitation, but the prospect of more tea was nice. It hadn't really occurred to her that it would be so much colder five hundred miles north. She smiled to herself as she followed Morag at a brisk march. If she'd come here with Ian, he'd have arrived with a full set of waterproofs and walking boots. Instead she had only an overnight bag and a suitcase, until her boxes arrived from home.

'If you take Thor,' Morag handed her a rope, attached to which was a solid blue-grey pony, 'I'll bring Mouse and Rhona, and we can take them down to the bottom field.'

Thor surveyed her through huge, liquid-brown eyes fringed with lashes that a supermodel would die for. His forelock reached down to his nose, like a 1980s pop star. Kate was in love. They clopped down the drive in a cloud of ponies' breath.

'So what brings you to Auchenmor?'

'Oh, I just fancied something different.' Kate attempted nonchalance. 'Bit of a chance to escape from reality.'

Morag looked at Kate and raised her eyebrows.

'Oh yes? What was his name then?' She laughed, clicking the gate shut and turning away from the field. 'I tell you what: why don't you tell me the whole story over breakfast. I like a wee bit of gossip with my bacon.'

Kate opened her mouth, then shut it. Jean had been right about everyone knowing everything. It was going to be excruciating if she had to tell the whole Ian saga to every person she met. It sounded a bit pathetic to say she'd escaped to the island to recover from breaking up with Ian – especially when the truth was that she didn't miss him at all.

Sitting at the table, frozen fingers hugging a cup of tea, Kate watched Morag prepare bacon and eggs. The kitchen was huge. A battered leather sofa in one corner was dominated by two Burmese cats, which had looked at her disdainfully when she'd entered. In contrast she'd been greeted effusively by Timmy, a skittering Jack Russell, and presented with a tea towel by Bert, a smiling Labrador retriever. Kate was desperate to investigate the huge bookcase, which was stuffed two layers deep in places. BBC Radio 4 was playing in the background, a soothing mutter that reminded her of her father.

As a child, she'd sit for hours in his study, drawing ponies on the back of discarded manuscripts, while he sat at his desk, always forgetting to drink his tea until it was cold. He'd been a huge giant of a dad, big shoulders in a long overcoat in winter, coming in from the office smelling of damp wool and buses and rainy, wintry Cambridge streets. Even as a little girl Kate had loved spending time in the office with him, charming his authors with her sweet, shy smile. She loved being flung up and caught in his big, capable hands, until one day she was thrown up in the air and he wasn't there to catch her. He'd walked out of the door, battered leather briefcase in hand, and never come home. Kate hadn't spoken for a year after the accident, stunned into silence by misery. Her mother, tortured with guilt at her last words to her husband being bitter ones, was suffocating in her need to prove herself a loving and ever-present parent. When Kate began speaking again, a year after her father's death, her mother saw that as confirmation that she was on the right track.

She's been smothering me ever since, thought Kate.

Looking out of the window, she could see ponies grazing and, beyond the woods, glimpses of a rocky outcrop reaching into the sea. She found herself feeling curiously at home.

'Here you are.' Morag slid a plate of bacon, eggs and

mushrooms across the table. 'Now eat up and tell me all. I need to live vicariously through you young people, now I'm an old lady.'

Morag, with her lined, still-beautiful, almost masculine face, didn't look like the sort of old lady who sat around drinking tea and waiting for gossip to come to her. Her dark eyes twinkled as she sat down opposite Kate, pouring the tea out of a huge Bridgewater pot. Despite Kate's misgivings, Morag seemed so straightforward and kind and kindred-spiritish that Kate found herself pouring out the whole story. How she'd met Ian at university and how his solid, comfortable nature had made her feel safe. How they'd ended up moving in together, not because it was romantic, but because Ian had been offered a job in Kate's home town of Cambridge and it seemed sensible. How being sensible had driven Kate slightly mad, and she'd found herself wanting to scream. How she'd ended up feeling trapped and lonely and unsure. How she was determined to spend time on the island trying to work out who she was, without the influence of a man. How she was looking forward to being single and living alone.

Morag listened intently, elbows on the table, silently topping up Kate's mug with tea, watching as the girl's breakfast grew cold.

'So here I am. I have three days a week to be a Girl Friday, although I still don't really know what that means, and the rest of the time I'm going to just be. That probably sounds a bit selfish, doesn't it?' Kate looked down at her breakfast. 'I'm sorry. You must think me very rude and self-obsessed. Your lovely cooking . . . '

Morag scooped up the plate. 'Five minutes in here,' she said, popping it into the bottom oven of the Aga, 'and it'll be as right as rain. And no, I don't think you're any of those things. I think you're very sensible.'

Morag sat down on the bench beside Kate, putting her hand on her arm and giving it a squeeze. Kate felt her eyes fill with unexpected tears.

'You're not the first person to find yourself drawn to Auchenmor. I think there's a wee bit of magic about this place. And, after thirty years of marriage, I can tell you that the first thing you need to do before you think about finding someone else is to work out who you are.'

'Is that what you did?' Kate wiped her eyes with her sleeve.

Morag smiled: a small, wry, remembering smile. 'Oh, you don't want to go listening to me. I did it all the wrong way round. I wouldn't recommend doing it my way.'

There was a tale there, but not one for today. Morag took her hand from Kate's arm with a final reassuring squeeze. She retrieved the breakfast from the warming oven, and the conversation turned to island life, Highland ponies and Kate's plans to redecorate the cottage. It was hard to believe that just twenty-four hours ago she'd been setting off from Cambridge.

An hour later, and clad in a pair of spare wellington boots and a padded coat ('I keep them here for Anna, my daughter-in-law, not that they get up here all that often,' Morag had explained, giving Kate a pile of thick jumpers, and a fruit cake at the same time), Kate returned to her cottage. Dropping off her gifts, she grabbed an apple from the fruit bowl, then locked the door of the cottage behind her. A strong wind had blown up out of nowhere, and she could hear the waves crashing down on the shore. She scrunched along the gravel pathway through the trees and down to have a look.

She could see something moving on the rocks as she walked closer. Slowing down, she realized it was a group of seals. They were staring at her with mild curiosity, but not making any attempts to move.

'Beautiful, aren't they?'

The voice behind her took her by surprise and she shrieked, jumping into the air.

As one, the seals plopped into the water, startled by the sudden sound.

Kate spun round.

'Sorry. I didn't mean to give you a fright,' said an impossibly gorgeous specimen of gorgeousness. Oops, thought Kate. Still, no harm in looking.

'Tom MacKelvie.' He held out his hand. 'I'm the game-keeper here at Duntarvie.'

Trying not to blush furiously at thoughts of Mellors, which were racing through her mind, Kate shook his hand.

'And yes, I've heard all the jokes about Lady Chatterley's lover,' Tom winked. 'Fortunately for me, there isn't a lady of the house and, no matter how many times he asks, I've told Roderick he's not my type.'

Kate laughed, trying to look as if the thought hadn't even crossed her mind. Tom was over six feet tall, broad-shouldered and managed to make a battered green shooting jersey look the height of style. He pushed up the sleeves of his sweater as he explained, showing off deeply tanned, muscular arms – the result of hours of physical work presumably, rather than evenings spent at the gym.

'We get a fair few seals on the island,' Tom broke through her musings, just in time. 'Although we don't usually see so many round this side. This time of year they're arriving to breed.' He pointed out a group of dark-grey heads, bobbing up and down in the water. 'The grey seal pups are born from now, in September, through to the middle of December. It's mainly grey seals we have living around the island.'

'They're beautiful.' Kate could have watched them all day. 'So graceful in the water.'

'They are indeed. Will you walk with me?'

Kate gulped. He was so incredibly handsome that her knees were having a wobbly moment. He looked like a film star, all bright-blue eyes and suntan and white teeth and dark hair and—

'Have you met Susan yet? I'm just going up for a cup of tea – why don't you come and say hello?' He turned and started stalking up the path on long legs, leaving Kate scuttling behind.

At this rate, Kate thought, I'll still be exploring the island by Christmas. And I have no idea who Susan is.

'No, I've met Morag, who cooked me a gorgeous breakfast; and Jean, who came over on the ferry to collect me last night. But that's it so far.' Kate puffed, trying to keep up. It was hard work, and she was feeling nervous at the thought of being bounced into another introduction. Everyone here seemed effortlessly confident, certain of themselves and their situation on the island.

'Oh, you'll be well fed, living round here. They'll be fattening you up for Christmas, that lot. Susan and Morag'll be in cahoots no doubt. They'll have you in a kilt in time for the Hogmanay ceilidh.'

Still trailing behind, Kate remembered her attempts at joining in the ceilidhs that had taken place during her time at Edinburgh University. There had been foot-tapping, mad music, a lot of whirling about, even more people yelling 'Wheech!' and quite a lot of falling over. That might have had something to do with the vast amounts of eye-watering malt whisky consumed.

'Daddy! Mummy, there's a lady here with Daddy. Look!'

Oh well. It was just as well she wasn't looking then, wasn't it? After all, going weak at the knees over the first gorgeous man she saw wasn't exactly part of the plan – even if he was ridiculously handsome, he was also very much attached. Kate suppressed a small sigh.

A small boy ran to the door, stared at her, then ran away down the toy-strewn hall, managing somehow to avoid breaking his neck in the process.

'I've brought you a waif and stray.' Tom kissed the tall, dark-haired woman who appeared in a doorway. 'I thought, after I'd nearly killed her with fright, that a cup of tea was the least we could do. Oh, and I've got us a wee bit of dinner.' With a flourish he pulled out a brace of pheasant from inside his coat. Ugh, thought Kate.

'I've just been talking about you,' said the woman, with a warm smile. 'Morag was riding by on Thor and we had a wee chat.' She stepped over a toy castle and kissed Kate on the cheek. 'Susan MacKelvie. Or Lady Chatterley, as I like to think of myself. I can't tell you how pleased I am to have someone our age living here.'

She led Kate through to the sitting room, which was painted white with stripped floorboards, modern furniture and huge, abstract paintings on every wall.

'Coffee? Tea? Gin?' Tom winked, putting his head through the door of the sitting room. 'I'll make them – you two sit down. Come on, Jamie, leave Mummy alone for five minutes.'

'Coffee?' Susan looked at Kate, who nodded. 'I need the caffeine to keep me awake. Oh, thank God. A sanity break.' She ran her fingers all the way through her long, dark hair. 'Tom always comes back, round about now, for a cup of tea. Some days I'm counting the minutes. The wee one is asleep in her cot, but Jamie never stops talking and it drives me round the bend. I just want five minutes' peace, like Mrs Large in the story . . .' She burst out laughing. 'Sorry. Here I am, ranting like a madwoman, and we've not even properly met. I've been so looking forward to having someone to talk to during the day who doesn't want to analyse the latest episode of *Thomas the Tank Engine*.'

Kate smiled, understanding. When the twins had been smaller, Emma had found it hard to cope with the incessant demands of small people and had been desperate for company, escaping most days to toddler groups and music classes – anything to avoid the endless hours until Sam returned.

She was still feeling faintly embarrassed at having swooned at Susan's husband, and was lost for words. Susan didn't seem to notice, and was happily filling her in on the things there were to do on the island (not much to speak of) and on the reasons why Kate must be insane to come and live here (countless).

'Oh, I don't really mean that. It's a gorgeous place. And with another grown-up to talk to, it'll be even nicer. And you're staying in Bruar Cottage all by yourself? Maybe I can sneak down with a bottle of wine and we can have a little house-warming party? I haven't had a girly evening for God knows how long.'

'Have you let Kate get a word in edgeways yet?' Tom appeared bearing a tray of coffees and a plate of delicious-looking shortbread.

'Um, maybe one or two,' laughed Susan. 'Now, it's

your turn, Kate. So, what on earth made you leave civilization and come up here to the ends of the earth?'

Realizing this question was going to be a frequent one, Kate took a breath and began again.

'I finished a job, and split up with my boyfriend, and thought it was time for a bit of a change. I spent four years living in Edinburgh, and I've always wanted to spend time on an island, and this seemed the ideal opportunity.' Kate was pleased with her summary, and wondered if it might be worth putting a piece to that effect in the local paper. It would seem that everyone on the island knew everything about everyone, so there was no point in trying to be enigmatic.

'Ooh, so you'll be on the hunt for someone new?' Susan's eyes lit up with the glint of the perennial matchmaker.

'Nope.' Kate shook her head, and took a slurp of coffee. 'I'm getting a dog instead.'

'A dog?' Susan grinned at her. 'Well, you've come to the right place.' Standing up, she called her little boy from his game in the hall.

'Jamie, come and show Kate what we've got in the garden.'

The little boy smiled at her shyly and took her hand. He led her through the kitchen and a back porch cluttered with wellington boots, raincoats and a filthy three-wheeled pushchair, into a fairy-tale garden. There was a playhouse that had been decorated by hand and was covered in fairies, toadstools and butterflies. Mirrored glass hung through the branches of an apple tree, and the air was filled with the sound of wind chimes.

'This is beautiful.' Kate stood, transfixed. She turned to Susan. 'It's like a secret world out here.'

'I don't get time to paint much any more, so I suppose the garden is my canvas at the moment. I can get it done while Jamie plays and Mhairi is in the pram.'

'Come on!' Jamie tugged at Kate's hand impatiently.

They went through a tall gate and into the second half of the garden. A stone building, traditionally constructed with a pointed roof and chimney, was fronted by a metal pen. This cage-like structure had a gate, which led to a sturdy, painted wooden door. Jamie opened the door, bursting with importance.

'You need to be quiet, 'cause they might be asleep.'

Inside the little building was a squirming, bouncing, yipping heap of liver-and-white springer-spaniel puppies, presided over by their very proud mother. Jamie was somehow managing to cuddle all the dogs at once.

'This is Tess. I think I've got it hard with two children – she has nine. Can you imagine?' laughed Susan.

She took a treat out of her pocket, and Tess hoovered it up in a second. She was wriggling with delight at the attention she was receiving, and looked as relieved as Susan had done to have a bit of adult company.

'Tom has bred from her a couple of times. The puppies go for silly money, but we always give a couple away to friends, because it's nice to keep them on the island.'

Kate's face burst into a huge grin.

'You mean . . . '

'Pick a pup – any pup,' Susan grinned back. 'All I ask in exchange is the right to escape down the road to yours with a bottle of something boozy of an evening. Deal?'

'Deal.' Kate put out her hand and shook on it, laughing.

'Right. This calls for a trip up to the metropolis of Kilmannan, I think. We'll go to the pet shop and get you what you need.'

Kate could hardly bear to drag herself away from Tess and her puppies, but Jamie was shooing her out of the door of the kennel and closing the door, looking very pleased with himself as he managed to turn the key.

On closer inspection the High Street of Kilmannan was even more tattered than it had appeared last night in the warmth of the evening sun.

'This place used to be one of the most popular tourist spots in Scotland, y'know,' Susan had explained, looking down the tired street. 'Back before everyone headed off to the Costa del Hot on holiday, my mum says it used to be heaving here every summer. Hard to believe, isn't it?'

'I can't believe how many of the shops are lying empty.' Kate peered in through the window of 'Annabel's Boutique', noticing the piles of mail mixed in with abandoned coat-hangers.

'This place needs a serious kick up the bum. I love it here – I'm sure there's more we could do to get people visiting the island. Hopefully Roddy's plans for the cottages will be a start.'

They'd bribed Jamie with the promise of an ice cream. He kept forgetting that, however, and was skittering around the pet shop knocking over tins of dog food, to the tutting disapproval of the owner.

Susan and Kate made their escape, giggling, with dog bowls and a collar and lead stuffed under Mhairi's mud-splattered pushchair.

'Jim Butcher, who runs that shop, used to be my geography teacher,' Susan explained, once they were out of earshot. 'He sent me to the rector for holding hands with Roderick under the desk in fifth year.'

'Roderick? As in "Lord of the Manor" Roderick?'

'The very one.' Susan winked at her and bumped the pushchair up the step and into the ice-cream parlour. The fittings were so ancient that they were now attractively retro in style. The tables were arranged in booths, with dark-red leather seats, and an original Wurlitzer jukebox at the far end of the room. They were the only people in there, and Jamie took full advantage of this, hurtling from one end of the cafe to the other, sliding across the polished floor on his knees.

'Susan MacKelvie. Where've ye been all ma life?' A beaming Italian man with a strong Glaswegian accent appeared.

'I was here on Tuesday, but you were probably up at the hotel bar having a sneaky pint,' said Susan. 'Bruno, this is Kate, who's moved into Bruar Cottage on the estate.'

Taking Kate's hand, he kissed it and then gave her a wink. '*Bellissima*. Guid tae meet ye, darlin'.'

'Don't you start,' snorted Susan. 'You'll be scaring her away when she's only just arrived. Jamie'll have his usual please, and can we have a couple of coffees. You've never tasted a coffee like Bruno makes – they're gorgeous.'

Kate was dying to hear more about the famous Roderick, her new employer. It was a relief when Susan picked up the thread of her story, having paused to arrange baby Mhairi under her jumper for a feed.

'Right.' She took a slurp of coffee. 'Roderick. Well, I've known him since we moved to the island when I was five. His parents used to bring him up here to the estate every summer. But he didn't go to school here until his mum died, when he was about fifteen.'

She paused to help Jamie poke a straw into his carton of apple juice.

'When she died at their house in England – Oxfordshire somewhere – his dad couldn't face living there, so they came up here.'

'Was she ill?'

'No, she fell down the stairs. I don't know what happened exactly. Sounded horrible, like something out of a fairy tale.'

Remembering the sudden emptiness that had fallen upon their family home, Kate felt a sudden pang of sympathy for her mysterious new boss. When her dad died, it was as if someone had put out a light. Nothing changed, and yet everything was different. She would get up for school, do her homework, have her friends round to play music and sleep over. It didn't occur to her for a long time that her mother's keenness to have Kate's friends round was out of over-protectiveness, and a desire to know where she was at all times.

Living in a small town, it was hard to break out of her mother's smothering embrace, but escaping to Edinburgh University had seemed the perfect opportunity. Her mum hadn't seen it as an escape, because Kate had been with Emma, her childhood best friend, the whole time.

In fact, Kate realized with a jolt, she'd headed up there and straight back home under her mother's watchful eye. This was the first time she'd flown solo, and while it was pretty terrifying being thrown in at the deep end of island life, she felt a sudden sense of pride. She was doing this without moral support, and there was nobody to hold her hand.

'So Roderick came up here and got a fair bit of stick, as you can imagine, having been the posh public-school boy up till then.' Susan absent-mindedly swirled her wooden stirrer through the coffee froth. 'But we were friends, and a wee bit more than that for a while, and eventually people just got used to him being around.'

'So where is his dad now?'

'He died of cancer a few years ago; it was very sudden. Only took a matter of weeks.'

'And now Roderick's in charge of the estate?'

'He is, and it's not in a good state, despite his best efforts. His father's heart was never in it, after his wife died, and Roderick has spent the last couple of years trying to get it back under control. There's a fishery and a wood-yard, and they're the main employers on the island. Without them, there are no jobs, and everyone will leave the island and the place will end up empty.'

'Oh,' Kate's face fell. 'So I've taken a job away from someone on the island?'

'Not at all. There's not many people would want to live in your cottage,' Susan said, raising her eyebrows. 'It's a bit – well, rustic. Most of the younger folk prefer to be here in the town, and not five miles away on a road with a bus that only comes past once a week.'

'Oh!' Kate put her hand over her mouth.

'What's the matter? Is it Jamie?' Susan spun round in her chair, expecting to see her toddler creating some kind of mess.

So much for going it alone. She hadn't thought this through at all. 'I don't have a car. There are no buses. And I'm living in the middle of nowhere!'

'Have you not got a car?' Susan asked.

'Nope. I left it with Ian.' Kate remembered her battered old Vauxhall. 'I told him he was welcome to it, because it kept breaking down at traffic lights.'

'Ah. Right.' Susan returned the sleeping baby to the pushchair, and wrapped Jamie up in his scarf and gloves. 'Next stop Jock's Cars then?'

Buying a car with Ian had been a long drawn-out process, involving the inevitable spreadsheet of cost-analysis pros and cons, miles to the gallon and other things, which Kate had found unbearably dull. She'd nodded and smiled, handed over half of the money and had driven whatever they'd ended up with. She couldn't help finding it amusing that, after all that analysis, they still ended up with a car that constantly broke down.

In comparison, buying a car on the island of Auchenmor was blissfully simple. With the money she'd received from Ian in lieu of the furniture, she was able to choose a car based on colour and shape, and the fact that it already had a dog guard fitted in the boot. Susan assured Kate that Jock wouldn't dream of selling her anything that wasn't reliable, and the grey-haired old man in a boiler suit had given her his word that the car was sound. He also had no problem with handing over a vehicle on the strength of a cheque.

Laughing to herself, Kate followed Susan, who drove like a maniac on the narrow island lanes, back to the estate, parking her car outside the cottage. Despite the reassurances that nobody here locked their vehicles, she double-checked the door before she walked away. Island life really was something else. The idea of walking into a garage, choosing a car and driving it home, without handing over hard cash, would be unthinkable back in Cambridge. It was like stepping back in time.

'I can't decide. They're all so beautiful.'

Kate was sitting on the floor of the kennel in a sea of fur, when a puppy chose her. Unlike the others, this one's face was almost all brown, but it looked as though someone had spilled a splash of white paint down one side of her muzzle. She was quieter than the others, and curled up on Kate's lap.

'This one. Now, quickly, get me out of here before I change my mind.'

Susan laughed and pulled her up from the floor with one hand. Kate's other hand curled around the soft, fat tummy of her little dog.

'The others are being homed over the weekend, so she'll be okay to go with you tonight.' Susan rummaged in a cupboard, pulling out a hot-water bottle. 'Tuck her up with this in her bed and she'll be fine.'

Kate had every intention of sneaking the puppy into bed with her, but took the hot-water bottle without argument.

'What's her name?' Jamie lay on the rug, letting the puppy chew his hair.

'Willow.' The name came out of nowhere, but suited her perfectly. Kate scooped her spaniel puppy into her arms, stroking her soft ears.

'Can we come and see her tomorrow?'

'You can come whenever you want, Jamie. Bring your mummy and daddy, too.'

'And Mhairi? She can't play with puppies because she's too little. Mummy said she's not allowed.'

'Mhairi, too. But you'll be in charge, because you're a grown-up boy. Mummy said you're going to be four on your birthday next week.'

'I think I'll be five. Five is bigger.' Jamie stood up on tiptoe. 'I'm quite big just now, look.'

'Enormous.' Kate laughed.

Susan reappeared from the baby's bedroom, creeping in with an expression of relief.

'Right, Jamie, I think a bit of *Thomas the Tank Engine* for you,' she switched on the television, 'and a wee sit-down for Mummy.' Susan looked suddenly exhausted, worn out by the needs of a sleepless baby, a little boy who was more than ready for school, and a whole kennel full of dogs. 'Do you want some more tea before you go?'

'Truly, no. But thanks.' Kate headed for the door, manoeuvring her way through the toy cars and assorted plastic. 'I'm awash with coffee as it is.'

Susan kissed her goodbye. The sun was setting on what had been another very long day, and Kate was dying to collapse in front of a fire and watch something mindless on television.

Her mobile beeped. Shuffling Willow under her arm, she managed to yank it out of her pocket:

Have you run off with a haggis? What's the news? I was
promised regular gossip updates.

Emma's texts always made her smile.

24 hours in: two new friends (no, you are NOT dumped), a
dog, a gorgeous gamekeeper (don't worry, married, so out
of bounds) and enough caffeine to send me into orbit.

'Ow!'

Not looking where she was going, Kate's ankle gave
way as she stepped into a pothole. With a gasp and a
yelp of surprise, she and Willow fell sprawling forward
into the mud and gravel of the drive. Somehow she'd
managed to avoid squashing Willow, or dropping her,
which was fortunate as a car was approaching at speed.

The Land Rover from last night, with the distinctive
DE 1 number plate, pulled up in front of her. Kate heard
the door hinges creak, and feet crunching towards her.

'Multitasking isn't going to be your strong point then,
I take it?'

Kate peered up from her landing place. Looking down
at her, dark brows in a line of disapproval, was the owner
of the voice. Tall, with dark hair flopping forward over
his eyes. Green wellingtons, of course. A pair of rather
muddy jeans, a navy-blue jumper, a checked shirt. He
held out a hand and hauled a filthy Kate and Willow
up from the ground.

Her phone, which had narrowly missed a puddle,

beeped indignantly. Her rescuer knelt down and picked
it up, glancing at the screen before handing it to Kate
with an expression she couldn't read.

Don't go falling madly in love with Sir Roderick of Posh, or
whatever he's called. You're not Cinderella.

'Sir Roderick of Posh: your new landlord, employer,
and definitely not Prince Charming.'

Fine pieces of gravel were falling gently, like rain,
from her hair. Willow was whimpering slightly. Kate
was tempted to join in.

'My friend Emma. I am *so* sorry. Oh God, I'm mortified. I'm so sorry. I mean . . . ' Kate was blushing furiously and, as ever, was unable to stop herself from
babbling in a crisis.

'I've been called far worse.' He raised an eyebrow.
'But you're not in the city now. We don't walk about
with our phones permanently glued to our ears round
here.'

Now he was admonishing her. And this after five
years of living with Ian, who could have won an Olympic
Gold in making her feel stupid. Her new employer was
obviously a pompous git who behaved in the same way.

'Come up to the house and I'll get Jean to take a look
at you – that was quite a fall.'

'I'm fine,' said Kate. 'I just need a hot bath.'

'I'd be happier if you did,' he said, in a don't-argue-
with-me sort of voice. 'I need you in one piece. I've got

61

plans for you.' He grabbed a pile of folders, throwing them onto the back seat of the car. With one word from their master, two sleek black Labradors leapt down from their vantage point on the front seat and were shut behind the dog-guard rail.

Feeling unable to object, Kate climbed into the Land Rover, trying not to wince. In protecting Willow, she'd fallen awkwardly on her left side, and her shoulder was beginning to ache badly. She could feel herself trembling slightly, and her teeth were chattering. She clutched onto the puppy for comfort.

Roderick edged the Land Rover round, expertly dodging the potholes on the way to the house. He didn't speak, giving Kate the chance to survey her new employer with a sideways glance. He seemed distracted, the frown still fixed in place and a nerve jumping in his cheek.

The Land Rover scrunched to a halt on the driveway. Kate looked up at Duntarvie House for the first time. Actual turrets, like a fairy-tale castle. Not just one, but loads of them. He lived in a blooming castle – no wonder her new boss seemed a bit snooty. It'd be hard to have any grasp of reality if you lived in a stately home.

The house was beautiful, a perfect example of the Scottish Baronial architecture her dad had loved. He'd taken her to Balmoral as a little girl, patiently explaining the characteristics of the castle. She could recognize the crow-stepped gables, the ornate cornices and the crenellated battlements of the central tower topped with another turret. There was even a flag. And gargoyles. It was utterly gorgeous, and quite ridiculous. Her shoulder was absolutely killing her, and everything – and everyone – she knew suddenly felt very distant.

'For goodness' sake, Roddy. What's been going on here?'

Jean opened the car door, taking in Kate's filthy clothes and pain-whitened face.

'You've been in the wars.' Scooping Willow out of Kate's hands, Jean passed the puppy to Roderick. Gently she then helped Kate out of the car.

Willow was lying upside down in Roderick's arms, squirming helplessly as he tickled her tummy.

Flirt, thought Kate, as she straightened up, gritting her teeth against the pain. 'I'm fine, really. It was only a tumble.'

Jean looked at her with motherly disapproval.

'Well, even so we'll get you inside and cleaned up, and then we'll decide.'

It was like being back home, with her mother lovingly railroading her. Kate allowed herself to be propelled across the gravel drive and up the stone stairs. Twin stone eagles guarded the steps, and above the door Kate noticed a crest carved into the stone. We're not in Kansas any more, Willow, she thought.

The hall of Duntarvie House was vast, with a parquet floor covered with a Turkish rug bigger than anything Kate had ever seen. There weren't any dead stags' heads that she could see, which was a relief, but ancient oil paintings of forbidding men in kilts indicated that the house had a long history. It smelled of wax polish and old oak and log fires. The staircase in front of her curled upwards, the banister spiralling towards a vaulted ceiling.

'Come away into the sitting room for a minute.' Jean propelled her into a chair and disappeared.

'Drink this. You're a bit shaken up, and it'll help.' Roderick handed her a glass of brandy, taking a step backwards and looking at her expectantly. She obediently drank the burning liquid, aware of his dark eyes watching. It seared down her throat, filling her with warmth.

'Where's Willow? I'm not much good at this dog-owning business, am I? She's been gone from her mother five minutes and I've tried to flatten her. And now she's gone AWOL.'

'She's in the kitchen.' Roderick leaned down, taking the glass from her hand. Kate caught a waft of his lemony aftershave. 'Jean's giving her some puppy food we had left over from Hugo – he's only just turned one. Not sure she'll eat much – I think she had a fright, too, looking at the state of your shirt.'

His expression was unreadable.

Kate looked down. It was possible to be more embarrassed after all: she was sitting on the posh sofa of a country house in a wee-soaked T-shirt. Time to escape. She tried to pull herself up, but her arm wouldn't co-operate and she slumped backwards into the chair.

'Stay where you are.'

Roderick strode out of the room and, with her good arm, Kate felt in her pocket for the offending phone. Feeling like a schoolgirl in danger of being caught out sending notes in class, she sent a surreptitious message to Emma:

Have made complete prat of myself. You would laugh.
I might later, too, if I don't throw myself off a cliff first.

Kate stuffed the phone back in her pocket as Jean reappeared, lips pursed, her head cocked sideways. She set down a tray with a pot of tea, and wrapped a blanket around Kate's shoulders.

'I'm running you a hot bath. I don't want you going home to the cottage tonight and sleeping on your own, when you've fallen down and hurt yourself.'

'That's lovely of you, but I really am fine.' Kate tried to shuffle forward out of the deep sofa, but winced at the pain. 'I need a sleep and a couple of painkillers.'

'Aye, and you'll get those here, and someone to keep an eye on you as well.' Jean poured her a cup of tea, before leaving Kate to survey the sitting room alone. It was tattered but beautiful, the walls panelled with wood, a threadbare rug by the fireplace. The table was piled with books and magazines – a strange, eclectic mixture of marine biology, interior decor and out-of-date copies of *Vogue* and *Hello!*

The door opened to the sound of Roderick and Jean

RACHAEL LUCAS

laughing together. Their easy familiarity caused another wave of homesickness to wash over Kate.

'One lesson you'll learn quickly,' Roderick said as he reappeared, holding Willow, now cradled in his arms like a baby and staring at him adoringly, 'is "Don't argue with Jean". Braver men than me have tried, and failed.'

'Och, away.' Jean was smiling at him with as much adoration as Willow. Roderick was clearly the apple of her eye, but Kate couldn't see the appeal. Admittedly he was more handsome than she'd expected, but, cosseted and living in a castle, Roderick clearly had no idea of how the other half lived.

'Leave Kate with me, Roddy, and I'll have a wee look at her shoulder now.'

'See what I mean? I'll take this little one away and get her settled.' He left, carrying the sleeping Willow in his arms. Typically upper-class, all horses and dogs and shooting.

'Let me have a look at that shoulder, Kate.' Jean gently lifted up the sleeve of her T-shirt, revealing a mass of stone scratches and the beginnings of some nasty bruising.

'Ow!' Looking at the mess of her arm, Kate felt a bit sick. It hurt a lot more now that she'd seen the damage.

'I was hoping to get you to see Duntarvie under slightly better circumstances, Kate, but welcome nonetheless. I hope you like it here.' Jean gave her a kind look.

'It's been a bit of a day. Car, people, puppy – and

now this. I have to keep reminding myself I was coming here for a bit of quiet.'

'Och, you'll not get that here on Auchenmor. There's always something going on.'

'So I see.' Kate tried to stand up, but her balance was definitely off-kilter.

'Sit yourself back down. I'm going to go and sort your bath out for you now, and I don't want you getting into any more trouble.'

Kate poured another cup of tea and watched the logs burning in the fireplace. It was very much like being in a faded country-house hotel, but this was someone's *home*. The idea of Roderick living alone in a place this size was insane. How on earth could he sleep at night in a house with countless empty bedrooms, and corridors just begging for ghosts to wander around them clanking chains – or whatever ghosts did these days. She shivered at the thought of it.

Jean reappeared, making Kate jump. 'Now, up to your bath, young lady, and no arguments.

The bathroom was huge, white and stark. But the bath was full to the brim with lavender-scented bubbles and, next to the towels, a pile of clothes lay folded neatly on a chair. Kate peered at them through the steam. What on earth? They were definitely her pyjamas, her dressing gown and her fluffy slippers. Someone – it must have been Jean, surely – had been back to the cottage and found them. Kate grimaced. The idea of someone going through her belongings, not to mention seeing the state of her already messed-up bedroom, was awful. Jean was right when she said there were no secrets on this island, she thought, clambering gingerly into the boiling hot water. At least she'd bought new pyjamas before she'd left Cambridge, instead of bringing the ancient scruffy nightshirt she'd worn while living with Ian. She leaned back, wincing with pain, and closed her eyes for just a second, luxuriating in the scented foam.

'Kate?'

A man's voice through the door woke her from her sleep. Heat-drunk and slightly shocked from the fall, she must have dozed off in the bath. It took a couple of moments before she could gather her thoughts to reply.

'Sorry, sorry. I'm here.'

'Glad to hear it.' Was that a note of humour underneath the clipped tone of voice? 'When you're ready, dinner's waiting, and there's a young lady here to see you.'

Kate pulled out the plug and climbed out of the bath. The soak and the painkillers had eased her stiff shoulder, which was already turning purple. With some difficulty she dried herself and managed to manoeuvre herself into her pyjamas. She folded up her dirty, torn clothes as best she could, leaving them on the chair with her phone, which had run out of charge in any case.

She left the brightly lit bathroom, her eyes taking a moment to adjust to the gloom of the corridor. A series of doors stretched before her, and the walls were hung with yet more of Roderick's ancestors. Turning for the stairs, she noticed that one of the doors was ajar. The temptation to peek inside was too much to resist. Heart pounding, she sneaked her head round the door. The room was ice-cold, with dust sheets covering the furniture. She withdrew with a shudder. Imagine *living* in this place. No wonder Roderick seemed a bit chilly – it probably seeped into his bones.

The stairs were the stuff of *Gone with the Wind*, but there was no dramatic entrance for Kate. She manoeuvred her way down cautiously, pausing as she reached to turn the handle of the sitting-room door. She looked down at her pyjamas and slippers – hardly suitable for dinner in such a grand house.

As if he'd sensed her presence, Roderick opened the door. He'd changed and shaved, and looked younger and less terrifying in a faded blue shirt and jeans. He was close enough that Kate could smell the citrus of his aftershave. His freshly washed hair was hanging in his eyes. He looked more like an advert for Barbour than the laird of a country estate that she'd imagined. She stood in the doorway, feeling extremely out of place.

'Kate. Well, it's nice to see what you actually look like when you're not covered in mud.' He flicked a glance towards her hand. 'No phone? Not got any urgent texts to send?'

'I left my phone with my things in the bathroom. Thought it might be a good idea to make it down the stairs without breaking my neck.'

He strode over to the bookshelves, where a bottle of whisky and two glasses stood on a tray. Pouring two huge measures, he handed her one and motioned for her to sit down. Easing herself into the chair, Kate took a sniff of the malt. She stifled a cough as the whisky fumes hit the back of her nose. She wiped her eyes.

Roderick sat down at the far end of the sofa.

'You've made quite the impression in twenty-four hours.'

The frown was back. Kate fiddled with her glass, looking down.

'I suppose we should be glad you're still with us. Jean told me you were planning to make your escape before you'd even set foot on the island.'

'I – no, I just . . . ' Kate stumbled over her words, not sure how to answer.

'Go on.' Roderick leaned forward, surveying her over the top of his glass. His dark eyes narrowed.

Without the stubble, Kate noticed, he had a bee-stung upper lip. It looked somehow vulnerable, and definitely at odds with his rather formal demeanour. She shook herself. This was her boss, a man who was used to getting what he wanted. And, right now, what he wanted was an answer.

'I'm not going anywhere.' Her voice was determined, and the last vestiges of doubt were gone.

Half-hiding her face behind her glass, she stared into the flames. If taking risks wasn't exactly her style – and, in the past, it hadn't been – she was going to show people she *could* do it. She'd jumped from one temp job to another in the last four years, and her lack of staying power was becoming a standing joke.

'You're building a patchwork CV,' Sam had teased her, recently. 'You can always say you'll try anything once.'

The joke had been a little too close to the bone. Kate, while laughing, had winced. And then there was the fleeting exchange of glances between Emma and her mother on the journey to Scotland when she'd mentioned staying for at least six months, if not more.

She put down her glass, resolute now. For once she was going to prove them wrong.

'I've brought your dinner through here.' Jean appeared in the doorway. 'I thought Kate would be more comfortable in the sitting room.'

Jean trundled in, pushing an ancient hostess trolley. It must have been in the family for generations. Kate wondered if Roderick had all his meals delivered by his stern-faced housekeeper rolling them into the sitting room, where he sat reading *The Shooting Times*, or whatever lairds read. Emma would have been giggling; it was just as well Kate had left her phone upstairs, or she'd have had to sneak a photograph. The whole thing was so far removed from reality.

'Join us, Jean?' He had picked up a folder and was scanning some figures, a distracted expression on his face. It wasn't quite a command, but Kate felt that the tone suggested he was used to people doing his bidding.

'No, I won't, thanks, Roddy. Hector will be wondering where I've got to.'

She set out plates heaped with shepherd's pie on the low oak table, giving Kate small comfort in the shape of a conciliatory smile. She wasn't even staying? Kate gave a small sigh.

'It's something easy for you to eat with one arm.'

Roderick looked up at Jean from his paperwork.

'Now, I've laid Kate's things in the green bedroom. I want her off to bed early, and I'll be in first thing to make sure she's all right.'

It was like being back with her mother. Kate caught Roderick's eye. Was that a hint of a twinkle there? He raised his eyebrows at her in mock-admonishment.

'Don't you worry. I'll have her off to bed as soon as she's finished dinner.' He stood up, dismissing his two dogs, which slunk off to their beds by the fire.

'See that she is. I don't want you young ones sitting up all night talking. Kate needs her rest.' Leaning over, Jean stroked the puppy, patted Kate on the knee and then straightened up. 'I'll see you in the morning.'

'Yes, ma'am.' Roderick shooed her out of the room gently, with Jean chuntering slightly as she headed for the door.

Kate couldn't quite catch what was said as they disappeared into the hall, but felt relieved to be off the hook when she heard the front door slam and the key turn in the lock.

Roderick pulled the door shut and, without speaking,

lifted the sleeping Willow from Kate's knee, putting her on the rug beside the fire. He placed a cushion behind Kate's back carefully, and set a wooden tray on her knee, complete with china plate and heavy silver cutlery, shaking out a linen napkin and laying it in her lap. His silence was unnerving. Kate was locked in a gigantic, quite possibly haunted house with a man she didn't know and only a sleeping spaniel puppy for protection. This place must have at least fifteen bedrooms, almost all of them uninhabited. It was seriously spooky, she thought, looking out of the window. It was pitch-black outside.

The whisky had dulled the ache in her shoulder, but left her incapable of small talk. She'd always struggled for the right thing to say in situations like this. She felt quite overawed.

'Um . . . '

'So . . .'

'You go first.'

'Lovely dinner,' said Kate desperately. She'd managed to scoop up a mouthful, but was too uncomfortable to eat, convinced that if she did so, she'd make one of those loud, gulpy swallowing noises, or choke.

Roderick had already half-finished his meal. He looked up from his plate and fixed her with dark brown eyes, his expression serious.

'I don't make a habit of scooping up stray girls and bringing them home to my lair, if that's what you're wondering.'

He seemed pretty convincing.

'That's a relief!' She pulled a wry face, before trying some of the dinner. It was utterly gorgeous, and she hadn't realized how hungry she was. It was a long time since she'd eaten anything proper. She'd arrived on the island and had survived on soup, coffee and tea. Added to the mixture, the whisky had warmed her stomach, but had left her distinctly light-headed.

Talking of which, Roderick was topping up her drink, unasked. At this rate she'd be unconscious soon. She scooped in another few mouthfuls of dinner, as ballast. In her post-university attempts to find a decent job, Kate had been subjected to some pretty odd new-girl inductions, but none of them had featured dinner in pyjamas with the boss in the first week.

Roderick was looking at her, his jaw set and his eyes narrowed. If he hadn't been so stern, Kate thought, he'd probably be quite nice-looking. Not in the same league as Tom, the film-star gamekeeper, mind you.

'The last girl we took on lasted a couple of weeks before she headed back down south – she couldn't cope. We have no end of southern softies turning up here on the island, hoping to "find themselves", or some nonsense like that.' His tone was cool.

Kate felt herself flushing. Leaning forward and gritting her teeth against the pain, she placed her tray carefully on the table in front of her. 'Well, I haven't come here to find myself, don't worry. And as it happens, I went to university in Edinburgh, so I'm used to the cold.'

The truth – which Roderick didn't need to hear right now, or ever – was that it had been far harder than she'd anticipated to find a decent job after university, and while she'd gathered a certain amount of useful skills doing telephone sales, inputting data for endless weeks for employment agencies, and performing countless other mind-numbing admin jobs, she was bored stiff. The thought of life on an island had been far preferable to the alternative. And didn't *everyone* secretly want to float around, discovering their inner artist and finding themselves? He clearly had no sense of adventure.

'Glad to hear it. The last thing we need is another one here today, gone tomorrow.' Roderick raked his fingers through his hair, frowning. The strain of running an estate showed on his face for a moment, and he gazed into the fire for a while before speaking. 'This place needs – well, I don't know what exactly. But if you're planning on making a run for it, I'd rather you just said now.'

'I'm not going anywhere.' Kate's voice was steady. She didn't have anywhere to go to, in reality, but that wasn't what he wanted to hear.

'Good.' Roderick poured some more whisky into their glasses. The effects of two hefty measures of malt were now making themselves felt. 'Here's to Duntarvie House.' He passed her the glass. 'You might just be the good-luck charm we need.'

Kate looked at him, confused.

'We've been given a grant – first time something has

gone right for I don't know how long. D'you know anything about doing up houses?'

Kate contemplated lying, but decided that she'd already done enough of that. She'd been a bit vague about her experience when she'd applied for the post, not really knowing what a Girl Friday position entailed, and her CV had been so disastrous that she'd been known in the past to do more editing and stretching of jobs than was strictly acceptable. There was something about Roderick – an old-before-his-time air – that made her admit the truth.

'Nothing at all.'

'Great! Me neither.' Bending down, he pulled out a leather-bound book from underneath the coffee table. He flipped open the pages, revealing beautiful pencil sketches of some island cottages, surrounded by tiny illustrations of seabirds, seals and eagles.

'Let me show you what I'm planning.'

His fingers were long, his hands broad and tanned from working outside. He pulled a pencil from his pocket, illustrating his point as he talked, drawing arrows, adding little details to the plans he had made. He explained that there was an opportunity for the ailing estate to make some money.

'What I plan is to renovate the old cow-byre and rent it out, along with a couple of old cottages on the west side of the island, which have been lying empty for years.' He tore out a sheet of paper, sketching his plans for the inside of the byre. 'We can turn it into a bunkhouse

– a hostel – for schools and colleges to use, and we can hire it out. They can come here and use it as a base for wildlife studies in the bay.'

'And my job is to renovate these cottages?' Exciting as the ideas were, Kate sounded dubious. Her DIY skills extended to painting, changing a plug and some extremely haphazard tiling.

'No, no. You're going to help me oversee the whole thing.'

'Oh,' Kate took a gulp of whisky. 'Yes. Of course I am.'

He grinned at her. 'But not until you get that shoulder sorted. I'll take you down to the surgery in the morning.'

4

Selkie Bay

A week later, with the strapping only just removed from her shoulder, Kate was busy overdoing things at the cottage. Her boxes of belongings had finally arrived, having been a victim of 'island time' – a phenomenon unknown to mainlanders, but very much a part of life on Auchenmor.

Jean's husband Hector, a man of few words but much kindness, had helped her to move the boxes from the wide hall of the cottage into their respective rooms. They seemed to have survived their unscheduled holiday in a storage unit near Glasgow, and it was bliss to stack her much-loved books and DVDs on the deep book-shelves on either side of the fireplace. Having been instructed that she wasn't to do a bit of work until she'd recovered, Kate had explored the grounds of Duntarvie house thoroughly, spending hours sitting on the tiny beach that looked out towards the mainland. She'd crept through the woodlands, catching wild deer unawares, and then collapsed back home by the fire, exhausted after broken nights with Willow, who was utterly adorable, but woke as often in the night as a newborn baby.

Kate hadn't caught a glimpse of Roderick since the morning he'd dropped her off at the surgery. Morag, who had taken to popping by for a cup of tea mid-morning, once she'd done the ponies, filled her in.

'According to Jean, he's off the island, seeing to the final details of this funding he's sorted for the cottages.' Morag's eyes swept around the room. 'You've made a good job of this kitchen. It's a lovely shade of blue.'

'I spent years living with Ian's taste for neutral colours,' Kate explained, opening a tin of biscuits. 'I think it's a little rebellion.'

'And you found it in the town? I have to confess I usually make a trip to the mainland when I'm planning any decorating.' Morag raised her eyebrows. 'I know we're supposed to support local business, but I draw the line there.'

'Ah. Phil in the hardware shop told me he hit the wrong button when he did his first online stock order. Apparently it should have been Marvellous Magnolia and not Morning Mist. He found three cans in the store-room, covered in dust.'

'Sounds like you've had a spot of luck, then. I still think you should have let Ted give you a hand with the painting. Dr Sergeant would have a fit if he knew what you'd been up to.'

'I didn't use my bad arm.' Kate laughed. 'And it's

not exactly the most perfect paint job you'll ever see – look!'

She pointed to the ceiling where several daubs of paint had missed their mark. Morag noticed, but didn't comment on, the fine blue specks that covered Kate's hair.

'Och, nobody looks up at the ceiling anyway.'

There was a scuffle as Willow, ears flapping, hurtled for the door, hearing approaching footsteps.

'Did someone say the kettle was on?'

Susan clattered through the doorway, nose pink with the cold. She scooped the excited puppy into her arms.

'You're not busy, are you, Kate?'

'I'm just making a pot of tea.' Kate pulled the mugs from the cupboard. 'I've been showing Morag my dodgy DIY.'

'Oops.' Susan slipped sideways on the kitchen floor. 'I think someone's had a little accident here.'

She laughed and grabbed a piece of kitchen roll, wiping up the mess with a practised hand. 'I can sympathize, Willow. Two children later, my pelvic floor's not what it was.'

'Away with you! You're only young,' Morag scoffed. 'Susan, have you seen what's on the front of the *Auchenmor Argus* this week? Come and have a look here – it's in my bag . . .'

Kate stood waiting for the kettle to boil, gazing out at the autumn morning. She was already learning that rumours and gossip made up the main fabric of island life, and she'd been initiated this week. Morag, keen to check she was settling in, had popped in daily. Susan and Jean were in and out too, passing by with just-baked scones and little gifts to make her feel at home. Kate had sat for hours, quietly listening, marvelling at the complicated interwoven relationships. Most of the time she hadn't a clue who Susan, Jean and Morag were discussing. But she'd been made welcome by the women of the Duntarvie estate, and it was clear they were keen to make her feel she belonged.

'Let me take that tea through to the sitting room for you.' Morag broke through Kate's thoughts, gathering together the pot, a jug of milk and some sugar onto a tray.

'Are you all ready for Jamie's party tomorrow, Susan?'

Kate sat down on the sofa, still guarding her sore shoulder. The painting had probably been a bit much, if she was honest with herself.

'Well, I've cleared out the bunker in the back garden, and I'm planning to hide in it, if that's what you mean.' Susan winked at Morag.

'Tom tells me you're covering the whole place with dinosaurs?'

'For my sins, yes. I'm nearly done. And I've cheated – they'd a perfect ready-made dinosaur cake in the supermarket, so no doubt there'll be words in the nursery-school playground about my domestic failings.'

Despite her jokes, Susan had worked hard to make Jamie's party perfect. Glad of a friend within walking distance, she'd been spending evenings in Kate's sitting room, painting giant dinosaur cutouts, occasionally stopping talking long enough to pause for breath. Then she'd say, 'I'm sorry, I'm talking your ear off, aren't I?' and would carry on being gloriously indiscreet.

Over the last few evenings, sharing the odd bottle of Chardonnay, Kate had heard about Susan and Tom's love life. Susan was an open book at the best of times. Once she'd had a glass of wine, her brain-to-mouth filter was non-existent. The unfortunate side-effect of this was that whenever Kate bumped into the gamekeeper, she flushed scarlet with embarrassment. She had thought it best not to mention to Susan that she'd swooned the first time she'd seen Tom. Susan seemed to be fairly matter-of-fact about the effect her husband had on women.

'As long as they're looking, not touching, I don't mind. I quite like other women perving over him.'

'And to think people accuse new parents of being staid and sensible and boring.'

'Never!' Susan had giggled, and poured another glass of wine for them both. 'We tend to take our fun where we find it. Mind you, it did ruin the mood a bit when Jamie started yelling, 'Daddy, I need a wee' outside the bathroom door when we were having a quickie.'

Kate shook herself, realizing she'd been daydreaming again. Morag was preparing to leave.

'I'm going over to the mainland to pick up a young-ster.'

Kate could see the outline of the Range Rover and horse trailer through the trees. Morag pulled on her coat.

'I'm away as well.' Susan rinsed out her mug and left it in the sink. 'I'll come down later after the little ones are in bed and get the decorations, if that's okay?'

'Perfect,' agreed Kate. 'I'm going into town to pick up some house-decorating magazines. I'm daydreaming about the cottages.'

'I'm not sure Roderick is thinking *Country Living* style; more "youth hostel for geography teachers".'

'Ah. Well, maybe I'll just have to persuade him.'

'Oh yes? Will you be using your womanly wiles?' Morag grinned. 'Taken a wee shine to our boss, have we?'

'Definitely not.' Kate was indignant. 'First of all, I'm having a year off men.'

Susan nodded, eyebrows raised, and looked disbelieving. 'Right you are.'

'Secondly, he made me feel about five years old when I did this,' and she motioned towards her shoulder.

Morag and Susan exchanged glances. Oops! Kate remembered she was talking about their friend.

'Sorry. I mean he definitely defrosted over a drink . . .'

'Yes, he'll do that,' said Susan, with a knowing look.

'. . . but I'm not even remotely interested in getting involved with anyone. Least of all my boss.'

'Ach well, you've not met Finn yet. Never mind Roddy Maxwell – you'll be under Finn's spell in a second.

You're exactly his type.' Susan pulled on her coat and slipped her woolly-socked feet into green wellington boots.

'Out!' laughed Kate, shooing her through the front door. 'I mean what I say. Noooo men.'

'We'll see about that.' Susan, and her cackle, disappeared up the driveway, echoing in the trees.

She returned at eight o'clock that night, blown in through the door by a sudden gust of wind, bringing a pile of the first autumn leaves with her. Willow barked excitedly and skittered around on the wooden floor, chasing them. A moment later she collapsed onto her bed, exhausted.

'She's just like a baby.'

'Aye, but she doesn't get you up in the night five times, like Mhairi did last night. I'm like the living dead.'

'Three times last night, so she's not much better,' said Kate, opening the fridge. 'I got us a little something to celebrate all your hard work.'

Susan had the corkscrew out of the drawer in a second. 'It'd be rude to refuse, wouldn't it?'

'Absolutely.'

They drank the first bottle of wine while piling up the dinosaurs in the hall. The glasses Kate had brought from Cambridge were huge and the wine soon disappeared. Opening the second bottle, she put on some music.

'Roddy loves The Killers, too, you know,' said Susan, with an angelic expression.

'Him and about five million other people.'

'I'm determined to get you paired off. A gorgeous girl like you, living in a romantic cottage like this, with a roaring fire and all this lovely orange carpet?'

'Mmm, nice.'

'Okay, we need to get you a furry rug.'

'Seventies. Even nicer. Am I going to be starring in a Barry White video?'

'Anyway. Stop changing the subject. You can't spend the next year on your own. It's not natural.' Susan was bobbing along to the music, slightly out of time, and flicking through a magazine.

'We don't all have the libido of a . . . of a . . . a *thing* with a big libido.'

'You're twenty-six. You're single,' Susan was pointing at her, or at least trying to, but the effect was ruined because she was aiming at the wall instead. 'You've spent the last five years of your life with a man who probably noted down on a spreadsheet how many times you had sex—'

Kate burst out laughing. 'You're not the first person to accuse him of that. I've got to get Emma over here, you'd love her.'

'And she'd agree with me. You need some nice therapeutic s—'

The doorbell rang.

Looking extremely windswept, very handsome and rather disapproving, Tom was standing on the doorstep with a baby-monitor in one hand and a torch in the other. It had come as a surprise to Kate how *dark* the darkness on the island was.

'It's half-past bloody eleven, they're going to be up at about five and I'm knackered.' He picked up the bags of Susan's paintings and passed his wife her coat. 'Sorry, Kate, but I know what this one's like. If I hadn't nipped out and got her just now, she'd be on the whisky and singing bloody Kylie Minogue songs at 2 a.m.'

'Karaoke! Ooh, we have to do that . . . ' Susan's eyes lit up.

'Maybe not tonight though, eh? Let's get you home.'

Tom set off up the path to their cottage, with a meandering Susan tottering on his arm. Kate watched them as Willow circled round the garden, chasing invisible night-time creatures. With the moon hidden, and no street lights outside the town, the island was blanketed in a velvety darkness. She whistled and Willow rushed to her heel. Kate locked the door and climbed hazily up the stairs to bed.

She was asleep, but someone was licking her face. And something had died in her mouth. And her head was pounding.

'Willow, ugh – stop it.' Kate half-opened her eyes. The puppy had managed to scramble onto her bed, complete with a half-chewed object.

'No! Oh no, Willow, my boot.'

Every night Kate had been scrupulous about putting anything remotely tasty out of reach of the razor-sharp spaniel teeth, but last night she'd staggered upstairs in her wine-soaked haze without doing the usual checks.

'Let's go and see what damage you've done.'

Willow's energy was exhausting to watch with a hangover. Kate followed her downstairs, only to discover that the puppy had also devoured a pair of shoes and Morag's leather gloves, which she'd left on the hall table yesterday.

After a jug of coffee, some toast and marmalade and a small lie-down on the couch, Kate felt almost human. Time to get ready for Jamie's birthday party, she thought, and hauled herself off the chair. She attempted to burn off the hangover with a scalding hot shower, which left her flushed and uncomfortable.

She rubbed at the misted-up bathroom window. The waves in her dark hair had sprung up with the steam of the shower. Kate twisted them up with a hair clip. She rubbed some foundation into her face, hoping it might stop her looking half-dead, and smudged black kohl eyeliner around her eyes.

'That'll do.' She felt a bit sick, and the steamy bathroom wasn't helping.

She grabbed last night's jeans from the chair in the corner of the bedroom and pulled them on. Perhaps sharing two bottles of wine hadn't been the best idea. Ugh! She pulled on a grey-and-white-striped top and covered it with a grey cardigan.

Her beloved boots were in pieces; it would have to be wellingtons. God! Her stomach churned, amplifying the hangover with a sudden feeling of dread at meeting a whole houseful of new people. She'd been lulled into a sense of belonging, pottering here at home, sharing chats with Jean, Susan and Morag. All the island gossip had been about other people, but she was suddenly hit with the realization that she was going to be on show – the new girl working at Duntarvie, another fly-by-night English girl who'd last a month, before giving up and going home.

Better make sure the socks are respectable, she thought, rejecting the first two pairs as unsuitable. If I'm going in, it's with my best socks on.

Kate stood on the narrow path outside the cottage, watching as Willow investigated the fresh scents of morning. Around the base of the trees, leaves lay in drifts. The puppy launched herself into them, barking with delight. The air was full of the scents of autumn; a bonfire was lit somewhere in the distance, and the faint smell reminded Kate of home, and of last year's fireworks in Emma and Sam's garden. She pulled out her phone, hit by a pang of homesickness:

> Trying to subdue hangover before facing dinosaur-fest with four-year-olds. Urgh!

Emma's reply flashed back, instantly:

> Ha! No escape from birthday-party hell. Grit teeth and think of gin. Or Colin Firth. Works for me, every time.

Kate laughed, surprising Willow, who rushed back from a particularly interesting smell to check on her mistress. It was the most beautiful, crisp late-September day. The cool air was the perfect hangover cure. She clipped on Willow's lead and walked up to the drive.

Cars were parked along the grass verge outside the long row of whitewashed cottages. A bunch of balloons tied to Susan and Tom's front door announced the birthday party. She opened the door, bracing herself.

The wall of noise hit her. Above her head were green, blue and yellow helium balloons, curled ribbons hanging beneath them. The walls were decorated with Susan's huge dinosaur pictures.

'Katie-Kate! It's my birthday. I am four,' Jamie rushed up to her, covered in chocolate, curls bobbing, green eyes sparkling with excitement and sugar overload. 'I'm big now – look.' He stood on tiptoe, wobbling.

'Let her get in the door first, Jamie,' said Tom, appearing from the kitchen and handing Kate a glass of orange juice. 'I'm assuming you don't want champagne, if you're in the same state as Susan?'

'I am *not* in a state. I'm just slightly delicate.' Susan, looking grey, emerged from the sitting room, closing the door on what sounded like a bloody massacre, complete with shrieks, whoops and yells.

'They're trying to break into the piñata. It's like the Battle of Culloden in there.' She leaned back against the door, pinning it shut. 'My head! I think my eyes are trying to burst forward out of my skull. I'm never drinking again.'

Tom raised his eyebrows at Kate. 'Slightly delicate, you say? I thought we Scots were the hardened drinkers?'

'All right, I admit it.' Susan slumped into a chair, head in her hands. 'I feel like death.'

'That's more like it. I'll make you a nice bacon roll when all this is over.' He leaned down and picked up Willow. 'I'll put her in the back room. She can stay there with Oliver.'

Oliver was their ancient golden retriever, an excellent nursemaid to Willow because he encouraged her to sleep. He wouldn't deign to spend time in the kennels with the working dogs, considering himself part of the family.

'Help!'

A muffled voice emitted from the sitting room. Susan held the door open for Kate.

'Ladies first.'

Kate walked into the room. There was an amorphous mass of small people, mainly boys, lying on the floor. The source of the sound couldn't be seen at first. She realized that underneath it all was a very squashed adult.

The mass swayed, then parted. Long legs appeared. Rumpled, with his dark hair sticking out untidily, Roderick emerged.

'Oh. Um, hello.' Well, this was unexpected.

'Do excuse me, I was being a diplodocus. The T. rexes were eating me alive.' He stood up, a rueful smile on his face. He ran a hand through his hair in a fruitless attempt to look less dishevelled. His collar was standing up on one side and his shirt sleeves were rolled up, revealing toned, tanned forearms.

He was her boss. She shouldn't be looking at his arms, and definitely should not be wanting to reach out and fix his collar. Kate found herself tongue-tied. A small girl was gnawing at his leg, apparently unaware that the game was over.

'That piñata is impossible to open. We've tried beating it with sticks, but it didn't work.' Susan entered the room, carrying an axe.

'Have you lot never heard of health-and-safety rules? You can't just—' gasped Kate, as her friend swung the axe forward, splitting the piñata so that the contents spilled out onto the floor.

'I just did. Now get out, quickly, or they'll really eat you alive.'

Kate and Roderick backed out rapidly as the children swooped down on the sweets and toys, squawking with delight. Marching back to the kitchen, Susan handed Kate the axe as she passed. She stood in the hall, holding it, nonplussed.

'Birthday parties are a bit more, er, vigorous on the island then?'

'Oh yes. They breed them tough up here.' Roderick lifted the axe out of her hand. 'Let me put that back outside.'

He strode out through the back door, leaving Kate

standing in the hall, mouth open. When he acted like a real person he was surprisingly lovely.

'I'd make a run for it, if I were you.' Susan popped her head out of the kitchen door. 'You've shown your face, and Jamie's so high on sugar he won't notice.'

She was holding a plate of mini sausage rolls. Popping one in her mouth, she offered the plate to Kate.

'Ugh, no. Still feeling a bit delicate.' What she needed was a bit of fresh air and a bacon roll, a duvet, a gallon of orange juice and *Calamity Jane* on DVD – that would do the trick.

'Me too. I'm hoping stodge will soak up the worst of the hangover.' Susan rearranged the sausage rolls into a spiral pattern, disguising the patches where she'd sampled her own cooking.

'Oi, you! Hands off.'

Roderick reappeared, pinching a couple more. He was followed by Tom, who helped himself to one.

'Every time – I don't know why I bother making party food, it's never the kids who eat it.'

Tom leaned over, kissing Susan on the cheek. 'Because it's delicious, and we get to have miniature sandwiches while they overload on cola bottles.'

They were revoltingly in love – it was adorable, but Kate sensed that Roderick was feeling as much of a spare part as she was. He cleared his throat.

'Would you mind if we did a runner then, Sus?'

'But I've only just arrived! I haven't even been

subjected to all the school-gate mothers yet, and I've got my best socks on, too.' Kate's protest drew an expression of confusion from Roderick and Tom.

'Nobody's going to notice if you two disappear – and you need a decent cup of coffee. Get out now, while you can,' Susan said firmly, handing Kate her coat. She gave Tom a sideways glance.

'If you're sure?' The prospect of curling up on the sofa was tempting.

Susan pushed Kate towards the door with a laugh. 'Get out, you two kids, and go have some fun. Leave us old married gits to do the boring stuff.'

'She's not going to take no for an answer.' Roderick helped Kate into her coat. Despite her protestations, the deeply ungorgeous present had already become a permanent fixture.

'I wouldn't argue with Susan when she's on a mission.' Tom opened the front door. 'Take that girl out, Roddy, and get her something to cure her hangover. I'll drop Willow off later.'

The door closed behind them.

'Well, that's us told.' Roderick shrugged on his coat. 'I'm sure you'd like to get back home, but if you're not busy, there's something I'd like to show you up at Selkie Bay.'

'Well, I did have a hot date with the best of Doris Day and a duvet, but I'm sure she'd let me off.'

'Come on, then.' He took her arm, in a curiously old-fashioned gesture. 'I'll take you up there, but, before I do, you look like you could do with a cup of coffee. Hard night, was it?' He couldn't help a smile.

'We accidentally drank a couple of bottles of wine.'

'Terrible when that happens. Just leapt down your throat, did they?' His tone was arch. Opening the door, he once again had to shove a newspaper, dog leads, a waterproof coat and assorted detritus onto the back seat before Kate could sit down. She watched in silence. Considering how posh his house was, the Land Rover was a disgrace. She climbed in.

They made their way down the drive, rhododendron leaves smacking wetly against the windows as Roderick dodged potholes by steering onto the overgrown verge. At one time the grass here had been manicured, maintained regularly by a team of gardeners. Kate had seen photographs of the estate in its prime along the walls of the kitchen – big black-and-white pictures of Roderick's relatives playing tennis in 1930s whites. The tennis court was completely wild now, the red ash surface swallowed up with mossy grass, the gate rusted shut.

'I must get this drive sorted.' He was talking half to himself. 'There always seems to be something else to pay for, though.'

Kate slid a look at him, sideways. The muscle in his cheek was jumping again, and his jaw was tense. She reached out, trying to placate him. 'Hopefully we'll get some money coming in, once the cottages and bunkhouse are rented out; that'll make a difference, won't it?'

'I hope so.' He sighed. 'The island economy is in a

hopeless state. Anything we can do to shore it up will help.'

He pulled up outside the cafe, opening the door for Kate and leaving the car unlocked. After numerous episodes of Susan, Morag and Jean all laughing at Kate assiduously locking the cottage every time she left it, she'd learned that on the island security seemed pretty low on the priority list.

'There are only three ferries a day going off the island, so I think we'd notice if someone was making away with our belongings,' Jean had explained, laughing. 'And I canna see anyone stealing a car – where would they hide it?'

'No Bruno.' Roderick read the sign on the window. '*Closed due to staff shortages*, my foot. He'll be watching the football up at the hotel bar.'

He fanned out his keys, selected one and opened the cafe door.

'Do you have a key for every building on the island?'

Roderick looked at her with curiosity. 'Why d'you say that?'

'Someone went into my cottage and got my clothes when I fell. And now you're letting yourself into a cafe.'

'Well, I am the Laird of Duntarvie.' He flicked his hair out of his eyes, turning on the lights.

Without seeing his face, Roderick's tone was impossible to judge. *Seriously?* Kate bristled. Just when she thought he'd unbuttoned a little.

Roderick fiddled with the set of keys, releasing one

and placing it on the Formica counter of the cafe. 'Just as well you'll be working outside most of the time, on the cottage redevelopment. If you can keep your desk up at Duntarvie in some sort of order, then nobody'll need to know how untidy you are in secret. Unless, that is, they end up in your bedroom.'

She was just about to open her mouth and tell him he was a raging hypocrite, considering the state of his car.

'I know what you're thinking. It's a disgrace. But you can talk – did you simply tip all your bags upside down as soon as you arrived at Bruar Cottage?'

Now he was looking down at her and laughing. He'd obviously been the one who'd rescued her things from the cottage when she first arrived.

Just because he's the Lord of the Manor, she told herself, you don't have to swoon every time he says something vaguely nice. We're not in a Disney film.

'Take a seat. I'll make you a coffee.' He motioned to one of the high stools by the counter. She perched on the red leather, tucking one foot behind the other on the metal bar. He switched on the Wurlitzer and the empty cafe filled with the sound of Otis Redding.

'Don't look so surprised.' Roderick was measuring beans, tipping them into the machine, filling the room with the delicious aroma of freshly ground coffee. Kate sat mesmerized, watching his hands twisting and flicking, swirling the milk in the metal jug as the steam hissed. 'There.' He handed her a cup of coffee, a leaf design swirled into the foam, and looked at her expectantly as she took a sip.

'It's perfect.'

He reached forward, wiping a smudge of foam from the end of her nose with a fingertip.

'Sorry,' said Kate, swiping at her nose again.

His dark eyes caught her grey ones, and her stomach jolted once again.

'Don't be. I always end up with coffee on my nose.' He was unsettling her. That was twice in one afternoon that she'd found herself distracted by her boss. There was something about him. Charisma perhaps, she thought, taking a sip and surveying him surreptitiously. Or maybe it was just a conditioned response to the landed gentry, which was a weird thought. Let's face it, a hundred years ago she'd probably have been working as a chambermaid, not being served coffee by the owner of the big house. But he did seem remarkably human for someone whose relatives probably hung out with the royal family.

He walked round to her side of the bar and sat down, taking a drink.

'So, you're a barista, as well as lord of all you survey?'

'I spent most of my time in here as a teenager,' he looked down into his cup. 'It was pretty miserable at home when we moved here from Oxfordshire.'

'Your mum.' The words were out before Kate could stop them. Without thinking, she put her hand on his arm. 'I'm sorry.'

He looked up at her, a strange expression on his face.

'Thank you.' His voice held a note of surprise, as if he hadn't expected sympathy.

'My dad died in an accident when I was ten. He argued with Mum, and stormed out of the house in a temper one morning.' Kate found herself filling the space with explanations. 'He was hit by a car while crossing the road and was killed instantly.'

'So you know.' He reached forward, fiddling with the wooden coffee stirrers, snapping several into pieces, creating tiny, bonfire-like heaps.

'I do.' Kate's voice, after a long silence, was flat. She suddenly felt a wave of homesickness for a life that hadn't existed for fifteen years.

Roderick smiled at her – a sad smile of shared loss and understanding.

He scooped up the shredded coffee stirrers into his hand. 'I'm sure Bruno only taught me how to make coffee because it kept me out of his hair. I spent most of the time being picked on at school for being posh. This was my escape.'

Roderick pushed back his chair, gathering their now-empty cups. He wiped down the surface, practised hands banging the coffee out of the filter, clearing up all evidence of their visit. Kate looked on. He was completely absorbed in what he was doing, happy in his work. His final act was to chalk a note for Bruno on the blackboard behind the bar: 'Hope the best team won.'

*

They climbed out of the car at Selkie Bay. In the distance Kate could see that the shingle beach was studded all over with rocks. Pulling on his coat, Roderick passed her a spare pair of gloves.

'It'll be freezing down there, and we might be a while.'

They climbed over rocks freckled with lichen, and down onto the rough sand. The tide was out, and seagulls were swooping down, searching for leftover morsels. As they walked across the beach, Kate realized that most of the rocks were moving. She turned to Roderick with a quizzical expression.

'A pod of seals hauled up here a couple of weeks ago. I thought you'd like to see the pups.'

'Oh! I saw some on the shore below Duntarvie House, the first morning I woke up here. They're so beautiful, aren't they?'

'I'm glad you like them.' Reaching into his pocket, he pulled out some binoculars. 'We can't get too close,' he explained. 'They can give you a nasty bite if they're upset, and at this time of the year they're pupping and going into moult.'

'I had no idea that seals moulted.'

'They do. Makes them really grumpy. It makes me laugh, watching them snap at each other.' Roderick was scanning the beach, searching. 'When I wasn't getting under Bruno's feet, I was up here, watching the seals. Look!'

He passed the binoculars to Kate, putting his hands

on her shoulders and turning her round gently until she was facing east.

'There's a cow with an unusual white splash on her back, can you see?'

'A cow? On the beach?'

'A female seal is known as a cow. A male is a bull, and the youngsters are pups.' There was laughter in his voice. 'Look, can you see where those gulls are landing?'

'I see her – she's rolling,' Kate adjusted the binoculars slightly, homing in on a shape beyond the adult seal. 'Oh, it's a baby!'

The pup was covered in a shaggy white coat. As Kate watched, it yawned, showing a coral-pink mouth.

'I've seen that cow here every year since I was fifteen. Seals can live for thirty years.'

Kate was transfixed. Ten minutes later she handed the binoculars back to Roderick. 'Sorry, I've hogged them. It's just that the seals are so beautiful. I could watch them for hours.'

Roderick raked his fingers through his hair and smiled lopsidedly. 'I thought you might think I was a bit of a geek.' He looked awkward, and suddenly young.

'Not at all. I spent my childhood collecting beetles.'

'As in creepy-crawlies, or as in toy cars?'

'Bugs.' She had no idea why she was sharing this information with him. It had been years since she'd even thought about her little collection of pet pests. 'I know, it sounds a bit bonkers. I kept them in little boxes and constantly got into trouble for having them escape all over the kitchen. Not quite so exotic, but we didn't have many seals in Essex.'

'Oh, you do,' Roderick said, boyish in his enthusiasm. 'I did some work down there a while back – you just need to head over to Foulness and . . . ' He paused for breath. 'Sorry. Anyway, as I was saying, about being a bit of a geek . . . '

Kate laughed.

'Come on then.' He strode ahead, beckoning her to follow. 'I'll show you my favourite place for watching them. It's where I'm going to have the hide built – the cottages aren't far from here, look.' He pointed to some grey stone buildings up on the hill.

They were much closer to the seals now, but hidden from sight by a stack of boulders. Creeping forwards, Kate slipped, falling backwards into Roderick's arms.

'Sorry, I missed my footing.' She pulled away, embarrassed.

'I'm not complaining.'

His amused tone sent an unexpected prickle of heat through Kate, flushing her face scarlet. She was suddenly very interested in the binocular straps, adjusting them with great concentration.

As if nothing had happened, Roderick pointed out the noses of a group of seals, bobbing up and down in the shallow water.

'They only sleep for ninety seconds at a time. That's a meeting of Insomniacs Anonymous out there.' He laughed. 'Come on, I'll take you up the hill and show you what we're dealing with.'

The cottages were tumbledown, but beautiful. Tussocks of grass grew in between the paving stones, and the little road that led to them was strewn with rusted, discarded farm machinery. The long, low byre, which was to become the student bunkhouse, was still full of straw.

'It's like a rural *Marie Celeste*.'

'It's sad, isn't it?' He gestured to the cottage in front of them, before pushing at the wooden door. Long shards of paint crackled to the ground. Inside, the cottage was floored with ancient linoleum, and the walls were covered in dated floral paper.

'This was lived in by a tenant farmer, who died when my father was still alive.' He held open the door to what had been the sitting room and kitchen. 'The other was rented to a family who decided to come and live the good life.' His voice was mocking. They made their way back through the door, standing on the step, taking in the view of Selkie Bay.

'And what happened to them?'

'One cold winter, and they'd had it. They were determined to be self-sufficient, but that only works if you're willing to eat a very limited diet.'

Kate gasped. 'They died?'

'No.' Roderick burst out laughing, startling a crow. It spiralled into the air, squawking in disgust. 'They legged it off the island. They got snowed in over here for about three days and had to live on turnips and pota-toes. I think they're living in an eco-house in Findhorn now.'

'There's a lot of work to do here, isn't there?' Kate poked at the wood of the window frame, which was spongy with age. 'So, working in island time, we're thinking these will be finished by about Christmas?'

'No chance! I've got a provisional booking from Glasgow University marine-biology department for next June.' The excitement was written on his face. 'My friend Sian Cowley is head lecturer there, and they're really keen to get over here and have a base for their studies. They want to see the behaviour of the common seals when they haul in to pup, and come back again this time next year to look at the grey seals.'

Kate rubbed her shoulder, absent-mindedly. 'Well, now I'm in one piece, perhaps it's time I started doing the work I'm supposed to do?'

'That's a great idea. Now let's collect that puppy of yours from Susan's and get you home.'

5

Fireworks

Kate found Roderick in the library, tapping a pen against his forehead in irritation.

'You okay?' He spun round to face her in the big leather chair. He rubbed his unshaven chin thoughtfully, not waiting for an answer. 'These grant applications will be the death of me.'

'We've had a report from some walkers of some sort of plastic netting washed up down on the shore. Can you take a look?'

'If it gets me out of this, definitely.' Roderick picked up his coat from the back of the battered leather sofa where he'd thrown it earlier. His dogs, eager for something to do, leapt to attention. 'Come, if you like?' His voice was casual. 'This time of year you might see the first of the Canada geese arriving. It's pretty impressive.'

The fire-regulation documents that she was reading on the computer were pretty poor competition, and she'd done enough for today in any case.

'Give me a second to grab my coat. I'll meet you outside.'

She shut down the laptop, waking Willow from her sleep with a jingling shake of her lead. By the time she made it outside, Roderick had already loaded the dogs into the back of the car. He held the door open for Kate, motioning for her to climb in. His manners were impeccable.

'I could do with checking how Billy's doing, on the floors in the cottages – could we stop in on the way back?' she asked.

'Of course.' He turned the key in the ignition.

Driving up towards the south of the island, they stopped the car to spy on a magnificent grey seal, which sat motionless, perched on a rock.

'She's on the equivalent of a coffee break,' Roderick explained. 'I'd say she's left her pup on the shore there and has nipped out for something to eat and a bit of a relax. They do it quite often.'

'And what happens to the pups?'

Roderick passed Kate the binoculars, sliding his seat back so that she could look past him. She leaned across for a closer look.

'Well, left to their own devices, they just snooze. The trouble comes, of course, if people spot a pup on the shore and assume it's been abandoned. As soon as they touch it, there's trouble.'

'Because the mother attacks?' Catching a scent of his aftershave, Kate had a sudden sense of just how closely she was leaning across him. She sat up with a start, passing back the binoculars, feeling awkward.

He looked at her with an amused expression. 'No, because she abandons the pup, and then you're in danger of it starving to death. The trouble is it's hard to explain to people that, once you touch that cute fluffy seal pup, you mark it with your scent and the mother won't go near it.'

'So rule number one is: never go near a seal pup?'

'You've got it.' He leaned over to put the binoculars into the glove compartment, just grazing her knee with his hand as he did so. Kate felt her heart thump slightly out of time as they drove in silence towards the furthest beach on the island.

Nethervannan was completely deserted, the walkers who had reported the trouble having long gone. One hand on his binoculars, Roderick scanned the water line. The tide was low.

'There it is. It's a bit of a walk – are you up for it?' He turned to Kate, who was fastening her coat against the biting wind.

'Of course.' She turned to summon Willow, but she was already a black speck, hurtling away to chase the waves with one of Roderick's Labradors in pursuit.

'Willow! Heel!' Kate yelled into the wind, hopelessly.

'Boris, leave it.' Hearing his master, Boris galloped back immediately. Willow, less impressively, carried on towards the water's edge.

'She's a model of disobedience.' Roderick laughed as Kate rummaged in her pocket for a treat, hoping to bribe the puppy back. Training was going well, but, faced with the excitement of a long stretch of beach, and a tide line scattered with the flotsam of an early winter storm, there was no competition.

Roderick tossed a stick towards the water, watching as his two black dogs pelted after it. With neither of them in a hurry to get back to work, he and Kate walked down to the shore in companionable silence.

It had been a month since Roderick had first shown Kate the buildings, and in that time workmen had gutted the two cottages, filling skips with ancient furniture and knocking out partition walls. Billy, the kind-eyed joker Kate had met on the ferry, was screwing down floor-boards, having stripped off the ugly linoleum. The floor underneath was mainly sound, and Billy had tidied it up with reclaimed oak boards.

'He's no working you too hard, is he then?' asked Billy sideways, through a mouthful of nails.

'Not at all.' Kate looked over at Roderick, who was smoothing the fresh plaster with his hand, admiring Billy's handiwork.

'Lady Muck here doesn't lift a finger,' he teased. 'I'll tell you what, if I'd known she was going to spend all her time reading *House Beautiful*, I'd have given the job to someone else.'

After more than a month of working with Roderick,

Kate still wasn't certain if he was serious, or if it was his strange sense of humour at play. He was impossible to read.

'Did ye no tell me there was only one applicant for the job?'

Always up for a bit of sport, Billy looked at Kate and winked.

'Yes. Well,' Roderick said, deadpan. 'She didn't know that.'

'*I've* already managed to secure two months of bookings for next summer, I'll have you know.'

'You have. In fact you've been doing far too much: the deal was three days of work a week, and the cottage in exchange.'

Kate didn't mind. Her plan for discovering herself and learning to paint had fallen by the wayside. Susan had brought her an easel and some acrylics, suggesting that she start with a landscape of the view from the rock-strewn beach below the cottage. She had tried to be encouraging. 'Look, it's just a case of *feeling* what you can see, and translating it onto canvas.'

Kate had looked at her painting with a snort of laughter. 'I can see – through the eyes of a seven-year-old. Seriously, Susan, this looks like something Jamie would do at pre-school. I don't think I've got the art gene.'

'It's not that bad . . . '

Picking up the brush, Kate had daubed a childish boat onto the seascape.

'Okay, you're right. Love you, but it's dreadful. Forget it! Your talents lie elsewhere. Let's go and get a coffee.'

And so art was forgotten. As for self-discovery – well, it was more fun spending time getting to know the islanders, with their dry sense of humour and quiet manner. The self-help books she'd ordered online lay neglected on the bookshelf.

'Don't worry, Billy. I'm having fun. I love it here.'

'You're no working her hard enough then.' Billy straightened, stretching his back with an audible crack and reaching in his pockets for a packet of cigarettes. 'I'll be done with this by the morn, Roddy.'

'We'll leave you to it then, Billy. I'll get this one home before it starts getting dark.'

Roderick reached out to guide Kate's elbow as they clambered out through the low cottage door into the yard. The cold hit instantly. Kate pulled her hands inside her sleeves, trying to hide them from the biting wind. At this time of year the winds from the Atlantic whipped in, sneaking through layers of clothing. The temperature on the uninhabited west side of the island could be lower than the east by a few degrees in winter. Kate felt sorry for the students who would be stuck out here for a week at a time. Even watching seals wasn't so much fun when your whole body was numb with cold.

Willow, on the other hand, had no such qualms. Released from the back of the car, she was dashing back and forth, nose questing the air. She paused for a moment, then scampered across the farmyard.

'Look at her searching. She'd have made a good hunting dog.'

'She's lovely. I still can't believe how far she can go without getting tired. Her energy is never-ending.' Kate whistled, bringing Willow hurtling back to heel.

'What a clever girl.' The puppy squirmed with pleasure as Roderick leaned down to stroke her soft coat. She looked moth-eaten with her baby fluff half-gone and her adult coat still growing. 'Good exercise for you, though, all this dog-walking.' He raised an enquiring eyebrow.

'Are you saying I need it?' Kate bristled slightly.

'No, but it'll not do your townie legs any harm to do a bit of walking.' Roderick cast a glance at Kate, wrapped up in her thick coat, jeans and walking boots.

'Sod off, you!' She pulled a face at him. When he was in this mood, with no sign of the aloof manner that could set her teeth on edge, it was easy to forget he was her boss.

'That's no way to talk to your employer.' He pulled the car keys out of his pocket and together they walked down to the coast road where the Land Rover was parked.

It was only half-past three, but already the sun blazed low in the sky – deep orange reflected onto an indigo sea. Kate looked down at the beach, unaware that Roderick was watching her as she stood enraptured by the beauty of the island sunset. She waited in silence, watching as the sun slipped below the sea after a final, dazzling burst of light.

'How could anyone want to live anywhere but here?' Eyes shining, she turned to Roderick, who was looking at her with a curious expression on his face.

'Are you looking forward to the bonfire tonight?'

'Can't wait,' Kate shivered. 'Though I'm worried I'll freeze. I've asked Emma to bring me up some jumpers when she comes next month.'

'You'll be acclimatised by then,' said Roderick. 'Let's get back to the house. I don't know about you, but I think my toes are frozen solid.'

Kate lifted Willow into the back seat and climbed into the front.

'There's one more thing we have to do. And I need you as backup,' Roderick told her, as he started the car. His mood had changed suddenly, and his silence was forbidding. His jaw was set hard, the amiable atmosphere between them lost. He frowned as he drove, thumbs drumming at the steering wheel. Shooting him the occasional covert glance, Kate sat in awkward silence. Were she to speak, she'd be shut down with monosyllabic answers – she'd learned that much. Perhaps she'd gone too far with the teasing comments, and he felt it inappropriate. It was two steps forward, one step back, getting to know Roderick. She'd seen him laughing and joking with Susan and Tom – in fact, with them he was always relaxed and comfortable. It must have been something she'd said. She swallowed uncomfortably. It was a long five-mile drive across the top of the island and down towards Kilmannan. They drove through the dusk in silence.

'Right. We're here.' He turned off the ignition and sat in the darkened car for a moment, eyes closed. 'And . . . ' said Roderick, tapping out a count of three on the steering wheel.

'Roddy! Where have you been hiding yourself?'

The car door was wrenched open. Pink lips were kissing him on the cheek, and he was being propelled up the stairs and through the half-glazed doors of the Bayview Hotel. He turned back and looked at Kate, eyes wide in mock-horror. Ah. Maybe it wasn't something she'd said, after all.

Clipping on Willow's lead, she trailed in behind, feeling like a spare part.

'So you're the lassie that's been taking our Roddy away from us?' The Glaswegian accent was shrill; the cerise lips set in a disapproving line. The woman had clearly been a real beauty in her youth, and was clinging onto the style she'd known and loved in the 1980s. She patted her expensive-looking blonde highlights.

That's not been done on the island. Kate found herself thinking of Sophisticutz, the salon on the High Street.

'Will you come inside?' Pausing with a proprietorial hand on the interior door, the woman eyed Kate coolly, the words belying her invitation.

'Now, Sandra, they can't hang about. Roderick's got an estate to look after,' said a gentle voice. Turning around gratefully, Kate caught the eye of a short, balding man in a golf sweater. He climbed up the stone steps of the hotel and gave her the ghost of a wink. He held out his hand.

'You'll be Kate?' he smiled. 'Murdo Gilfillan. Owner of the Bayview, husband of the lovely Sandra.'

The lovely Sandra collected herself visibly, exhaling through disapproving nostrils.

'Very nice to meet you,' she said in clipped tones, which implied the opposite. She flicked an invisible speck of dust from her cream satin blouse. Her nails, Kate noticed, matched her lipstick.

'I just wanted to have a quick word about the fireworks tonight,' said Roderick.

'Everything's under control,' replied Murdo. 'We've got the cake, and Finn's going to bring his bagpipes, so all you have to do is make sure she's here on time.'

Kate turned to Roderick, wondering what was going on. Her head was spinning. For every moment that she felt she was getting a handle on island life, another came along when she realized she hadn't a clue what was going on and she was lost again. It was a never-ending game of catch-up, like trying to keep up with *EastEnders* now that she didn't have Sky Plus – only there were no summaries in the weekend edition of the local paper. More's the pity, thought Kate.

'It's Jean's birthday tomorrow – she's sixty. I thought as we'd all be gathered for Bonfire Night, we'd have a little celebration,' Roderick explained.

'Her birthday? You're joking!' Kate screwed up her

face in impatience, throwing her hands in the air. 'It's four o'clock on an island with about three shops, and you didn't think to mention it?' She blurted out the words before she could stop herself.

'You never asked,' said Roderick mildly. 'I was quite impressed with myself for sorting out a party.'

Men! She couldn't even look to Sandra for commiseration. Head cocked slightly to one side, pink-lipsticked mouth pursed in an expression of prim satisfaction, Sandra made a little 'hmm' of smugness. So much for the sisterhood.

Roderick scratched his head in puzzlement.

Murdo chortled, giving him a nudge. 'You'll never please them, man, believe me. I've tried and failed for many a year.'

Roderick shrugged, his expression helpless. 'I didn't even think about a present. I'm sure you can find something in town.'

Kate gave a gusty sigh of exasperation.

Unable to resist the opportunity for a boast, Sandra ushered them into the hotel. 'We've got a *lovely* present for Jean. Come away through and I'll show you the spread we've put on.'

She took Kate's elbow and led her, with an unwilling Willow trailing behind, into the lounge bar. The walls were papered with dark-green paper, the carpet was tartan and, in celebration of Jean's birthday, there were huge tartan ribbons festooned above the polished mahogany bar.

'Murdo has this place gleaming like a new pin.' Sandra preened, like a smug hen. 'And I've made my Coronation Chicken – I know how much you love it, Roddy.'

'Oh yes.' His tone gave nothing away, but Kate had a suspicion he was trying not to laugh.

'You can see the mainland from here on a clear day,' said Murdo, slipping behind the bar. 'It's a fine spot. Now, will you join me in a wee something?'

'I'm driving,' said Roderick. 'But our Kate's developed a bit of a taste for whisky since she's been here. When she's not on the wine, that is.'

She shot him a glance. Sometimes it was hard to tell whether or not he was joking.

'It's a bit early for that, don't you think?' Sandra's expression was disapproving. 'I don't like to drink much, myself, as you know, Roddy. All those empty calories.'

Kate sucked in her stomach, without thinking. She could feel Sandra's eyes upon her.

'A girl after my own heart.' Murdo reached up to the shelf, moving a photograph of a blonde girl in traditional Highland dress to reach behind it for something. Kate sneaked a closer look. The girl would have been quite beautiful, were it not for a slight curl to the nostril, which gave the impression she'd recently smelled something quite unpleasant. She had to be related to Sandra. Kate covered her smile with a hand, disguising it as a cough.

Murdo opened a bottle and poured a hefty measure

of whisky into a crystal glass. 'Slàinte.' He raised his glass to her and took a sip, eyes closed in appreciation.

Kate followed suit, feeling the liquid warmth travel through her body. Despite the baking heat in the bar, her fingers and toes were still frozen.

'Will you have another?'

'Thank you, but we ought to be getting back.' She looked down, realizing that the tension on Willow's lead had slackened. The puppy had slipped her new, too-big collar and was squatting in a corner with an expression of relief, which rapidly changed to guilt.

Sandra, who had been straightening the serried ranks of glasses on a table in front of the bar, shrieked with horror.

'Get that creature out of here. My new carpet!'

'I'm so sorry.' Kate scooped up the cringing Willow and rushed out into the freezing air.

'Don't be,' said Roderick's amused voice in her ear. 'Extra treats for you tonight, Willow. What a good girl!'

'We'll see you at seven.' Murdo stood silhouetted in the hotel doorway, whisky glass in hand.

Looking through the window as the Land Rover crunched down the drive, Kate could see Sandra beetling through the bar, bucket and cleaning liquid in hand, looking furious.

'She didn't seem all that friendly, for a landlady.'

'Ah. It's a long story. And we've got a firework display to get to.'

*

Having soaked for far too long in a boiling hot bath, Kate was scarlet in the face and had no time left to straighten her hair. She swiped green eyeshadow over her lids and smudged on some eyeliner. Her mother had sent her some thermal underwear, and she pulled it on, looking at herself in the ancient, freckled mirror. The vest and long johns clung to her, giving her the appearance of an overstuffed sausage. The woman on the packaging – long blonde hair tumbling carelessly – managed to look effortlessly sexy and radiate an aura of ski-chalet chic. Kate looked more like a draught-excluder cushion. She laughed at her reflection. Willow barked excitedly at the sound.

'Sorry, darling, you're going back to Susan tonight. I don't want you to be frightened by all that noise.'

She picked up her jeans from the tangle of clothes at the end of her bed. An old, long-sleeved T-shirt, a sweatshirt and a thick fleece completed the outfit. She caught another glimpse of herself in the mirror. Her hair had a kink in it from her ponytail band. She was definitely putting on weight – it was all those cakes Morag kept feeding her. Combined with the Michelin Man layers, Kate reflected that it was just as well she was off men.

'I'm not exactly chic, am I?'

Willow didn't reply. Kate popped on her coat and wellington boots, twisted her hair up into a woolly hat and they set off for Susan and Tom's cottage.

'Fireworts, fireworts, fireworts,' Jamie crowed, opening the door.

'Oh God, he's going into orbit himself,' laughed Susan, welcoming Kate and Willow into the chaos.

'Willow will be fine in there tonight. Mum's going to stay here with Mhairi, because she's too wee. And, even better still, Dad's going to take Jamie back afterwards, so we can stay and have a dance.'

'Dance?' Kate looked blank.

'The party at the Bayview afterwards. I thought you said on the phone you were there this afternoon?'

'I did,' said Kate, horror suddenly dawning on her. 'I was so busy thinking of what to wear to keep warm, I sort of forgot that bit.'

'Ah.' Susan nodded. 'So you haven't gone for anything like this?' She lifted up her fleece to reveal a tight black, sparkly vest, which clung to her flat stomach and stopped short of her slim hips.

'Er, no.' Kate unzipped her coat. 'More this.' She lifted up her sweatshirt, showing off her deeply unbeautiful cotton thermals.

'Oops!' Susan laughed. 'Nip down and grab something. I'll shove Jamie in the car and drag Tom away from the computer.'

'Aha, my fellow whisky-lover. Let me get you a wee dram to warm you up.' Murdo spotted Kate as she climbed down from Tom's huge four-wheel drive. He was carrying a tray full of steaming mugs.

'Mulled wine, yum. Thank you!' Susan lifted Jamie out of the car and grabbed a drink.

'I'm going to find Dad, make sure we've got a good spot at the front to watch the fireworks. I'll save you a space,' Susan said.

The grounds of the hotel were packed. Most of the island's population was there, laughing, stamping their feet and waiting for the fireworks to begin. Jamie's eyes were huge, and he was so excited that he appeared to have lost the power of speech.

'Come away in with me, Kate.' Murdo was in good spirits, probably because Sandra was nowhere to be seen, thought Kate.

He pushed at a well-disguised panelled door in the hall. Inside she found Roderick sitting opposite Bruno, long legs in jeans, stretched out in front of a log fire. He was wearing a checked shirt and thick woollen sweater, freshly shaved, his cheekbones deeply shadowed by the firelight. He raised his glass to her in greeting.

'You found our hiding place.' He moved over on the sofa, patting the space beside him.

'Kate,' Bruno took her coat. 'Sit yersel down and get warm.'

She felt as if she'd sneaked into a corner of a gentlemen's club. The little room was tiny, with two sofas facing each other. The walls were panelled with dark wood, and a stag's head leered down at her. It seemed picky to point out that she was already more than warm, having dressed for freezing temperatures, but having ended up in a centrally heated room with a blazing open fire.

'I'll join you for a quick top-up.' Murdo reappeared, bearing a bottle of Jura. 'Sandra's got her knickers in a twist about everything being perfect. If I stay still too long, she'll be tying a tartan ribbon round my head.'

Feeling outnumbered by the men and ignoring Roderick's invitation to sit down, Kate perched on the arm of the sofa. The room was small and hot, and she could feel herself beginning to melt under her many layers. Sitting in uncomfortably close proximity to her somewhat temperamental boss was the last thing she needed. She sipped her drink, the peaty warmth of the malt burning her throat and making her cough.

'Ye're no on duty now, hen. You can relax,' Bruno laughed.

'I can't. I have so many layers on my legs don't bend,' explained Kate, flushing as they all exploded with laughter.

'It's not even that cold tonight,' Roderick placed his glass on the tray and stood up, holding out his hand. 'Up you come, it's nearly seven – time for Jean's surprise.'

In the field behind the hotel people had gathered in a semicircle, keeping their distance from the unlit bonfire. Kate and Roderick joined Jean and her husband Hector.

Murdo was weaving up the path with a loudhailer in his hand.

'He's lethal with that thing,' Jean laughed. 'I thought Sandra hid it after the Highland Games last year?'

'He found it in the wardrobe in the spare room,' explained Roderick.

'Herself will not be happy about that, I'm thinking.'

'Take a look.' Roderick pointed at Sandra, who was storming across the field after Murdo, a thunderous expression on her face. 'I think Murdo is about to be put back in his box, don't you?'

The loudhailer squawked.

'LADIES – hang on, that's a bitty loud . . . ' Murdo fiddled with a button. 'Ladies and gentlemen. I'm about to have this loudhailer snatched off me by my good lady wife, who thinks I'm going to embarrass her again.'

The islanders around the bonfire erupted in laughter.

'So, without further ado, let's have a countdown to the Auchenmor fireworks. Get OFF, Sandra.' He batted at his wife ineffectually as she grappled with him, seizing the loudhailer and beetling away.

'What exactly happened at the Games?' As the rest of the islanders were counting down from ten, Kate turned to Roderick, intrigued.

'Murdo had one too many to drink. And Sandra, as usual, was complaining,' Roderick leaned forward, his mouth close to her ear, to make himself heard over the yelling crowd. She could hear the smile in his voice. 'He decided he'd had enough and tried to auction her off to the highest bidder.'

Kate's laughter was drowned out by the first fireworks. The crowd had pressed forward with the excitement. Sensing Roderick's body just inches away, she stood, frozen to the spot. He was so close that she could feel his breath on her hair. Despite the crowds, the moment seemed strangely intimate.

When the last rocket had shot into the air, Roderick squeezed past her and darted out of sight. He re-emerged holding the loudhailer and flicking it on.

'I wanted to take a moment to say thank you to someone very dear to me,' he began.

Standing beside Roderick with a lemon-sucking expression, Sandra shot Kate a narrow-eyed glance of dislike. It was picked up by Jean, who gave Kate's arm a reassuring squeeze.

'Don't you worry yourself about *her*.'

Kate laughed in surprise.

'She's got tickets on herself, that one,' Jean sniffed disapprovingly.

'She doesn't like a lot of fuss,' continued Roderick, his voice echoing across the field. 'So this is for you, Jean.'

Out of the shadows came the sound of bagpipes. The piper strolled forward, clad in a kilt and a thick woollen sweater. The low bass drone filled the night air. Kate turned to a speechless Jean, who was flapping her hands in front of her eyes, trying in vain to stem the tears.

'Go on then,' said Kate, pushing Jean gently forward. 'Enjoy your moment.'

The piper's tune changed. Kate realized with delight that the Highland melody had been replaced by 'Happy Birthday'. Roderick turned to Murdo, who had reappeared bearing a birthday cake. The candles flickered, lighting up Roderick's face. He looked across at Kate, caught her eye and smiled. He put the loudhailer to his mouth and turned back to the crowd.

'Three cheers,' he roused the islanders, who yelled in response. 'And now, Jean, if you'll do the honours?'

He passed her a wooden stake, topped with a petrol-soaked rag. Murdo struck a match. The crowd roared again as he leapt back, swearing, at the sudden whoosh.

Jean circled the bonfire, methodically lighting her way around it, before throwing the lit torch onto the effigy of Guy Fawkes. She beamed at Roderick, who gave her a wink and smiled.

'Get yourself inside and I'll buy you and Hector a drink,' he instructed her.

Kate turned, looking around for Susan now that the crowd had thinned. Parents were carrying tired, protesting children away from the field, looking forward to tucking them up, sitting down in front of the television and having some time to themselves.

'I can't see Susan,' she stood on tiptoe, peering through the darkness. 'She said to wait for her outside.'

'Ah,' said Roderick, pointing into the darkness. 'She asked me to mention that her dad was going back with Jamie, so the two of them have a night off. She's away with the fairies.'

Kate looked at him, puzzled.

'Come a bit closer and I'll show you,' he explained. Torch in hand, he led her away from the bonfire and into the darkness.

123

As Kate drew closer to the edge of the field, she could see the outline of a twisted hawthorn tree, festooned with torn pieces of rag. She turned to Roderick.

'What on earth is that?'

'It's the clootie well. I won't take you any closer at the moment, in case we disturb the young lovers.'

'So why is the tree covered in bits of cloth?'

'Well, tradition says that if you tie a piece of the cloth to the tree and make a wish, the fairies will grant it before the cloth wears out,' Roderick said. 'People used to do it when their family members were ill, but nowadays it's more likely to be teenagers making wishes about the person they fancy. And of course it's also a place where they can hide and nobody knows what they're up to.'

'Hmm,' said Kate, teasing. 'That's interesting. Maybe I'll be coming back here to make a wish myself one day.'

'Oh yes?' Roderick laughed at her.

'Morag says this island is magical.' Kate was thoughtful. 'It's certainly cast a spell over me. I love it here.'

Roderick stared at her for a long moment, a strange expression on his face. Kate could feel a blush rising on her own face, hidden by the moonlight.

'Bugger off, you two,' came a voice from the darkness. 'You're as bad as the children. Can we not have a snog in peace?'

'You'll be wanting to change?' Somehow Sandra managed to beam at Roderick and glare at Kate simultaneously. 'If you follow me upstairs, I'll show you where to go.'

I bet you'd love to, thought Kate. Roderick ducked back through the wall into the men-only hiding space, leaving her to climb the stairs behind Sandra, stiff-legged in her thick layers of clothing.

'You can leave your things in here, and I'm assuming,' Sandra paused to cast a disdainful glance up and down Kate, taking in her mismatched, lumpy appearance, 'you brought something else to wear?'

'I've got my things here, yes.' Refusing to rise to the bait, Kate patted her bag, reassuring herself that she definitely *had* remembered the change of clothes.

'I'll leave you to it, then. The bathroom is just there.'

Slipping off her boots, Kate surveyed the hotel room. The bed was covered in heaps of discarded clothes, the floor strewn with boots and wellingtons. It looked as if the whole island had thrown off their sensible winter layers. It was lucky she and Roderick had spent the time after the fireworks ended walking over the field to the clootie well, or she'd have been changing amongst the chaos of a crowd of excited islanders.

Locking herself in the bathroom, she pulled out the contents of her shoulder bag. Removing the long johns from under her black jeans, she peeled off layers of vest, jumper and fleece, stuffing them in haphazardly. She slipped on her top, a shimmering grey cowl-necked vest. It was an old favourite, and she thanked the gods of clothing that it had been the first thing she'd grabbed when she ran down to the cottage earlier. Slipping on her black heels, which had managed to survive puppy-attack, she surveyed her outfit. A bit plain, perhaps, but definitely an improvement on the overstuffed-pillow look. She clipped on her favourite silver bracelet, ran her fingers through her hair, sprayed on a ton of deodor-ant, reapplied some lip gloss, eyeliner and mascara, then grimaced at herself in the mirror. Without the gregari-ous Susan to keep her company and make her laugh, she wasn't really looking forward to the party.

'Wow!' Roderick was standing at the bottom of the stairs, watching as she made her way down. He gave a low whistle. 'I'm now officially off-duty. Shall we have that drink we were offered earlier?'

Kate was relieved, and touched. Everyone on the island, with the notable exception of Sandra, had been welcoming and kind, but walking alone into a noisy, thronging party full of drunken islanders had been a terrifying prospect.

'Sit yourself down here.' Roderick pulled out a chair for Kate. 'I'll go and get those drinks for Jean and Hector.'

The room was heaving with people, all of them far more dressed up than Kate. She twiddled her hair, checking her phone out of habit. No messages. Of course there wouldn't be – the hotel, being Victorian, had thick walls that were impervious to mobile signals, so she couldn't even text Emma for moral support. Sitting on the chair alone, she felt conspicuously lacking in friends, and suddenly aware of how far from home she was. She searched the room for a familiar face. The sound of excited Scottish voices, blended with the music from the disco in the corner, was deafening. Having cast off their reserved nature along with their layers of clothing, the islanders seemed determined to have a good time.

She jumped as cold lips kissed her on the cheek.

'Morag!'

'You look very beautiful, young lady,' said Morag gravely, turning to the bearded man on her left. 'Doesn't she, Ted?'

'As always.' Ted's eyes twinkled with pleasure.

As soon as they'd met, the gentle Ted had recognized a kindred spirit. Delighted to be sharing the contents of his huge bookshelves with Kate, he'd spent hours discussing the book world. In his previous life he'd worked at a big London publishing house and had known, and worked with, Kate's dad. Because of this, he felt a little bit like home to Kate. He'd shared stories of mutual friends, giving her a feeling of rootedness and security that she hadn't realized she missed. He'd reminded her so much of her dad, with his warm nature, amused eyes watching the world quietly.

'That silver grey matches the colour of your eyes,' said Morag, reaching forward and feeling the soft metallic material between her fingers. 'Very pretty. You'll be the catch of the night.'

Kate smiled, but said nothing. She had no desire to be the catch of this, or any other, night. She was enjoying the peace of her uncomplicated life, and her nights in bed reading until 2 a.m., sleeping star-shaped in the bed. Even Emma's text the other day hadn't shaken her:

> Gossip update – Ian is going out with woman from his office. Met him in the Feathers. He's a fast mover.

She'd known Ian wouldn't be alone for long, and had wondered what she would feel when he moved on. The answer was nothing, as she had been relieved to discover. With the music pounding in the little hotel bar, that life felt very far away.

'Kate?' Morag broke through her thoughts, leaning in to be heard over the pounding music of the disco. 'You're away in a dream – oh, here's Roddy.'

'I wasn't sure which you'd prefer, so I got a couple of everything.' Placing a clinking tray of drinks on the table, he leaned down, kissing Morag on the cheek. 'Hello, you. You can all take your pick.'

He sat down opposite them, long legs folding underneath the tiny bar table. He handed a whisky to Ted, taking one for himself and nodding a silent toast.

Kate reached forward, helping herself to a glass of whisky. The first one, before the fireworks, had filled her with a warm glow. Whisky was definitely growing on her. Ted smiled at her approvingly. 'I do like a woman who enjoys a good single malt. And a beautiful one, at that.' Ted smiled at Roddy, half-raising a sly eyebrow. 'Does she not look lovely tonight?'

Ted and Morag were looking between her and Roderick with expectation.

'She scrubs up pretty well, considering I'm used to seeing her in jeans and a fleece.' Roderick looked a little awkward, avoiding Kate's eye. Morag shot Ted a half-smile, raising an eyebrow.

The music ended, and the DJ beckoned Roderick over.

'He's a good boy, that one.' Ted nodded towards the little makeshift podium where Roderick was now deep in conversation with the guy behind the speakers.

'They both are. Finn's a handful, mind you. You'll find out for yourself soon enough, Kate.'

Kate followed Ted's gaze, flushing slightly when Roderick and the DJ both looked up at the same time, looking directly at her. The DJ, who had the same cheeky expression as a young Ewan McGregor, raised one eyebrow and said something to Roderick, who recoiled slightly, shaking his head as his friend nodded, and laughing.

'Right then, you lot,' boomed the DJ's voice through the loudspeaker. 'So we've got a new girl here tonight.'

Roderick looked over at her with an apologetic expression. What on earth was he up to?

'Time to show Kate from England what we can do.' The voice began again. 'Anyone up for a wee bit of a whirl round the dance floor? One for the oldies now, but you can join in if you went to Kilmannan Academy and remember the steps from Scottish country-dance lessons with Mrs Duff . . .'

And with that, the bagpipe music had started and the room, full of Scottish people on their third drink, inhibitions lowered, was a whirl of laughter. Ted and Morag were up, marching their way round the dance floor, and Kate was alone again, but this time with curious eyes upon her as she sat, pretending to look at her phone, at the table.

'I'm *so* sorry, Kate.' Appearing through the melee, Roderick sat down beside her. 'It's Finn – he's another one who's unstoppable with a microphone in his hand.'

'It's fine.' It wasn't, and she really wanted to disappear.

'He was trying to make you feel at home. He's a bit like a Labrador puppy, he tends to bounce over everyone.' Roderick put a reassuring hand on her knee, then pulled it away almost instantly as if she was red-hot. 'Sorry.' He shifted sideways in his chair, taking a gulp of his drink.

'It's okay – I just hadn't expected to have the entire room sizing me up as the new girl. Some of those women make Sandra look downright friendly.'

'Ah, yes. I know islanders have a reputation for being warm and open, and all that – but there's a few of them who've got a bit of an axe to grind with me.'

'Really?' She couldn't keep the surprise from her voice. He might be the laird of the island, and have long sweeping eyelashes, and Slavic cheekbones above dark stubble, and – hang on, that was the whisky talking –

he might be all those things, but he didn't strike her as being the island Lothario.

'It's a long story. Not for tonight.' He closed down the conversation with a distinct edge to his voice, a muscle twitching in his jaw. He glanced involuntarily towards the bar and the portrait of Sandra's identikit daughter.

At a loss for something to do, Kate took an eye-wateringly huge swig of her whisky. The resultant coughing fit, complete with nostrils flaring and a feeling that her head was going to fall off, was enough to take her mind off the conversation.

'Anyway,' Roderick handed her a glass of water, looking both amused and concerned, 'I came over to ask if you'd like to join me for a dance. Morag and Ted won't get off our backs until we do.'

Accidentally inhaling the second glass of whisky had worked wonders – and she'd already made herself look like an idiot. She was practically blowing steam out of her nostrils. 'Oh, go on then. Why not?'

'If you want a lift home, Ted's got the van. He's taking everyone from the estate. It'll be a bit of a squash, mind, and highly illegal.'

Standing at the sink in the hotel toilets, Kate looked up as Morag's head appeared round the door. It was the end of a long night, her head was spinning and while she felt half-envious of the gang that she'd heard planning to head into Kilmannan for an impromptu house-party, she was secretly looking forward to a huge glass of water and bed.

'That would be lovely. Just give me two minutes.'

Kate splashed her scarlet face once more with cold water. She was baking hot, after dancing for what felt like hours. It had been surprising to see Roderick helpless with laughter, as Morag, Ted and eventually Jean fruitlessly attempted to teach her an Eightsome Reel. It was a dance designed to confuse anyone who didn't have Scottish blood in their veins.

Passing a gang of revellers who were still going strong, she climbed up the staircase to find her things. The room was deserted now, and she grabbed her bag from the back of the wardrobe where she'd stashed it, out of sight. Almost all of the coats, fleeces and boots had gone, with a slightly unsteady-on-the-feet stream of people walking down the road into the town of Kilmannan. She walked down the stairs, looking through the window of the lounge, spotting Bruno, Murdo and Ted deep in conversation by the bar, Murdo polishing glasses, never off-duty.

She heard a metallic slither and a chink, and looked down. Her silver bracelet had fallen off. Not surprising, given the amount of whirling about I've done tonight, she thought, bending down to pick it up from the tartan carpet in the hotel lobby. Straightening up, she didn't notice Roderick open the hidden door in front of her.

'Oof!' She walked right into him and looked up, ready

to make a joke. He took her wrist, pulling her gently into the tiny, firelit room. Pushing the door shut, he turned, facing her. He took in a breath, not saying a word for a long moment. He was so close that she could feel the heat of his body. He lifted his hand and traced her jawbone with his finger. Kate's heart was pounding. He tipped up her chin, gently. He was looking directly into her eyes and her legs were going to give way. She bit her lower lip, trying to steady herself.

Roderick's mouth was almost on hers. He caught a curl of her hair that had broken free, tucking it behind her ear. He kissed her gently, pulled back and looked at her.

'I've wanted to do that all evening.'

And then he kissed her again, and this time her hands were wrapping around his back, feeling the muscles beneath the shirt, her heart still thumping, pulling him closer, feeling his body pushing against hers. Fingers were tangled in her hair, the wood-panelled wall was pressing into her back—

'Put her down!'

They pulled apart with a start. Bruno had burst into the room, sizing up the scene with a burst of laughter.

'Yer carriage is here, Cinderella.' He gave an enormous wink. 'That's if ye still want a lift home?'

'Oh – yes.' Kate took a step sideways and straightened her top, her legs still decidedly wobbly. 'Yes, that would probably be a good thing.'

Roderick caught her eye. He ran his hand through

his hair, leaving it sticking up untidily. His eyes were glittering, and he was slightly out of breath.

'Indeed,' Bruno remarked, looking at Roderick.

The journey home, crammed like sardines in the van, was awkward. Roderick sat opposite, making polite conversation with Morag. Every time they went over a pothole, his knee touched hers and she felt a spark of what she realized, worryingly, was lust. For her boss.

Oh God. Oh God, oh God, oh God!

Have just had accidental snog with Prince Charming.
Oops!

Back in the cottage, having been walked home by an unknowing and solicitous Ted, she lay in bed with her phone. It was 3 a.m. and she had been lying awake for the last hour, half-hoping that Roderick would bang on the door in a masterful manner, then remembering that she was supposed to be having a year off men.

But that kiss. She sighed, remembering, and switched off the light.

The room flashed brightly for a second as her phone beeped, disturbing her:

What happened to Mrs No-Men-for-a-Year-I'm-Wearing-a-Chastity-Belt? Need details but it's the middle of the night!
Call me tomorrow. Em x

6

The Secret

'It's a terrible shame.' Jean's voice carried through from the kitchen as Kate floated into Duntarvie House. Jean put down the telephone and sat heavily at the table. Her face was grim.

'What is?' asked Kate. She looked around, half-hoping to see Roderick, half-dreading the sight of his face.

'There's been heavy rain in Oxfordshire for days now. The river burst its banks last night. Oak House is in a terrible state, apparently.'

'The Maxwells' family house?' A wave of disappointment hit her. She already knew the answer before she asked. 'Where's Roderick?'

'He's gone . . .' Jean waved her arm distractedly in the direction of the sea, sifting through some paperwork, searching for something. 'Caught the first boat off the island this morning when he got the call.'

'Oh.' Kate felt herself come down to earth with a thud.

'He's left instructions that I've to help you wherever

I can. You're really just chasing up decorators and ordering furniture now, though, aren't you?' Jean gathered the paperwork, which had been left strewn across the table, probably by Roderick as he scrabbled to get the problem sorted. She placed it back in a green file entitled 'Paperwork: England'.

'Something like that,' replied Kate vaguely. 'I'll be fine.' A small sigh escaped her, unbidden. There was a tiny and deliciously illogical part of her mind that had played and replayed the kiss as she lay in bed that morning; and while she stood under the shower until the hot water ran out; and again as she walked down the estate road to the big house. Kate had been surprised by her response to Roderick. She'd spent so long convincing herself – and everyone – that she was having a year off from men. Now she was here, having been kissed very thoroughly, and he was halfway to England. Typical.

She watched in silence as Jean comforted herself with the familiar ritual of making tea, rinsing out the pot with scalding water, adding the leaves, covering the pot.

'So how long do you think Roderick will be away?' She was trying to keep her voice level, fiddling with teaspoons and folding napkins.

'Well, as you know, Oak House is rented out, and has been since his mother died, and he hasn't been back there since.' Jean poured out the tea, adding milk. 'So he'll maybe have some sorting-out to do. It's time he got it done, really.'

'He hasn't been back? Not once?'

'Never.' She passed a mug across the table. 'It was certainly too hard for his father, and I think as time went on, Roderick found it easier to forget about the house and what happened there.'

Warming her hands on the mug, Kate looked at Jean, wondering if it was safe to ask.

'What was she like, his mother?'

'Annabel?' Jean stood up, cup in hand, motioning for Kate to follow her. She passed through a second door in the kitchen into what Kate had always assumed was a pantry.

In all the time that she'd been on the island she'd never seen around the whole of Duntarvie House. The promised tour had never happened after she hurt her shoulder, and she'd settled into a routine of working at the old oak desk in the sitting room, where there was a phone, a computer and a view across the gardens and down to the sea. It suited her to work in there, where the fire was always lit and Jean was close at hand, ready with a pot of tea and a bit of a chat. Roderick would wander in and out, often working on the sofa, legs stretched out, dogs at his feet.

The rest of the house was still a mystery to her, and she didn't feel comfortable asking for a chance to look around it alone – besides, she was still a bit freaked out by the idea of all those spooky old rooms covered with dust sheets, full of memories.

It wasn't a pantry, however, but a wood-panelled

corridor, and Jean opened another door. Inside was a library, packed on all sides from floor to ceiling. Kate gasped. She could lose herself for weeks in here. It had a delicious, musty, old-book smell, and there was a fireplace beside which was a huge, comfortable leather armchair and a window that looked out across the gardens of Duntarvie House. There was a proper, huge, old-fashioned mahogany desk, complete with a brass desk lamp, a leather blotter and a beautiful leather office chair.

Jean took a key from a pot on a shelf, unlocked a long drawer and pulled it open. Inside lay a stack of enlarged black-and-white photos, obviously taken by a professional, now browning and curled at the edges.

'Here she is, look.' She lifted up a photograph, handing it to Kate.

The woman in the photograph had long, smooth, pale-blonde hair. She was wearing a straw hat and a strapless sundress. She was probably in her mid-thirties, with the bone structure of a model. She was looking sideways at the camera, a cat-like smile playing at her lips, her eyes sparkling with mischief. She looked as if she could be a handful, Kate thought.

'She's beautiful,' she said. 'But why are all her photographs kept in a drawer?'

'I think it was too painful for James, Roderick's father, to remember.' Jean shook her head, lips pursed. 'He burnt every photograph he had of her. These are the only ones that survive.'

Kate thought of her own mother, and of the countless framed photographs that lined the walls of their pink cottage in Saffron Walden. Her mum had never remarried following her father's death.

'There is nobody who comes close to your father,' her mother would say, briskly, whenever the subject was raised. Kate had given up asking now, and it was clear that her charities, her part-time library job and her friendships were enough.

'He must have been devastated.'

'Och no, Kate.' Leaning forward conspiratorially, looking around the empty room as if expecting ghosts to appear and chastise her for speaking out of turn, Jean explained. 'He was furious. Roderick's mother was with another man when she died.'

'I thought she fell down the stairs at home?'

'She did.' Jean raised her eyebrows. 'But she wasn't on her own when it happened. She'd been having an affair with the Right Honourable Ivar Cornwall.'

'The MP?' Kate was astounded. He was renowned for his dedication to family life. Having come late to parenthood with his first daughter at the age of forty-one, he was notoriously outspoken on the need for politicians to lead by example. He was photographed regularly with his much-younger wife, their five beautiful golden-haired children and numerous dogs, outside his family house near Oxford.

'The very one.' Jean took the photograph. 'He was

there when it happened. It was all hushed up. Money can buy a way out of most problems.'

'My God!' Kate was horrified. 'Does Roderick know?'

'He does now, yes. He found these photographs and some letters locked in a drawer, and confronted his father. For a long time he was a very angry young man.'

'So that's why they moved up here to Auchenmor,' mused Kate. 'To escape from all of it.'

'That's right. His father had been good friends with Ivar Cornwall, and they moved in the same circles. It would have been too painful. After the funeral they upped and left.'

Kate was intrigued. 'I can't believe he just walked away from everything.'

'Aye, but the Maxwells have a stubborn streak, right enough.' Jean closed the library door behind them and they walked back to the kitchen.

Kate gulped down the cold remains of her tea and popped her mug in the dishwasher. Billy would be waiting for her up at the cottages. 'I'll see you later, Jean. And don't worry, I won't breathe a word.'

On the west coast of the island the sky was a vibrant blue. Kate was sitting on a rock, watching the seals, and trying not to think about Roderick and the kiss. She was failing miserably. Picking up a handful of stones, she threw them across the beach, startling a flock of sea-gulls, which soared, squawking, into the sky. It had been stupid to kiss him, or to let herself be kissed by him:

she wasn't quite sure which it had been. A bit of both, she supposed. But now she was sitting on a rock on what was effectively *his* island, feeling like an idiot.

She felt her phone vibrate before it began to ring. Pulling it out of her pocket, she looked down and felt her stomach falling to the floor.

Roderick.

Oh, help. Oh God. Oh no!

'Hello.' Her voice came out as an unappealing squeak.

'Kate.'

Oh God. Oh, help. 'Hello.'

'Sorry, I don't have long. I gather Jean's told you what's happened.' His voice was clipped and brusque, and he sounded very far away.

She closed her eyes, feeling a blush spread from her forehead to her toes and back again.

'She has,' she replied. Come on, she thought, sort yourself out. If he can do business-like, so can you. 'I've been to the cottages today, and the glaziers are in.'

'Great.' He sounded more like himself. 'Can I leave you to sort out the barn with Billy?'

'That's fine. I took a call this morning.' She couldn't help herself, she was smiling. 'And guess what? I've got a booking for the big cottage over Christmas and New Year.'

'Really?'

She could hear a smile in his voice.

'That's amazing. Well done, Kate, you're doing a wonderful job.'

Thanks, thought Kate, but now you're talking to me like an employee, and last night you had me up against a wall. A thrill of excitement shot from her toes up through her whole body before she gathered herself.

'Kate? This line is terrible. I can't hear you at all.'

'Sorry. I mean, thank you. I'm glad you're pleased.' The conversation was painfully stilted. 'Anyway, if everything goes to plan, the cottages will easily be finished by then. The tiler from the mainland is doing the kitchen tomorrow.'

'Perfect. Right then, if you've got everything under control, I'm going to go,' he said. 'It sounds like you don't need me, so I'll be in touch once I've got Oak House sorted.'

His voice was cool and distracted. He obviously had no plans to mention anything at all. It was pretty clear how Roderick planned to handle last night.

'Take care, Kate. I've told Jean to keep you on the straight and narrow.'

'How long will—' she started the sentence, but he was gone. She closed her eyes in horror and despair, and sat on the rock until long after the sun had set.

At home Willow, irate at having been left alone for three hours, had eaten half of Kate's iPod. Retrieving the tangled mess of wire and plastic from the dog bed, Kate didn't have the heart to tell her off. She grabbed her lead and a torch and set off into the darkness to walk the puppy.

*

'Aha, a wanderer in the night.'

Kate heard Ted's voice before she saw him. 'Bloody hell! You made me jump.'

'Bit late for a dog-walk, isn't it?'

'She ate my iPod. I spent three hours sitting on a stone at Selkie Bay wondering how I ended up here, and when I got home she'd weed on the floor in disgust and taken it out on my iPod.'

'Come on, you.' Ted whistled to his dogs, which came hurtling up, panting, with Willow orbiting them in excitement, a blur of ears and fur. 'Morag's got the kettle on, and she's been baking. You look like you could do with a piece of cake.'

He put an arm around her, and they trudged round the corner to the stable yard. The security lights flashed on automatically. With a groan and a clatter of hooves, Thor appeared at his stable door, eyes blinking in the unexpected light, silver forelock festooned with wood shavings.

'I'll take the dogs in. Someone's got up just to see you – go and say hello.' Ted took Willow's lead out of Kate's hand, leaving her alone in the yard.

Thor whickered at her. She reached for his velvety muzzle, cupping it gently in her hand. He nudged her, his big head swinging forward, then reached down, whiffling her pockets, hoping for treats. She pulled out a packet of mints, and he took one gently from her outstretched palm. Burying her face in his neck, curling her arms into his long, thick mane, Kate recalled

143

that life as a pony-mad teenager had been a lot less complicated.

'I'm sticking to horses from now on,' she muttered into his long mane.

'Kettle's boiled,' called Ted through the kitchen window.

Inside Morag had laid the table with tea, cake, scones and home-made jam. She patted the bench, inviting Kate to join her.

'So, I hear you had a good time at the fireworks last night?' asked Morag guilelessly.

'Lovely,' Kate took a sip of tea, and choked. It was boiling hot. 'Nice to see the islanders letting their hair down.'

'Indeed it was. And you young ones had a good time, by all accounts?'

'It was fun, yes.'

There was an elephant in the room, and Kate was trying to ignore it. Morag stared at Ted pointedly, eyebrows raised over her reading glasses. He looked back at her, puzzled, before glancing at Kate with a little 'Oh' of understanding.

'D'you know,' he said casually, 'I might take this into the sitting room. I'd like to catch the evening news.' He ambled out, newspaper under one arm, glasses tucked into his shirt pocket, cup of tea in hand.

'So here we are then.' Kate leaned down to stroke Willow, avoiding Morag's eye. The elephant marched across the room and sat down beside her on the bench.

'A wee bird tells me that you and Master Roderick were caught in a compromising position?'

'Oh God!' Kate looked up at Morag, her face screwed up in embarrassment. 'Is Bruno going to tell the entire island? I don't think I can bear it if he does. I feel like such a fool.'

'Hush yourself.' Morag covered Kate's hand with her own, and looked into her eyes. 'Bruno mentioned it to me because he suspected I'd be the one left picking up the pieces.'

Kate pulled her hand away, suddenly rigid. 'Really? Is Roderick in the habit of kissing girls and then pretending it didn't happen?'

'Not exactly, no,' said Morag opaquely.

Kate frowned at her.

'But once in a while he chooses to exercise his *droit de seigneur*?'

'The Lord of the Manor's right to sleep with whom he chooses?' Morag chuckled, a sudden shout of laughter, which startled the sleeping Willow. 'Lord, no – that's not Roddy at all.' She reached over, slicing a scone and buttering it thoughtfully. 'He *was* in a relationship. They broke up about six months ago.'

Kate waited as Morag chewed and swallowed.

'There was never any chance of it going anywhere. Everyone – well, almost everyone – who knew them could see they were ill-matched.'

'Huh!' snorted Kate. 'Was her blood not blue enough?'

Morag smiled. 'Nothing like that. Fiona and Roddy had known each other all their lives, like most of the young people on this island. After his father died he was a lost soul. I don't think it took much for him to be railroaded into a relationship.'

'And then he dumped her, once he'd had enough?' Putting two and two together, Kate was seeing another side to Roderick, one she didn't much like.

'Now, Kate, that's unfair,' Morag chided. 'Fiona is more than capable of fighting her own corner. She worked her way in no time from writing a schoolgirl's column in the *Auchenmor Argus* to editor of the paper. She was spotted as a rising star and offered a job on one of the big papers in Glasgow. She worked her way up pretty fast, but Fiona doesn't take any prisoners.'

'And Roderick wouldn't go with her?'

'So I believe. But I think he saw it as a lucky escape. Our Fiona was always a bit of a madam, but working as a journalist has brought out the worst in her.' Morag looked disapproving.

'In what way?'

'Och, nothing I can put a finger on. But she'd step on her own granny to get to a story.'

Kate managed a laugh at the image. 'Well, as nobody knows about my little incident with Roderick, and he seems to be determined to pretend it didn't happen, I'm just going to forget it. I'm supposed to be having a year off men.' Her words sounded a lot more convincing than they felt. Remembering his words in her ear, it was difficult to believe it had meant nothing to him. But he was so mercurial in temperament.

'Mmm. I don't know about you, but as soon as I mention the word "diet",' Morag looked down at her slim horsewoman's hips and completely flat stomach, 'I find myself with my nose in the biscuit tin.'

'Point taken,' laughed Kate. 'Maybe I'll just swear off accidental kisses with people at parties.'

'Ooh, no.' Morag shook a finger, jokingly. 'I want to hear of lots of accidental kisses in secret corners. You're young, and you need to be having fun.'

'I promise.' Watching her expression, Kate sensed that Morag could see straight through her false conviction.

'You need to go have some fun, Kate. Don't worry yourself pining after Roderick, if he's not here. There's been enough pining over Maxwell men, if you ask me.'

Suddenly feeling the effects of a late night, Kate yawned. Morag stood up, gathering dogs, and saw her home.

7

On a Mission

Oh God, my idea of hell is a dinner party. Kate put down her mobile and let out a wail. Willow, who was gnawing companionably on a seaside spade, jumped up into her lap.

She was trying desperately to pin up her hair, but it was slipping, too clean, out of the clips. She rammed in another five, wincing as she jabbed herself in the scalp. That would have to do. Picking up a bottle of dark nail varnish, she painted her nails, hiding the crescents of paint from her DIY efforts.

Sitting on the bed waiting for the varnish to dry, her thoughts turned to Roderick. In the three weeks since he left the island, Kate had spoken to him only a handful of times. He was preoccupied, dealing with the effects of the flood, and their conversations had been brief. Between them, Kate and Jean had organized Billy and his companions, until the cottages were ahead of schedule.

'It's a right mess down there,' Jean had explained. 'I spoke to him yesterday evening – they can't do anything without permission from the relevant authorities, because Oak House is a listed building.'

'Will he be gone much longer?' Kate had tried to sound casual.

'A good while, I think,' Jean had glanced up sharply, hearing the tone of Kate's voice.

Plenty of time to forget about a slightly tipsy kiss. That's if he even remembered it in the first place, Kate suddenly realized with relief.

Unsure of what to wear tonight, she'd received a flurry of texts from Emma, full of helpful links to websites selling farmers' overalls and green wellies. In the end Kate had taken her first trip off the island, venturing into Glasgow. The noise of the traffic, the lights, the people everywhere – she'd only been gone a couple of months and already life on the mainland seemed chaotic, noisy and over-rated. Sitting in a packed cafe, drinking a disgusting latte that bore no relation to Bruno's coffee, Kate had realized she was desperate to get back.

Back at the cottage, nails now dry, she pulled on the dress. It was beautiful: dark-grey lace, with a deep V-neckline. Kate tugged at the hem, convinced it had been longer in the shop. She wiggled her toes, admiring the sheen of her legs, encased for once not in jeans or leggings, but sheer black tights. She picked up her very high, very expensive and completely impractical black suede shoes, giving herself one last look in the mirror.

'Not bad. Shame there's nobody to notice it,' she

remarked to Willow. The puppy paused from her chewing and thumped her tail appreciatively.

'Right, let's get you downstairs.'

Stopping to grab a bottle of wine from the fridge, Kate didn't notice that she'd left her shoes lying on the kitchen floor. Settling Willow in her basket with a raw-hide chew bone, she grabbed her handbag, stuffing in the box of chocolates and bottle of wine she'd chosen, and slipped her feet into wellington boots to walk up to Morag's house.

Thor was hanging out of his stable longingly. Kate blew him a kiss.

'Good look!' laughed Tom, opening the door to Stable Cottage. Just inside the hall, taking off his Barbour jacket, was a tall, burly, strangely familiar man. Kate wondered if there was something in the water on the island that made them all so bloody good-looking.

'I'm not keeping the wellies on. Give me a second to change my – oh God, my shoes!' Kate started to laugh. 'I've left them at the cottage. I can't spend the evening in stockinged feet.'

'Did someone mention stockings?'

'Oh, for goodness' sake, Finn, we can't take you anywhere.' Tom turned to the man behind him, punching him on the arm. 'Kate, this is Finn. Finn – Kate.'

The burly stranger stepped forward, leaning down and kissing her, his fair stubbled cheek smelling of bonfires and cold winter air. He was wearing a faded blue shirt, which, Kate noticed, matched his eyes.

'He's jealous because I've got all the lines, and now that he's an old married man he's lost his touch.'

'Bugger off,' laughed Tom. 'Make yourself useful, Finn. Nip down to Kate's house – she's in Bruar Cottage – and get her shoes while I pour her a drink.'

Finn turned to Kate, holding out his hand. 'Of course I will. Do you have the keys?'

Kate pulled them out of her bag and then paused for a second, her hand in mid-air.

'Earth to Kate?' Finn looked at her, quizzically.

'I'll go.' In the split second it had taken to retrieve the keys, a vision of her bedroom had flashed in front of Kate's eyes. The chair was covered in a mountain of clothes, the bed was unmade, hairdryer and straightener wires snarled in a tangle, and the contents of her make-up bag were strewn across the floor.

'You're not walking down there in the dark on your own.'

'I just walked up on my own,' she pointed out reasonably, but Finn had already shrugged on his coat. He held out her waterproof jacket. Fastening it, she caught him looking down. It hung as low as the hem of her dress. She looked like a deranged bucolic flasher. In tights.

'Tom was right. It *is* a good look.' Holding open the door, Finn flashed her a grin, eyes crinkling at the corners. 'Hold my arm, I'll keep you safe.'

There was no moon, but Finn clearly knew the road well. Kate had stumbled several times on the way up, even with the aid of her torch.

'You're settling in then?' She definitely recognized him from somewhere, but couldn't place him. His accent was beautiful, and it seemed to resonate somewhere just below her navel.

'I am. It's beautiful here – oops!' Kate lurched sideways, almost falling into another pothole, but Finn had caught her. His arms were solid with muscle. Not, thought Kate, that she was noticing. And she was definitely ignoring the fact that he'd now slipped a casual arm around her waist. He seemed remarkably comfortable in his own skin.

'I didn't get a chance to say hello at the bonfire. I had my hands full.'

Ah, that was why he was familiar. He was the piper who had played at the fireworks, and then afterwards spent the evening behind the decks of the disco, with a crowd of girls gathered around him. Not surprisingly, she thought, because not only was he ridiculously handsome, but his turn at the disco had shown him to have a nice line in self-deprecating humour.

'Here we are,' he broke into her musings. He took her hand, gently untangling the keys from her icy fingers. 'Your hands are freezing.'

'Stay here in the hall,' said Kate, kicking a pile of non-specific stuff under the chair with a practised foot. She opened the kitchen door. 'Shit!'

'What's happened?' Finn was at her side in a second. He looked down and roared with laughter.

Willow was lying upside down, fast asleep, one expensive suede shoe in her bed and the gnawed remains of the other strewn across the floor.

'Stockings it is then,' said Finn innocently, turning to her with a wink.

God, he was gorgeous. If she'd been Susan, she would probably have reached up, snogged him and dragged him into the sitting room, but that wasn't exactly Kate's style. Oh no, she thought, much better to be picked up by her employer, snogged in a moment of passion, then discarded and forgotten about. She narrowed her eyes, thinking of Roderick. He was clearly determined to pretend that nothing had happened. Perhaps she should take a leaf out of his book. She retrieved what was left of the shoes, put them into the bin and rescued her flat silver pumps from the cupboard in the hall.

Finn was remarkably easy company. They walked back up to the cottage together, chatting about his part-time job at the Duntarvie estate wood-yard and how it funded his true love, which was sculpture.

'So the wooden carvings in the big house – they're yours?'

'They are. When I finished art school I came back here. Roddy's dad bought my first few works, and did a lot off the island to publicize my work. He was a good man, James.'

They opened the door into the hall.

'We don't know if anything went on between her and Roddy.' Tom's voice carried through from the open door of the kitchen. Kate felt herself blushing in horror. 'And even if it did, he's not here, and Kate looks to me like she could do with a—'

'Lovely walk in the fresh air with her local artist?' Finn called through from the hall, giving her a wink. Kate shuffled off her wellington boots and slipped on her silver pumps. Finn took her coat and hung it with his own on a peg in the hall, before guiding her, a warm hand on her hip, into the room.

'That,' said Ted, pouring them both a glass of wine, 'is precisely what we were about to say.'

Leaving Morag, large glass of white in hand, chatting to Susan and stirring some risotto in the kitchen, Ted rounded up the dinner guests and sent them into the dining room. Four people were already sitting down, chatting comfortably.

'Kate, you know Helen and George from the end cottage.'

Kate had bumped into the gentle, quiet Helen a few times, when out walking Willow. She was a florist with her own little shop in town, and had a beautiful cottage garden, which somehow managed to look immaculate, even in depressingly brown November. She stood up, kissing Kate warmly on the cheek.

'Lovely to have a chance to talk without your mad puppy dashing off.'

'I know – she's worse than wee Jamie. She's like an unguided missile.'

George, Helen's husband, ran the fishery, and was Bruno's football-loving partner in crime. Kate had met him several times in the cafe; he jumped up, kissing her on the cheek. He gave Finn a knowing nod.

'You've got yourself a date for tonight then, Finn?'

'I can but hope, George.' His tone was self-deprecating but humorous. He gave her a wink. 'You're blushing, Kate.'

'I'm not,' she lied.

Finn moved in, his mouth close to her ear. 'I'll have to try a bit harder then.'

That voice. In a split second she could hear Emma saying, 'Go on then, do it.' She hid her smirk behind her hand. Finn's straightforward flirting seemed to be contagious.

'And this is Michael,' continued Ted, bringing her back to earth. 'He lives in Kilmannan and owns the IT company up on the hill. This is his wife Georgia: she's English as well.'

'We can compare notes,' said Georgia, 'on island time, and the weird sense of humour, and learning to love whisky, and living in a place where the supermarket runs out of bags because the boat can't get over because of the storms.'

A smile of complicity passed between them. Georgia reminded her of friends back home, and it put Kate at her ease.

'And not having a cinema, and the pub opening whenever it wants, and everyone knowing what you're up to, *all* the time,' added Kate. 'And people assuming you'll have loads in common with someone, just because they're

English, too.' The words tumbled out with a sense of relief. She hadn't realized until now that she'd been holding her breath, watching her step, especially since the night of the fireworks. Much as she was growing to love the island, it was lovely to feel that someone understood just where she was coming from. Coffee and cake with Georgia once in a while might help keep her feet on the ground.

Ted gave her a gentle poke in the ribs. 'Come on, you, it's not that bad. We did our stint living down south, remember.'

'Oh, I know.' Kate felt a sudden pang for Cambridge, the familiar cobbled streets and the shops, and the heaps of bicycles stacked against every railing. She sipped her wine, musing. 'It's just: *everything* here is so different.'

Georgia rolled her eyes. 'It's that fish-out-of-water thing, isn't it? You're always slightly on your guard, never quite getting a handle on the island customs. Depends on how long you're staying, but it does get easier.'

Half-listening to Ted, Kate sat, deep in thought. She'd vowed she'd stay at least six months. With Roderick gone, that seemed feasible. But he was so changeable, and she had no idea what the atmosphere would be like when – or if – he returned. He might decide to stay down there.

'It's worse for me, Kate.' She shook herself out of her reverie, hearing her name. Georgia was leaning over, topping up her wine glass. 'I'm the head teacher of the secondary school, so I'm always on my best behaviour. The only chance I have to misbehave is when I'm out here in the sticks.'

'Well, here's to being naughty when nobody's looking,' said Kate, clinking her glass against Georgia's.

Finn raised his eyebrows at the two women, but said nothing.

'Oh yes? This night's getting interesting already.' Ted pulled out a chair at the huge mahogany table. It was set beautifully with old silver tableware mixed with bone china, and with a huge, low floral centrepiece, created by Helen.

It was amazing, Kate thought later, as she ricocheted gently against the doorframe on the way to the loo, how easy everyone was to talk to after some wine. Maybe it was having a bit of English moral support in Georgia, or being in a smaller gathering, but she felt this time she wasn't sitting on the sidelines, but was a real member of the group. The contrast between this and her memory of sitting awkwardly at the table on the night of the fire-works was huge. The only awkward part was the fact that every time she looked at Finn she was overwhelmed by an urge to rip off all his clothes in a most un-Kate-like manner.

Texting from the loo . . . Have had wine, and am thinking I might be a Bad Girl tonight. Just, you know, as a sort of scientific experiment?

157

They'd made their way through to the sitting room, where a fire was lit and two huge white sofas faced each other. Ted had already collapsed into one and was snoring gently.

'Every bloody time,' sighed Morag, tucking a crocheted blanket around him and pulling off his shoes. 'That'll be him for the night. I apologize in advance for the snores.'

The door slammed. Susan and Tom had sloped off home to take advantage of a child-free evening. Helen was curled up on the sofa next to Finn, chatting to Georgia about funding for the arts on the island. The other men had disappeared outside to look at a new greenhouse.

Kate sat down on the only remaining patch of sofa, which was unexpectedly low. She landed perilously close to Finn, her thigh touching his.

'Hello.'

Oh, he could read the ingredients on a cereal packet and make it sound filthy.

'D'you want a bit more wine?' he asked, stretching forward for the bottle, shirt riding up to reveal a smooth, tanned back.

'Actually, no.' She was tempted to reach up inside the shirt. 'I think maybe I should go. I need to let Willow out.' She started to haul herself out of the depths of the sofa.

He stood up. 'I'll take you home.'

Kate climbed out of the couch and tugged at the hem of her dress, which had ridden up to show rather too much thigh.

'Thanks, Morag.' He smiled. 'I'll see you in a bit.'

'I'll leave the door unlocked then.'

Kate looked at him, eyebrows raised.

'I'm staying with Morag tonight – there's no way I'll get a taxi at this time. They never come out here to the estate, if they can help it.'

As they stepped out into the cold, he reached for her hand.

'I don't want you falling over, now.'

His fingers laced in between hers, and she felt the edge of his thumb gently rubbing her palm. But he said nothing. They walked in silence.

They arrived at the cottage. Kate untangled her fingers, turned to face him and stood, hand on the door.

'Would you like some coffee?'

She sounded ridiculous. She wasn't very good at this.

'I thought a sophisticated town girl like you would have better lines than that,' said Finn, his mouth curling into a smile.

'I'm not in the habit of this sort of thing,' replied Kate. 'But I keep telling myself: you only live once. And I'm not looking for anything serious, because I'm not interested in a relationship.'

'Just as well.' He raised an eyebrow.

'Okay.' Kate gave a small smile, looking up at him.

He was awfully like a young Ewan McGregor, and the wine had given her courage and . . .

He reached across, moving a strand of hair from her lips, tucking it behind her ear with a practised gesture. 'Are you flirting with me?'

'I don't know. Am I?'

'I'd say so.' Finn took the keys from her hand and opened the door.

She let Willow out, watching silently from the front door as the puppy galloped around the garden, barking with excitement.

'I'll put the kettle on then, shall I?' Finn called from the kitchen. 'For coffee?'

Willow bounded back up, holding a rubber chew. She hurtled into the kitchen. Kate closed the door and stood in the darkened hall, heart pounding, wondering what she was doing. Being human, she decided. Doing what everyone else had been doing while she was slowly dying of boredom for the last five years.

Finn emerged from the sitting room. 'I've lit the fire. And your coffee is waiting.' He walked forward into the dark hall. 'I can leave, if you want,' he said gently.

Now or never, Kate thought.

'I don't want.' She dropped the keys on the table. He was standing right in front of her. She reached up with one hand, feeling the stubble on his cheek.

He leaned down. With his mouth millimetres away from hers, he spoke.

'Kate.'

She could feel his breath on her face.

'Yes?'

Finn's mouth curled into a smile. 'Are you flirting with me again?'

Her hands were on his hips, catching at the belt hooks, pulling him towards her, reaching into his shirt, pulling it free from his jeans.

He pulled back, breathing fast. His expression was teasing. 'I think you might be, you know.'

As he reached behind her head, the remaining clips gave way as he tangled his fingers in her hair, tipping her head back gently. He bent, kissing either side of her mouth – two unexpectedly gentle kisses, which left her with goosebumps.

'Come with me.' He took her hand, pulling her through the darkened hall and into the room. As he passed the kitchen, he pulled the door closed on Willow, winking at Kate as he did so. 'Now sit here.' He pulled her down onto the couch.

Somehow she was unfastening his shirt buttons, her eyes not moving from his, running her finger along the smooth line of hair that led down from his navel.

'You are definitely flirting.' His voice sounded breathy.

Kate felt rather pleased with herself. 'I am, aren't I?'

He ran his finger along her jawline, reminding her of Bonfire Night and Roderick. She took a sharp intake of breath. 'I can't do this.'

'You can't?' Finn looked at her levelly, smoothing

back her hair, running his hand gently down her back.

'I shouldn't.'

'Ah. That's not quite the same as "can't".'

True. Kate thought again of her five years of being sensible, and of being unceremoniously dumped by Roderick before anything had even happened. In the flickering light of the fire she took in Finn's laughing eyes, the ruffled sandy hair, the rueful smile.

'No.' She leaned forward, unfastening the final button of his shirt. 'I suppose it isn't, is it?'

He laughed, and pulled her into his arms.

Kate's head was thumping. Willow was barking furiously at a knocking on the door. Kate pulled on her pyjama bottoms and grabbed a T-shirt. Hair flying, she ran down the stairs. She opened the kitchen door and Willow hurtled across the hall, yelping with joy. The puppy was leaping up and down with excitement as Kate fumbled with the key, her fingers as hungover as the rest of her. She pulled the stiff door open.

'Kate.'

Roderick stood there, eyes hollow with tiredness, a quarter-inch of dark shadow on his cheeks. He looked stressed, and tired, and beautiful.

Kate felt her disobedient stomach lurch with happiness.

'I've just got off the boat. I know it's early, but I thought you'd be up with Willow.'

The puppy was there, circling his feet, ecstatic with happiness and barking madly.

'At least someone is pleased to see me,' he said ruefully, leaning down to tickle her tummy.

'I am. I mean, I'm not . . . I'm just – it's just I wasn't expecting . . . ' she said.

'I shouldn't have come. I'm sorry.' He half-turned.

She caught his arm. 'No. Don't go. I just didn't expect you to appear. You didn't . . .' She wasn't sure where to begin.

'I've had a lot to sort out.' He ran his fingers through his hair. 'It's a long story. I'll explain, but not now.'

'I . . .' She stood on the doorstep, open-mouthed with horror, excitement and mortification, shivering with cold and shock in her pyjama trousers.

'I missed you, Kate.' He looked almost surprised that he'd said it out loud. He took a step forward, so close that his foot was in between hers. There was something strangely intimate about that one step. Kate looked down at their feet, not saying anything. They were so close. He looked at her mouth, then her eyes.

She looked away, flushing, suddenly flooded with embarrassment.

'Kate . . .'

He caught her chin with his finger, turning her face back so that he was looking into her eyes. His hand was shaking.

He moved a fraction closer, his glance moving slowly from her eyes to her mouth, then back again. And his mouth was only a hair's breadth from hers, and he was—

'Any chance of that coffee now, Kate?' Finn, clad only in a pair of jeans, thundered down the stairs.

Roderick stepped back as if scalded.

'Morning, Roddy,' Finn said cheerfully. 'Back on the first ferry, I see? You didn't say you were working today, Kate. That's going to be a bugger, if your hangover is anything like mine.'

Kate stood, slack-jawed, incapable of speech.

'I'm so sorry.' Roderick's voice was flat, his face instantly tight and closed. 'I had no idea you had company.'

'Dinner party up at Morag and Ted's house last night,' Finn informed him, oblivious to everything.

'Of course.'

Kate was still dumbstruck, but managed to shut her mouth.

'Kate, I'll stick the kettle on. Roddy, a quick coffee?'

'I don't think so, no.' Roderick leaned down, patting goodbye to the ecstatically squirming Willow. 'I'll leave you two to it then, shall I?'

'It's not what it looks like.' She realized, as soon as the words were out, that they sounded hollow.

'It's not up to me what it looks like,' remarked Roderick, his mouth set in a thin line. 'You're a free agent.' He straightened up, turned and stalked down the drive.

'Got any marmalade, Kate?'

She stood in the kitchen with her head in her hands. Finn was helping himself to breakfast, apparently unaware that Kate was having a minor nervous breakdown right next to him. He was actually *humming* to himself as he clattered around, opening and shutting drawers, finding teaspoons and mugs as the kettle boiled. Was he completely blind? She exhaled slowly, a huge out-breath of mortified horror, which caused him to look up.

'Toast?' He held out a slice, thickly buttered and dripping with marmalade.

'I'm not really hungry.'

'I'll have yours.' He plonked it on a tray alongside the teapot and mugs, pushing open the kitchen door with his foot. 'We can watch a bit of crap morning television, and you can stop being embarrassed.'

She followed him through to the sitting room mutely, and curled up in a corner of the sofa, huddled beneath a blanket, abject with misery.

'Bloody hell, Kate, was it that bad?' Finn passed her a mug of tea. She shook her head as he offered her sugar.

'It's hideous,' she said. 'Of all the things to happen – on a scale of one to ten for awfulness – I'd rate it about a fifteen.'

Finn pulled a face. 'I'm going to have to brush up on my technique. Maybe it's a bit too country bumpkin for a sophisticated city chick like you?'

The penny dropped and Kate burst out laughing,

despite her misery. 'Oh God, Finn. No, you were very – oh God, I've forgotten about last night.' She flushed scarlet. 'And now I'm embarrassed about that, too.'

'No need.'

'I was drunk and I tore your shirt off like a fiend.'

'Not at all. You weren't that drunk, and you did unfasten the buttons very politely.'

Oh God, oh God!

'But more to the point,' he teased, 'I was very what? Good? Amazing?'

'You were very good. It was very good. I mean, thank you for a lovely night. But oh, nooo.' Kate emitted a howl of despair, head in her hands. 'It's not that.' She plucked at the blanket. She could see Finn's mind working slowly.

'You and Roddy?'

'There isn't any me and Roddy – well, there certainly won't be now.'

'Bloody hell, Kate.' He looked at her with sudden recognition, blue eyes softening.

'I know,' she said, miserably.

Having explained the whole making-friends-having-fun-going-to-bonfire-accidental-snog scenario to Finn, Kate found she felt slightly better. Watching him flick through the channels before settling on an episode of *Friends*, she realized who he reminded her of – he was Joey. Gorgeous, well aware of the effect he had on women, but more interested in the chase than the morning after. He'd clearly had so many morning-afters that he didn't feel the slightest pang of guilt. He was like a Labrador puppy, happily bounding from one person to the next, sharing his affections.

'Well, if it's Roddy you're after, it'd be pointless working on a plot to make him realize what he's missing by snogging me,' he said, with a rueful grin. 'I think we've already covered that one.'

Kate cringed, remembering the expression on Roderick's face. Somehow she suspected he wasn't the sort to respond to that sort of game-playing, in any case.

'So what do I do?'

'Nothing at the moment. You need to carry on working, get out, have some fun, let him see you're not bothered.' Finn took a final swig of tea.

'I can't see how that'll work.'

'You're a gorgeous girl, Kate, and I'm not going to tread on anyone's toes.' Finn answered her dubious look. 'We had a great night last night, but it was a wee bit of fun. If you're serious about Roddy, you go for it.'

'You don't think he'll have written me off after this morning?' She felt a tiny glimmer of hope. Finn and Roderick had been friends since childhood – surely he had some idea how his friend thought?

'I think he's the opposite of me. There's a lot more going on under the surface. I'm more your what-you-see-is-what-you-get kind of bloke.' He stood up, stretching. 'It might surprise you to hear that I'm univer-sally regarded as being the island's agony uncle. Trust me. I know my stuff. There's not much I haven't seen.'

'Okay, I'll give you till Christmas.' Unconvinced, Kate gathered the tea things and took them back to the kitchen.

Kate wasn't working. She spent the day skulking around miserably, having a hot bath (after fixing the temperamental water heater, again), eating chocolate and watching *Bridget Jones's Diary* on DVD. It wasn't the same without Emma, and it wasn't half as much fun finding herself in the part of Bridget, with Roderick as the gorgeous Darcy. Susan was too busy juggling small people to come and keep her company, and Kate didn't have the energy to deal with an excited Jamie, who was spending all his waking hours planning his Christmas list.

For the first time since she'd been on the island, Kate felt lonely, and miserable.

> Am in cottage with only log fire and dog and DVDs for company. Cheer me up?

She hit Send, and waited for Emma's response.

> Cheer you up? What happened to your mission to be a Very Bad Girl last night?

> Bad Idea.

Kate sent the two-word response to Emma and closed her eyes, lying back on the rug by the fire.

Hello? I am stuck here with the entrails of three laptops and two squabbling children. I need to live vicariously.

Despite herself, Kate smiled.

Okay, brief summary. Ended up back here with Finn the Foxy Piper.

Aha. So why the bad idea?

Woke up in bed with Highland Adonis. But then

Willow leapt onto Kate's lap, so she accidentally sent the message.

You realized he was a woman? Come on, this is like pulling teeth.

Then the door went and it was Sir Roderick of Posh, aka Mr I'm-not-going-to-fancy-you-just-because-you-snogged-me-up-against-a-wall (am having slight problem with that).

COME on! These texts are taking way too long and I am panting with excitement, as you appear to be living in a Jilly Cooper novel.

And then Sir R of P was there, just about to snog me, clearly having realized I am a morsel of foxy gorgeousness, when lo and behold, Finn the Hot Piper appears.

SHIT!

Er, yes. In just a pair of jeans. With a big 'Yes, we did' sign above his head.

And then what? Tell me they stripped, and fought for you whilst wearing kilts and waving daggers (pant, pant)?

Er, no. Sir R of P legged it in disgust, and Finn made me breakfast. And has now decided it's his mission in life to act as matchmaker.

Obviously. OMG! Now that's cleared up, I must help Katharine with her spellings. It's all glamour round here. Call you later. Love you xxx

Kate rolled onto her back and lay for a long time, staring at the ceiling.

8

First Impressions

'So, all that's left to do is the bunkhouse.' Closing the door of the holiday cottage, Kate hugged the clipboard to her chest for comfort. The atmosphere was almost as chilly as the weather.

Having been left without Roderick's backup, she'd found herself far more involved in the cottage renovations than she'd expected. With Jean's comforting support in the background, she'd chosen colour schemes and furnishings that she would have picked, had she been decorating her own cottage from scratch. The wooden floors had been polished and the dated kitchen cupboards replaced with wooden cabinets in muted shades of grey. The trouble was that returning to her cottage, alone, was becoming less and less appealing. Where it had seemed comfortingly untidy, it now felt lonely, set apart from the cosy group of cottages up the lane. Having thrown herself into work, Kate had seen her own decorating plans fall by the wayside. She felt alone, despite her new friends, and thoughts of escaping back to Cambridge were sneaking into her mind at inopportune moments.

'Thank you, Kate,' said Roderick stiffly, jingling his car keys. 'You've done a wonderful job, hasn't she, Jean?'

'That she has.' Jean reached across and gave Kate's arm a little squeeze. 'Shall we christen it with a cup of tea? I've got everything we need in the car.'

'No, thank you,' said Roderick quickly, just as Kate's mouth was also opening to make an excuse. 'I need to get back.'

Jean looked at the two of them, but said nothing. She'd heard all about the situation with Finn. He was prone to popping in to warm himself over the Aga with a cup of tea when he was working on the estate. Typical of men, there was no atmosphere between him and Roderick, but Jean thought that Roderick was behaving like a spoilt child, expecting to put down a toy, leave it for a month, then return to find it in exactly the same place. Smiling to herself at what the ever-more independent Kate would think about being called a toy, she decided to make herself a cup of tea, even if nobody else wanted one.

Kate marched away from the house, throwing her clipboard onto the back seat of her car, and changed her shoes for wellington boots. It was a bitter December day and the wind was whipping in from the Atlantic. She wrapped her scarf round her nose and pulled on a hat.

'Sorry, darling, you can't come down to Selkie Bay, you'll be eaten alive,' she said to Willow, closing her into her dog cage.

Locking the car, she clambered over the rocks and

down onto the long, deserted beach. In the distance she could see the grey mounds. Even now she couldn't quite make out if they were stones or seals, but the familiar banana shape of one gave it away. Sitting down on a rocky ledge, she pulled her binoculars out of her pocket.

I have binoculars. It's official, thought Kate, I'm a seal nerd. She scanned the beach. Since the first day that Roderick had spent time teaching her all about the seals' behaviour, she'd loved coming to Selkie Bay with a flask of coffee, her hands warm in fingerless gloves.

A group of three seal pups were exploring a rock pool, watched from a distance by their mothers, who floated, noses above the water, in the waves. Kate watched them sniffing each other, biting and ducking. All of their play was vital, teaching the pups how to survive in the wilds of the winter sea. She sat observing them until her legs were stiff with cold and her cheeks were frozen by the wind.

As she stood to leave, slowly unfolding her legs, Kate saw something hurtling across the beach. It was a tiny dog, heading straight for a group of seals with their pups.

'Blossom! Come back here!'

Kate wheeled round, hearing a familiar voice carrying on the wind. Sandra, dressed in a pair of floral welling-tons, a very clean Barbour and a pair of immaculate moleskin trousers, was speed-walking towards her.

'Call her away from the seals – she'll scare them,' yelled Kate desperately.

'Blossom! Blossom, come here at once!' Sandra squawked, but the terrier wasn't listening. Kate was running forward onto the beach, calling the dog, groping in her pockets for the treats she used when training Willow.

'Come! Blossom, come!' Kate called again in a sing-song voice, and the dog stopped barking, turning to her with an ear cocked. It was hard to be heard with the wind whipping past, but she shouted desperately, and finally the terrier cantered up the beach towards her, sitting down and taking a treat as if she deserved it.

Sandra was ranting at the dog, and at Kate, but it was falling on deaf ears. She hadn't noticed, but Kate was staring out to the edge of the water. Dozens of seals were dragging themselves over the rocks to escape the threat. Tears stung her eyes. The seals were rushing, not looking where they were going on the rocky shoreline. Kate remembered Roderick's explanation of the damage that could be caused to their fins and their undersides as a result. She turned to Sandra in fury.

'Why did you let her off the lead here? Don't you know dogs aren't allowed on the beach when the seals are hauled out?'

'She's not my dog,' snapped Sandra defensively.

Kate shook her head, too upset to speak. She stood silently and watched the last few seals slip into the safety of the waves. Sandra slunk off, taking the disgruntled Blossom with her.

The best thing to do with seals is leave them to it,

Kate could imagine Roderick saying. She stood for a few moments, watching as the shape of Sandra grew smaller as she scuttled up the beach. The tiny speck climbed into her car and drove off.

'Stupid humans,' said Kate out loud. She turned and headed for the car, and her little dog, safely locked away out of reach of the seals.

Back at the cottage that night, Kate slept badly. She lay awake watching the digital numbers on her alarm clock as they slipped from 2.00, to 3.00, to 4.00. When she finally succumbed to sleep, she dreamed of seals, and of Roderick telling her off for letting Willow chase them. Her alarm dragged her awake at half-past seven. Heavy-legged with exhaustion, she stumbled downstairs, letting Willow out into the garden. As the spaniel explored the latest delicious smells, Kate boiled the kettle.

'I'm putting a lot of faith in this cup of coffee,' she said as the puppy came back and leapt into her arms, snuggling up like a wriggling hot-water bottle. 'Maybe just five minutes in bed, and then we'll get up properly. Come on, Willow.'

Kate was dreaming again. Roderick was there, and Willow was in her arms.

'I'm sorry for being such a pompous arse,' he smiled.

In the dream Kate was effortlessly chic, legs clad in black jeans that weren't covered in dog fur, in a beau-tifully ironed and expensive-looking shirt, and her hair was smooth and immaculate. She swished her dream hair, which was salon-thick and glossy.

'I forgive you,' said Dream Kate, magnanimously.

Roderick bent down, and licked her face lovingly.

'Ugh. Ugh! Willow – ugh, stop it!'

Sensing that her mistress had dozed off, Willow had decided to wake her with an impromptu face-washing session.

'Bleargh! Dog breath.'

All traces of dog slobber gone, and at least some of the tiredness washed away in a scalding hot shower, Kate whistled to Willow and decided to walk the five minutes up to Duntarvie House. She had some final preparations to make before the arrival of the first cottage residents, and Jean had instructed her to come armed with plans for the Hogmanay ceilidh. Unfortunately Kate's only experience of ceilidhs had been of drunken whirling and looking up men's kilts at university. She'd managed to gloss over that fact with Jean, who was fizzing with excitement in a most uncharacteristic manner. She was spending most of her time looking at kilt catalogues, and trying to persuade Kate that she should wear traditional Highland dress to the party.

'Morning.' Clipped, brusque and incredibly irritating, Roderick opened the door to the house.

'Just about.' Kate smothered a yawn. She bent down, unclipping Willow, who hurtled through the hall to find Roderick's dogs. She skittered on the parquet floor and disappeared out of sight. Roderick smiled at Willow fondly, then shook himself.

'Right, Kate, we need to discuss the practicalities of this cottage let.'

All we ever discuss now are practicalities, thought Kate. 'Yes, we do. And I need to talk to Jean about New Year's Eve.'

'Hogmanay,' he reminded her, with a tiny ghost of a smile.

'It's the same thing,' snapped Kate.

'It most certainly is not, as you'll see.'

'I'm not sure I will. I'm going home for Christmas, and I'm not sure I'll come back before New Year.' Ha, thought Kate, I'm going to call it that, to piss him off.

'But you have to!' The words burst out of Roderick's mouth. He reined himself in, taking a sharp intake of breath. 'You can't miss your first ceilidh here at the house. Jean would be devastated.'

'Would she?' said Kate, non-committally.

'Kate, you're here. Wonderful,' exclaimed Jean, as they walked into the kitchen.

Oh God, thought Kate. Jean was armed with more bloody kilt brochures and a slightly manic air.

'I ordered some snippets, so we could see which colours suited you.' She brandished a handful of hairy tartan at Kate. 'Now, come over here to the mirror and we can have a look.'

'But I'm not Scottish. And my surname is Jarvis.'

Jean beamed.

'Aha, but that's the beauty of tartan. Your name comes under the Stirling District clan.' She reached forward, holding the piece of itchy material against Kate's cheek and turning her to the mirror. 'Now look at that. That yellow looks an absolute treat with your pale skin.'

Speechless, Kate looked at herself in the mirror. The material made her look ghostly white, and her freckles stood out as if each one had been painted on. Oh, help! And Jean was looking at her with anticipation and glee.

'It's . . . very . . . striking.'

In the mirror she caught a glimpse of Roderick leaving the room. Kate could swear he was laughing, but when he returned a few moments later he looked as buttoned-up as ever.

'Now then, if you two have finished your fashion show,' he slid a glance at Kate, 'we'll have a quick check over the final details for the cottages.'

It was agreed that Kate would drive over to the cottages after a supermarket visit. All three of them were desperately keen for the first cottage guests to have a trouble-free stay. Kate's shopping list included a bottle of malt whisky from the distillery on the island, flowers for the kitchen and the basics: bread, milk, cheese, coffee and tea.

'R–Roderick,' she stumbled slightly. There was something about just saying his name that made her feel embarrassed. 'I forgot to say – when I was at the beach yesterday, Sandra let a lunatic dog loose. It scared the seals and they all headed back to sea.'

'That bloody woman,' said Roderick, slamming down his coffee. 'She has no sense. I'll take a drive up later and have a look at the seals.' He gathered up a pile of paperwork and stormed out of the room, thunder-faced.

Jean sneaked a look at Kate, and raised her eyebrows.

'Now then, young lady. What's this I hear about you sneaking away for Christmas?'

'It's . . . well, I'd like to see my mum,' muttered Kate, thinking that she sounded about five. 'And . . .'

'And it's a bitty awkward here, with Roderick being such a pain in the backside?' finished Jean.

'Jean!' Kate laughed. 'But yes, that's it, really. I mean, the cottages are nearly done, the bunkhouse will be finished by February . . .' She tailed off, biting her lip.

'I'd be very sad to see you go.'

'I didn't say I was going.'

Jean's face was grave. 'You don't have to. I was young once, remember.' She reached across the table, taking Kate's hand. 'Roderick is a lovely young man; he's like a son to me. But he's proud, and stubborn, and the circumstances of his mother's death affected him.'

Kate put her head in her hands, remembering his face that morning at the cottage.

'We were thinking that he'd seen sense after Bonfire Night,' said Jean gently.

'Oh God,' groaned Kate, head still in her hands. 'Did Bruno tell the entire island?'

'That he did not. But after Roderick – well, I could say after he saw the light about Fiona, but maybe that's a wee bit unfair . . . We were so glad he'd seen sense. The two of you would make a great pair.'

Kate sighed, unconvinced. 'He didn't seem to think so, Jean. He legged it off the island and never mentioned it again.'

'He did, and that was a mistake. He's his father's son. Takes too long to make a decision, and then ends up having it made for him.'

Kate's interest was piqued and she looked up at Jean. 'Am I missing something?'

'Och, you've not taken long to pick up the ways of this place,' laughed Jean. 'I'll put the kettle on and tell you the whole saga.'

Kate parked herself next to the Aga, pulling up another chair for her feet. 'I love a saga.'

'Right then,' said Jean, arranging the teapot on the table and covering it with an embroidered tea cosy. 'I think a long story like this needs a wee bit of cake. Hold on.'

She leapt up from the table, returning with a tartan tin filled with a sticky, heavily perfumed gingerbread.

'It was like this. Long ago – we're talking probably a good thirty-five years – James, Roderick's father, was secretly in love with a young girl from the island. She was beautiful and wild and funny, and she loved him back. They were the greatest of friends.'

Kate cut a second slice of cake, and ate it mindlessly as she listened to Jean continue the tale. She was a born storyteller, the soft island lilt giving the narrative a fairy-tale quality.

'But James was shy, and he never let on how he felt. And after a couple of years the young girl grew tired of waiting for him to declare his feelings.'

'Jean!' exclaimed Kate, suddenly realizing, 'it was you!'

'It was not.' Jean took a long drink of tea and continued. 'Meanwhile there was another man, a quiet, thoughtful man, who also loved the girl. He didn't have a grand castle to offer her, but he was kind, and hard-working, and he was good.'

Kate rolled her eyes, thinking of her life with Ian. 'He sounds a bit . . . well, dull.'

'Ach, you young things are all the same. There's nothing wrong with a quiet life. Anyway. So the young girl went to James and told him that another man was in love with her, but that she had feelings for him.'

'She was hoping he'd declare undying love?'

'But he never did. I suppose he wasn't sure how she felt, and he wasn't willing to take a risk and get it wrong. So he congratulated her, and offered her Duntarvie House for the wedding.'

Kate sighed. 'That's so sad.'

'Indeed it is. Because we all know what happened next. Suddenly realizing that he'd missed the boat, James married the next girl who came along, who just happened to be Miss Annabel Farquhar. And, as you know, that didn't end well.'

'But what happened to the girl? Did she leave the island?'

'She did that. She went away to London with her good man and lived there for many years. But when James died a few years back, he left her a house on the island in his will and she came back.'

'And she's still here?'

'She is. And she's my dearest friend.'

'Morag?' Kate gasped.

Jean nodded slightly. 'James left her the stables and his horses, knowing how much she'd always loved Highland ponies.'

'Oh, that's so sad.'

'And a lesson that a certain young laird would do well to remember.'

A tear sneaked out of the corner of Kate's eye, and she wiped it away quickly before Jean could see, standing up and warming her hands on the Aga.

'You know, Roderick came to the cottage the morning he arrived back from England,' said Kate.

'Did he indeed.' She looked at Kate, not letting on. 'That was bad timing, that's all. You're a young girl – you're entitled to a wee bit of fun now and again.' Jean's eyes twinkled. 'And I tell you what, Finn McArthur's a good-looking young man. If I was thirty years younger—'

'Jean!' Kate burst out laughing.

'You just wait, young lady. You'll wake up one day

and be sixty – and you'll not feel much different from the way you do at twenty-five.'

If I carry on at this rate, I'll still be single, too, Kate thought.

She stood up, making to clear away the cups. 'Look at the time. I'm sorry, Jean, I'd better get to the super-market, much as I'd love to sit here all day.'

Jean smiled at her fondly. 'Leave that, I'll sort it out. Now, don't you go worrying your head about Roderick. Give him a bit of time.'

Kate grimaced. Whilst it was lovely to have someone to confide in, there was something excruciating about having her feelings out there in the open. Until now she hadn't even really admitted them to herself. Her chest throbbed with a raw, lonely, miserable ache. It was only ten o'clock and already what she wanted to do was sneak home and climb into bed.

'Can I leave Willow with you, Jean?' Kate didn't have the heart to deal with the rambunctious bouncing of her little dog around the shops, no matter how gorgeous she was.

'Course you can, dear. I'll take her out when I walk Roddy's two later.'

Kate plonked the bags of shopping down on the table. She'd spent a bit more money than she'd planned in town. She'd driven to the little distillery and picked up a bottle of whisky, had a chat and a coffee with Bruno, then collected a beautiful crunchy loaf from the bakery, and had a lovely chat with Helen while she put together a beautiful bouquet of flowers for their guest, who was proving to be a bit of a mystery.

'And you've no idea who's staying?' Helen had asked, snipping eucalyptus leaves.

'Not a clue. It was booked by one of those corporate concierge services. There's nothing other than a company name. I think it was a Glasgow number.'

'Very odd.'

'Well, it's perfectly normal for anywhere else, but odd for the island of Auchenmor – I've only been here three months, and I've already caught the nosiness bug. Back in Cambridge I was never interested in other people's comings and goings like this.' Kate had been fiddling with a roll of raffia and it had unfurled all over the floor. She was trying to put it back without Helen noticing.

'Give me that. What are you doing? You're making a right dog's dinner of it.'

'Oops!'

Following that, Kate had popped into the supermarket to get the bare essentials.

'All right gorgeous?'

A familiar husky voice caused her to spin round in the bakery aisle. She flushed scarlet at the sight of Finn, who grinned at her broadly, taking the heavy basket of shopping out of her hands.

'Have you been behaving yourself?'

'Of course.' She sounded a bit stiff and formal. It was more awkward than she'd expected, bumping into him.

He seemed completely at ease, presumably because one-night stands were more of a regular occurrence in his world.

He fell into step beside her as she wandered the aisles of the supermarket. His big mouth stretched open in a huge yawn, his fair hair and blond stubble making him look like a young lion.

'Sorry, excuse me. I'm knackered – got a couple of sculpture commissions, and I'm busy with the forestry at this time of year as well.'

'Aren't you ever tempted to get an exhibition together over on the mainland?' Kate plopped a bottle of washing-up liquid into the basket, alongside a couple of packs of scented tea-lights. The cottage was going to look gorgeous. She hoped their first guest would appreciate all the little touches she'd done to make it feel like a cosy retreat.

'No chance to get the work done – I'd need a decent six-month run at it, and unless I win the lottery, there's no way I can give up working for Roddy. I need the estate as much as they need someone running the forestry.'

He grabbed the bottle of lemonade he'd come in for, tucking it under his arm. 'Got everything?'

'Thanks – do you want me to take that?' She motioned to the shopping basket.

'You're fine.' He plonked it down on the conveyor, helpfully unloading the items one by one. Feeling a bit of a spare part, Kate fiddled with her purse.

It slipped out of her hands, falling to the ground with a thump, the catch bursting open. Coins spun across the floor.

Finn knelt down at the same moment she did, gathering handfuls of pennies. He leaned in towards her, eager for news.

'Any word on you and Roddy? I haven't heard anything through the jungle drums.'

'There is no me and Roddy.' Kate pulled a shut-up face at him. The last thing she wanted was everyone knowing what had happened.

'Not yet.' He gave her a wink.

'Finn, you're impossible.' Kate stood up, laughing despite herself.

The woman behind the checkout gave her a curious look. 'Eighteen pounds forty-two, hen.'

Finn gathered the bags of shopping, insisting on taking them out to the car. He slammed the boot shut, giving a piratical grin.

'Y'know, Kate, it must get a bit boring out there in the sticks by yourself. If you ever fancy a bit of company . . .'

Kate blushed again. 'I don't think so, Finn. But thanks for the offer.'

'Any time, darling.' And, with a cheeky grin, he was gone.

She stopped at New Farm for half a dozen blue, white and brown speckled eggs on the way across the island to the cottages. There was something about old-fashioned shopping that made her feel like a proper islander, regardless of the fact that the proper islanders like Jean were ecstatic about the sterile new supermarket.

Kate placed the bread on the wooden chopping board, the cheese, butter and milk in the fridge, and the whisky on the table. She stood for a moment, wondering whether to leave the bread knife out, but decided there was something a bit mass-murdererish about it, and shoved it back in the drawer. She plonked the flowers on the coffee table. Helen, knowing that Kate's flower-arranging skills were minimal, had made her up a ready-tied arrangement, with a vase to plonk them in. Kate lit the wood-burning stove and stepped back, admiring her handiwork. The cottage looked beautiful: homely, cosy, understated and classic. Kate could quite happily have moved in herself. Smiling, she turned for the door.

As she turned the handle, she felt the door being pushed hard from the outside.

'Good God! You'd think they'd manage to get the front door right,' came a voice from outside. 'I mean, have they not heard about first impressions?'

Kate let go of the door and stepped back just in time as it swung open, nearly hitting her in the face.

'And who are you?' demanded the voice.

It was attached to a prim-mouthed, slightly pinched-looking woman of around the same age as Kate. Her long blonde hair had been ironed poker-straight and expensively highlighted. Her eyebrows had been plucked into obedience and stood to attention above ice-blue eyes. The voice, and its body, stood waiting for a response.

Kate gulped slightly. 'I'm Kate. I work with . . . I work for . . . the Duntarvie estate.'

'Fiona darling, will you take Blossom while I unload the Range Rover?' A familiar voice fluted through the room, one that it took Kate a moment to recognize.

'Oh, hello, Kate. You'll have met Fiona then?'

Sandra appeared in the room, towed by an over-excited Blossom. The dog sniffed at the table, circuited the room and promptly peed with excitement by the arm of the sofa. Kate cringed.

'Naughty Blossom!' said Fiona, sounding not at all put out. 'I'm sure you've got something to clean that up, haven't you?' She turned to Kate, smiling at her.

That's more of a smirk than a smile, thought Kate, but the customer is always right. She reached into the cupboard under the sink and pulled out a bottle of all-purpose cleaner and a J-cloth.

'That's absolutely fine,' she said, through gritted teeth. 'Everyone has a little accident now and then.'

Fiona laughed, a fluting and unpleasant sound. 'Oh, it's more than now and then with my little Blossom, but never mind, darling.' She reached down for the dog, stroking her on the head. 'It's only a rented house anyway.'

'Yes,' said Sandra, disapprovingly, 'and your father and I have no idea why you've come all the way out here. We could easily have let down one of the hotel guests and told them there was a problem with the room. I hate to think of you out here on your own.'

Fiona looked at Sandra and winked. 'Ah well, Mother, I'm hoping not to be on my own all Christmas.'

Kate was in the garden, putting the wee-soaked cloth in the bin, when she realized. Inside the cottage was *the* Fiona: the one who'd been in a relationship with Roderick; the one who'd left the island to be a journalist; the one from whom he'd split up and who'd put him off women altogether. She felt a little pang of disappointment, realizing that Roderick was obviously as shallow as most of the men she'd met, and that he'd fallen for Fiona's brittle blonde looks. The fact that she had no personality, and a mouth like a cat's bum, seemed to have passed him by.

Kate was still smiling to herself at that thought when she returned to the cottage kitchen to retrieve her bag.

'Look what they've left: that bloody rock-hard bread from Paine's the baker,' Fiona was complaining as Kate walked in. 'What the hell is wrong with good old Mother's Pride?'

Rather than get into a disagreement, Kate grabbed her bag and, after making her goodbyes, left the cottage. The sun was low in the sky, but there was just time, she decided, to take a quick look down at the beach and check the seals. She pulled on her wellies and grabbed her binoculars from the car, before marching off, muttering to herself about Lady Muck, and her badly behaved dog peeing on her furniture.

The beach was deserted. Kate scanned the whole stretch of rocky sand for signs of the seals, but there were none. Blossom's rampage around the beach had clearly disturbed them. Without the seals, the beach seemed bleak and empty. Kate walked down towards the shoreline, scanning for any signs of the familiar faces poking out of the sea, but there was nothing. She sat down on a rocky outcrop, deciding to watch the sunset. Bloody Fiona was vile, she thought, and God knows what Roderick ever saw in her – besides, obviously, the swishy blonde hair, the slim perfect figure, the immaculate clothes and the aura of entitlement. She reached down to the side of the rock, aiming for a stone to throw in the water. Her hand touched something furry and icy cold and she leapt up, screaming.

She peered over the side of the rock. Lying there, not moving, was a seal pup. It looked at her and tried to roll over, but only managed to flap its flippers feebly.

Disaster! She remembered Roderick's first rule: never touch a seal. Only he hadn't mentioned anything about accidental seal-groping. Kate leaned over the side of the rock, this time being careful not to get in the pup's eyeline. Its skin looked too big and its eyes were dull and lifeless.

She ran up the beach, cursing herself for leaving her phone in the car. Blooming island life, thought Kate: a year ago I'd have had that phone fired up and ready to go in my jeans pocket.

She was rummaging desperately through the detritus

in the footwell of her car when she heard Roderick's voice.

'Looking for something?' He sounded faintly amused.

'My phone. But you're here now – are you psychic? I'm impressed.'

Roderick looked at her with a curious expression. 'I said I was going to come out and check on the seals after bloody Sandra let her bloody dog loose on the beach.'

'Not Sandra's dog,' said Kate, unthinking. Roderick snapped her a quick look, but said nothing.

'Whatever. Have you been down to the shore?'

'They're gone – well, all of them but one, a pup. I found it by mistake. I assume its mother has gone fishing or something, but I'm scared she'll be put off by my smell on her baby.'

'I don't think so. Can you show me where it is?'

Kate took Roderick down to the shore, leading him to the rocks, where the seal pup was still lying on its side. It looked up at him through huge brown eyes, but made no attempt to move. Even to Kate's inexpert eye it looked dreadful.

'Hello, little one,' said Roderick, in a gentle voice. 'Let's have a look at you.'

He pulled on some gloves and softly ran his hands down the pup's sides. 'This pup is dehydrated, I'd say, and hasn't fed for a few days. You remember I said that newborn pups need thousands of calories a day? It doesn't take long before starvation takes effect.'

191

Kate found her eyes were filling with tears, but she batted them away. 'Poor little chick.'

'Yep, and now we need to work out what to do.'

'You can't leave it here – it's so cold at night,' pleaded Kate. 'Can't we take it back to the house?'

'Absolutely not. The first thing we need to do is call Seal Rescue and tell them what's happened.' He patted his pockets, hopefully. 'Can I borrow your phone? I think I've left mine back at the house.'

He tapped a number from memory into the keypad.

'Reception's hopeless on this side of the island.' He looked at the phone, irritably. 'Mark, it's Roddy. I've got a grey here, probably no more than a week old, maybe two – it's dehydrated, I'd say it hasn't fed for a while . . . '

He paused, eyes closed and concentrating, while the person on the other end of the line spoke. Kate stuffed her hands in her pockets before she could reach out and run her fingers through Roddy's hair, which was ruffling in the wind.

'Right, that's fine. Yep, I know it's not exactly standard procedure, but I'm worried about this one making it through the night. Okay, we'll take it from here.'

Roderick switched off the phone, then took a couple of photographs of the seal. 'I need to text these to Mark, so he can see what we're dealing with.'

'What happens now?' Kate asked, as Roderick handed her back the mobile, having sent the messages.

'Mark works at the Seal Sanctuary on the mainland. I've had to take abandoned pups over to him before. They do a wonderful job, caring for them, bringing them on and then releasing them back into the wild when they're ready. Usually we'd watch an abandoned pup from a distance for a day or so, before we made any decisions about what to do. But I don't think this little one will last another day, and I think that, given what happened yesterday, there's no chance the mum is coming back.'

Kate took a sharp intake of breath. 'That bloody dog.'

'Never mind the dog,' said Roderick with feeling. 'The owner's even worse. Come with me.'

He turned, stalking up the beach at speed. Kate marched along beside him. 'So what happens now?'

'We'll get it off the island and to the sanctuary. Judging by the look of it, I'd say it's only a week or so old – you can still see the dried-up umbilical cord. But its eyes are dull. I'm worried we might be too late.'

Kate dug her fingernails into her palms to stop the tears that were threatening to escape. Roderick leaned into the back of his Land Rover, pulling out what looked like an Ikea shopping bag, but fluorescent orange instead of the familiar blue.

'We need to get the pup in here, and get down to the ferry – if get a move on, we'll catch the four o'clock.'

Together they ran back down the beach, scrambling across the rocks to the pup's hiding place. The light was failing rapidly, darkness creeping across the sky.

'Hold the bag open – now, this might be a bit of a struggle.'

Kate looked at the seal pup, which was lying passively beside the rocks, and looked back at Roderick, one eyebrow raised.

'A struggle?'

'Watch.'

He moved stealthily, gloved hands reaching down to grab the pup. As he did so, the seal flipped over with a sudden last burst of defiance, yowling and snapping. With practised ease, Roderick scooped the pup across and into the open bag.

'Feisty little thing.' His eyes met Kate's and he smiled: the first genuine smile Kate had seen from him in weeks. 'You take that handle, I'll take this one. The bag is deep, to stop the pup from getting out.'

'They can't jump, can they?'

'You'll be amazed what an angry seal can do. I've rescued a few injured ones from this beach who've not been happy. And, believe me, you don't want to find out what a seal bite feels like.'

'Ouch!'

He smiled ruefully. 'Let's just say I've been there, and it's not pleasant.'

They reached the top of the beach, where Roderick's Land Rover was pulled in on the grass verge. Kate looked up the hill at the cottages, where the light was glowing gently through the windows. A furl of smoke twisted gently from the chimney. Following her gaze, Roderick looked up at the cottage.

'That's Sandra's car. What's she doing there?' He was trying with one hand to release his car keys from the back of his jeans. The seal bag was wriggling impatiently.

'Our first visitor is Fiona Gilfillan. I assumed you knew?' said Kate.

Roderick closed his eyes and groaned. 'You are joking?' He opened his eyes and looked at Kate, hopefully. 'You're not. You're telling me that Fiona and Sandra are sitting up there in our cottage?'

Kate's stomach did an Olympic-sized back-flip. *Our* cottage.

'They are. Large as life and twice as—' Kate stopped herself. By no stretch of the imagination could the polished, glamorous Fiona be called ugly.

'Ah. This day gets better and better.' Roderick flicked open the back door, pulling out a cat basket. 'Right then, little one, let's decant you into this.'

'Is this something you make a habit of?' asked Kate, watching as he deftly slid the furry contents of the seal bag into the cat carrier and closed the door.

'Seal-rescuing – just another service I provide.' He reached into his pocket, pulling out his wallet, and flipped it open, pulling out a card. 'Roderick Maxwell, certified Marine Mammal Medic, at your service.'

'You're a vet?' Kate was astounded.

'No, I'm not a vet. I'm a qualified Medic – the British

Divers' Marine Life Rescue organization trains members of the public. Our job is to look out for stranded mammals and do what we can for them.'

'So not just seals then?'

'No, we're trained to help with beached whales, porpoises, dolphins and seals,' said Roderick, throwing her the empty seal bag. 'Let's go.'

'My car – won't they wonder why I've left it sitting on the road?'

'Sandra and Fiona, no,' he said shortly. 'They're too wrapped up in themselves to notice anything. Why don't you ring Murdo up at the hotel, let him know?'

'Too late.' Kate pointed at the two women speed-walking down the lane from the cottages. 'I think we've been spotted.'

'Roddy! You dark horse, were you coming out here to surprise me?'

Fiona was at the window of the car, tapping it with perfectly manicured scarlet nails. Roderick sighed and pressed a button, so that the window opened fully. 'Fiona.'

'You came all the way out here to welcome me, and I thought you were still sulking.'

'I'm not sulking,' said Roderick, his voice measured and patient. 'Look, Fiona, we have to get going. Your mother let that lunatic dog of yours loose on the beach and it caused the seals to stampede.'

Fiona leaned inside the window, kissing Roderick on the cheek. 'That naughty dog. Sweet of you to give me

a puppy, Roddy, but I'm not really the dog-training type.'
She looked up, catching sight of Kate for the first time.
'Oh.' Her nose wrinkled slightly. 'I see. Have I been
replaced already?'

'Of course not,' said Roderick, rather too emphati-
cally for Kate's liking. Was she such a hideous prospect?
'Kate works for me – and she's helped rescue this seal
pup. Now we must go: we have to catch the four o'clock
ferry.'

'You must come up to the hotel for drinks,' Fiona
was saying, but Roderick had already started the engine
and was driving away, leaving her mouthing furiously.

9

A Rescue

They sat in silence all the way to the ferry. Roderick drove on to the boat, grim-faced. The seal pup had stopped crying for its mother, which was a relief, because Kate was worried that the eerie, child-like noise was going to arouse suspicions on the boat about their motives.

'Is it breathing?' Kate was too scared to look closely.

'It's fine.' Roderick closed the door of the carrier. 'We'll be there in forty minutes, and Mark is waiting for us with everything it needs. Now we need to get you sorted out.'

'Me?' Kate was baffled. Roderick shut the door and locked the Land Rover.

'Your lips are blue.' He looked at her face, placing his scarf around her neck. 'You've been out in the cold for so long, your hands are blocks of ice.' He took both of her hands and cupped them inside his. They were burning hot. Kate had been so wrapped up in rescuing the seal that she hadn't noticed she'd spent the best part of an hour standing on a remote beach with the Atlantic wind whipping in on her.

'Shall we get a cup of tea?'

'I think that would be an idea,' said Roderick, gently letting go of her frozen hands.

It felt strange being on the ferry with him. He ushered her into a corner, next to a radiator, and disappeared, returning a couple of minutes later with a pot of tea and a couple of warm fleece blankets.

'Where did you get those from?' Kate nursed the hot teacup, feeling warmth slowly seeping back into her bones. It was amazing how cold that island could be.

'Aha. It's all about who you know,' Roderick tapped his nose. 'I've been here fifteen years, remember – there's not a ferry worker I don't know by name. And believe me, when you've been stuck out here on the sea for six hours because it's too rough to dock, you need blankets to keep the cold off.'

Kate pulled the blanket closer around her shoulders. 'It's amazing, really, isn't it? Most of us consider ourselves island dwellers, just by virtue of living in Britain. But we have no idea what it's really like.'

'Ah, but we're the lucky ones,' said Roderick.

'Thank you for travelling with Caledonian MacBrayne. The ferry will be docking shortly. Please make your way back to your vehicle.'

Kate had fallen asleep, lulled by the repetitive hum of the boat's engine.

The clipped voice of the recorded announcement woke her up. Oh God, she was leaning on Roderick's shoulder. Worse still, she realized, closing her mouth, which was dry as parchment, she'd obviously been snoring. Attractive! She rubbed her eyes furiously and sat up.

'Oh.' She was dazed and took a moment to place herself. 'It's the boat – every time I get on it, I conk out, instantly. I'm sorry, I must have fallen asleep for a minute.'

Roderick rolled his eyes. 'Twenty actually, and by God, you can't half snore.'

Kate emitted a vague sort of harrumphing noise and scrambled up, escaping to the loo.

Looking at herself in the mirror, she was horrified, but not surprised, to discover that her crumpled face was imprinted with the rib of Roderick's jumper. Her eyeliner was non-existent on one eye, and smudged on the other. She made a vague attempt to make herself respectable and set off downstairs to find the Land Rover.

'The pup's fine,' said Roderick, as she opened the car door. 'I've checked. Still sleeping.'

The ferry pulled into the dock, and Kate tapped her fingers impatiently on the dashboard as they waited for all the cars and lorries in front to unload. It seemed to take forever. Finally they rolled off the ferry and up the ramp onto the mainland. Roderick turned the car left into a car park, where a battered four-wheel drive was waiting.

'Mark, hello.' Roderick jumped out of the car. 'This is Kate. She found the pup, and she saw the disturbance yesterday.'

Mark grinned at her and held out a filthy hand. 'Might be a bit fishy, it's just been feeding time. But lovely to meet you, Kate.' He turned to Roderick, who was opening the back of the Land Rover. 'Bit late in the season for a grey, isn't it?'

'I thought so, too. But this little one is still hanging on, even if its mother has legged it.' Roderick opened the carrier, and Mark peered in. Still nervous in case her pup hadn't made it, Kate hung back.

'Let's get it back to the sanctuary. We can get some food down it and see how we're doing. Melanie's back home, getting all the stuff ready for a tube feed.'

Phew, still alive then, thought Kate. They climbed back into the Land Rover and followed Mark out of town. They drove in silence for a couple of miles, then Roderick indicated right and pulled over, through a wooden gate. The Seal Sanctuary sign was tattered and weathered by the elements, and the buildings had seen better days. Inside one of them they found Melanie, Mark's wife. As she expertly scooped up the seal, weighed it, then placed it down on the table, she explained how they'd ended up on the west coast of Scotland, saving seals.

'I was taking a year out from teaching biology at secondary school, and Mark was a chemist for a big pharmaceutical company. We came up here on holiday, saw the seals and fell in love.'

Roderick glanced at Kate quickly. She felt herself blushing, and looked down at her feet. Mark raised his eyebrows at Melanie. The whole thing happened in a split second, but was excruciating.

'How's Fiona?'

'Mark! Roderick's here to deliver us a seal pup, not to discuss his love life.' Melanie shot him a warning look.

'Fiona is fine,' said Roderick. 'But we're not – well, we went our separate ways a few months ago.' He looked pained. No matter what he said, he must still have feelings for her.

Kate stood up. 'Melanie, have you got many other animals in at the moment?' Her voice sounded brittle and higher than normal.

'Yes, we have eight grey seals that came in earlier in the season, and a common seal that was found about half a mile from the sea, shuffling along the main road.' She poured a foul-smelling, yellow-grey sludge into a container, mixing it expertly. 'This is what we feed them – it stinks, but it does the trick. Let me get this little chick sorted and then I'll show you round.'

Melanie and Mark worked together as a team, seemingly knowing what had to be done without using words. One held down the pup, and the other manoeuvred the feeding tube down the throat of the startled seal.

'It's easy enough when they're quiet, but when they get a bit bigger, mealtime is a bit hairy,' said Mark, holding the pup steady as the liquid poured down her throat. After a few moments of struggling, she remained still.

'What is it?'

'It's an electrolyte supplement. After that, she'll go onto a combination of fish oil, high-protein milk supplement and a vitamin mixture. It'll build her up pretty quickly; she'll be catching fish on her own before you know it.' Melanie gently pulled the tube out. 'There you are, little one. We have to stop off the tube as it's coming back out, to make sure no liquid makes its way down into the lungs.' She picked up the seal pup and placed it in a pen. 'There you go, darling.'

'Look at that – she's picked up already.' Mark smiled at the pup, beckoning Kate over. 'What are you going to call her, Kate? It's the finder's privilege.'

Kate looked into the seal kennel. The seal's dark, liquid eyes were brighter already. As she watched, the pup rolled onto her side and began sucking on her flipper.

'Flora.'

'A good Scottish name,' nodded Melanie. 'Now let's give her a bit of peace, and I'll show you round.'

Melanie and Mark offered to put them up for the night, but with no bag, and feeling worried about Willow, Kate really wanted to get home. With promises of daily updates on Flora's progress, they left the mainland, managing to catch the last ferry home with seconds to spare.

If I'm honest with myself, Kate thought, what I want to do is lie on the couch with a glass of wine and my nice fire, and contemplate ways to bump off the vile Fiona.

'Penny for your thoughts?' said Roderick, inter-rupting her daydream.

'I was just thinking about, um . . . ' Kate plucked an idea out of her head, desperately, '. . . New Year.'

'Mmm. It should be good.' Roderick looked over at her. 'You will come back for it, won't you? I'd like you to see a proper island Hogmanay.' Seemingly not thinking, he said, 'You think Bonfire Night was some-thing. Wait until you see the islanders really let their hair down.'

Kate's eyes widened, as Roderick realized his mistake. They looked at each other for a never-ending awkward moment. She decided to bluff her way out of it and continue with the fabrication that nothing had happened.

'It sounds interesting.'

'That's one word for it.' The relief in his tone was evident as he continued, 'It's the biggest night of the year here on the island, and you'll be expected to be suitably impressed.'

Pulling her cold hands inside her sleeves, Kate thought for a moment. 'I'm not going to get away with not coming to it, am I?'

'Nope.' He smiled at her. 'If you don't get back up here by the thirtieth of December, Jean will be beetling down the M1 to collect you herself.'

10

Christmas in Cambridge

Bruno's cafe was decorated for Christmas. The ceiling was adorned with crepe-paper hangings in vibrant, clashing colours, and he had Elvis's *Christmas Album* on a constant loop on the Wurlitzer. Behind the Formica counter, he was making coffee, wearing a Father Christmas hat.

'I'll be home for Christmas,' he crooned, looking up at Kate. 'When are you away?'

'Tomorrow, on the 6 a.m. ferry.'

'Early tae bed for you tonight?' He passed over her coffee with a flourish.

The froth on the top was decorated with a swirl in the shape of a Christmas tree.

'How do you do that?' marvelled Kate, as was expected of her. 'No, not an early night. Susan and Tom have invited me round for Christmas drinks. Worst-case scenario, I can sleep on the train down to Cambridge.'

'Just mind ye take a bit of water wi' it – that ferry is no fun wi' a sore heid. Believe me, there's no an islander that wouldna say the same.'

Kate saluted him, laughing. 'Yes, sir.'

'And ye'll be back for Hogmanay?' Bruno wiped an invisible speck from the worktop with a bar cloth.

'I don't have any choice. Jean has issued an edict.'

'Best ye're back here in plenty of time, hen. I wouldna cross that one – she's fierce.'

The hedges outside Susan and Tom's house were woven with fairy lights, which sparkled in the dark. On the icy footpath, tiny waxed paper bags, each one with a tea-light in the base, lit the way to the front door, which was decked with a huge, simple wreath of holly, hung on a deep-red ribbon. Kate opened the door and was hit with a blast of cinnamon, cloves and something alcoholic.

'Hello, stranger.' Tom kissed her cheek. 'You're freezing. Come in, let me take your coat. Susan's making mulled wine.'

In the kitchen Susan was standing, half-empty bottle of brandy in hand. Morag was at the table, holding a drowsing baby Mhairi. Through the hall Kate could hear the shouts of Jamie and Ted playing a game of tennis on the Wii.

'I'm afraid my hand slipped when I was adding a tot of brandy to the mulled wine,' said Susan, with a conspiratorial grin. 'It's now like rocket fuel. D'you want some?'

'I'd love some. I've been warned by Bruno that I'm not to drink too much, though, or I'll be dying on the six o'clock ferry in the morning.'

'Ah,' said Ted, coming into the room with Jamie on his shoulders. 'But a hungover ferry journey is a rite of passage. We've all done it, haven't we?'

The room filled with groans of reminiscence.

'I'll just have one,' said Kate firmly. She was trying to ignore a slight feeling of disappointment. Half of her had been hoping that Roderick would have been there, given his close friendship with Tom and Susan. But perhaps, she realized, they hadn't invited him, knowing it might be awkward.

Morag put the baby down to bed. Tom lifted a protesting Jamie off Ted's shoulders, saying, 'Bed for you too, young man.'

Kate blew Jamie a kiss. 'I've a special present in my bag for you – I'll leave it under the Christmas tree. You can tell me what you think when I get back from England.'

Jamie, eyes heavy with sleep, blew her a kiss back. 'Night-night, Katie-Kate.'

'Right then,' said Susan gleefully, 'Let the party commence.' She ladled the steaming hot mulled wine into huge, heavy glasses, each of which appeared to be wearing a little woollen coat. Kate took her drink and peered at the woollen attachment.

'It's Helen's idea. It keeps them warm for longer,' explained Susan, laughing. 'Wait till you're outside watching the fireworks and you'll see the point of them.'

'Fireworks?'

'Aye, it's our little tradition – Christmas Day is for

the children, so we take it in turns to have drinks at someone's house the week before. The fireworks started off as sparklers, but somehow over the years it snow-balled.'

'Is that your idea of a Christmas pun?' Kate groaned.

'Ha. No, but it's a good one,' said Susan.

There was a soft knock at the door, and suddenly the long hall was full of more visitors. Finn, a box under his arm, leaned over and kissed Kate hello. His face was cold. Remembering his recent half-proposition, she blushed.

'All right, gorgeous?' He gave her a wink.

'Roddy, will you take my coat?'

The voice filled Kate with horror. Oh please, no, she thought, looking past Finn. But oh God, yes, it was. Standing in the hall with a fur hat on top of her golden hair, thin-lipped mouth pouting (not a good look, thought Kate) was Fiona. And behind her . . .

'Kate.' Roderick, strangely, looked pleased to see her. He leaned forward and kissed her in greeting. It was the first sign of affection he'd shown since his return from Oxfordshire, and the briefest kiss on her cheek made her stomach disappear through her feet.

Perhaps he's got a weird firework-fetish, she thought, and started to giggle.

'Are you all right?' He looked at her, puzzled.

'Fine. Sorry, I was thinking about something.'

'I'll have a vodka and tonic,' announced Fiona breezily, as she walked past Kate.

Kate looked round to see if there was anyone else at whom she could have been aiming the request, but the hall was empty. Finn was standing in the kitchen with Morag, and the others had made their way to the sitting room.

'I don't think there is any – at least, I don't know where it is. There's mulled wine,' said Kate, trying to be helpful.

'Well, don't you think you should find out that sort of thing at the beginning of the night?' snapped Fiona.

'Fiona! This isn't Kate's house. Why on earth would you expect her to know where the drinks are kept?' Roderick looked over Fiona's shoulder at Kate, pulling an embarrassed face.

'Is she not working tonight?'

Hello, thought Kate, I am actually standing right here.

'Kate?' Roderick burst out laughing. 'Why on earth would she be working here? She's friends with Tom and Susan – she's here as a guest.'

'Oh. I assumed, with what she was wearing,' Fiona looked Kate up and down, taking in the black jeans and black polo neck, 'that they'd borrowed her from you for the night.'

Kate snorted. Roderick, sensing mutiny in the ranks, ushered Fiona through into the sitting room, throwing an apologetic look over his shoulder as he did so.

'That bloody cow!' Kate stormed into the kitchen, pouring herself a large top-up of the now-cooling mulled wine. She gulped it all, and slammed down her glass.

'Fiona,' said Finn and Morag in unison.

'She's vicious.' Kate held out her glass.

Morag filled it to the brim, her face thunderous. 'Aye, well, you don't want to get on the wrong side of her.'

'Do you think she and Roderick are back together?' The thought make Kate feel quite ill.

Finn shook his head violently. 'I can't see it. But let's face it, the stakes are fairly high with Roderick. She'll not give up that easily.'

Morag nodded. 'And that's what worries me. Fiona doesn't want Roddy because she loves him; she wants the house and the land and the cachet of being the laird's wife.'

'Right enough,' nodded Finn. 'I tell you what, Kate, we were so pleased to get shot of her when she got the job on the mainland, I wanted to fly over to Glasgow and thank the newspaper editor myself.'

'Och now, Finn, she's not a bad girl at heart. She's just spoilt.' Morag gave him a little poke in the ribs. 'Mind you, the local paper has been a much nicer read since she gave up as editor,' she admitted. 'If I wanted an exposé every week, I'd read the red-tops.'

Kate, by this time halfway down her third mulled wine, was feeling distinctly light-headed. She twirled the cinnamon stick in her drink, watching the dark whirlpool, daydreaming.

'Kate?'

'Hmm? Oh. So Fiona left to work for a national paper?'

'Sandra was over the moon,' said Finn. 'Fiona was

determined that Roderick would come with her and get someone in to run the estate day-to-day. But he dug in his heels and refused, so she upped sticks and went to Glasgow without him.'

'So why is she back now?'

'Well, I think her plan fell through.' Morag continued the tale. 'I think she thought she'd storm off and Roderick would follow her. But she underestimated his love for this place.'

'And the fact that he probably thought he had a lucky escape,' added Finn, in an undertone.

'There's that as well,' Morag laughed. 'Finn, your glass is empty. Here you go.' She topped it up.

'Are you trying to get me drunk?'

'Behave yourself, Finn McArthur.'

'Can't blame me for trying. You're a good-looking woman for your age.' He winked at her.

'Bloody hell, Finn,' laughed Kate, the wine loosening her tongue. 'I can't believe I fell for your lines. Talk about cheesy.'

He pulled her into his arms, grinning hugely, and bent her backwards in a parody of a stage kiss, so that she gasped as his laughing mouth was almost on hers. 'Admit it, you want me.'

'Don't mind me,' said Fiona crisply. 'I only came to find out if there was any chance of getting a drink around here. It was Christmas *drinks* that we were invited to, after all.'

'Fiona, my dear,' Morag sloshed some mulled wine

into a glass, scooping in some fruit and a cinnamon stick. 'How thoughtless of Kate.'

Fiona sniffed disapprovingly in Kate's direction. The humour in Morag's voice was lost on her. 'I'll take a drink for Roddy. Where on earth are Tom and Susan? It's supposed to be their party and they're nowhere to be seen.'

'Probably sneaked upstairs for a quickie, knowing them,' whispered Finn as Fiona stalked out of the room, glasses in hand.

'We can't hide in the kitchen all night.' Kate unwillingly put her glass on the worktop. 'Plus Fiona thinks I'm the hired help.' Brightening at her own joke, she pulled a face. 'I need to get in there and refresh the glasses.'

The sitting room looked beautiful. Susan had strung fairy lights around the windows, and each of her huge, abstract paintings was festooned with swathes of pine, which together with the enormous tree in the corner filled the room with the smell of Christmas. The log fire was crackling, and an excited Jamie had already hung stockings by the fireplace, complete with strange little offerings. Kate bent down to look at a letter, held in place by a Playmobil knight, a marble and a small wooden box full of paperclips.

'Don't ask,' laughed Susan, who appeared out of nowhere, crouching down to join Kate by the fireplace. 'Every night Jamie leaves a little note for Father Christmas, and a collection of assorted tat. We're running out of hiding places for all the stuff, and Tom's on strike and refusing to write any more letters back from Santa.'

Kate stood up. Roderick was sitting in the corner of the sofa, with Fiona perched over him on the arm of the chair. She was flirting hard, playing with her hair, flicking imaginary specks of dust off his shirt, twirling the cinnamon stick in her drink to show off her beautifully manicured scarlet nails.

'Poor bugger looks terrified, don't you think?' grinned Finn, joining her by the fire.

As they looked over at them, Kate watched Fiona lean across Roderick, whispering something in his ear. His face registered surprise. He caught Kate's eye, then his glance darted across to Finn and back again. Fiona sat up, looking at Kate with a satisfied smirk.

'Right, everyone, the little ones are sleeping – let's see how long it takes before we wake them up with my fireworks display,' said Tom, coming in from the hall.

Morag had settled herself by the fire and looked distinctly unexcited at the prospect. She was dragged, mock-grumbling, out of her chair by Ted.

'I should have gone up to the big house with Jean and the dogs. She's up there by a roaring fire watching *It's A Wonderful Life* on DVD,' she muttered to Kate as they stood in the field behind the cottages. Kate glanced through the darkness at her friend. Strange to think that the big house, and the land they were standing on, all could have been Morag's. Now wasn't the time, but one day she'd ask how it felt.

'What about the ponies?'

'They're in the far field – they won't hear a thing. Especially as I've stuffed their lugs with cotton wool.' Morag clinked her glass against Kate's and laughed.

Tom's fireworks weren't on the same scale as the huge display up at the hotel, but the Christmassy atmosphere and the ever-flowing mulled wine and port kept everyone warm and happy. Kate couldn't help noticing that Roderick was keeping his distance from her, and that the vile Fiona was draping herself across him at every opportunity. She was even insinuating her way into his arms; Kate could see her shivering ostentatiously and cuddling up to him.

'You're away in a dream,' said Morag, taking her arm. 'Thinking of home?'

'Yes,' lied Kate. 'It'll be nice to see my mum, and to catch up with Emma and Sam.'

Actually she hadn't given it much thought, once the tickets had been booked. It had been cheaper to go by train than to drive, and the prospect of a few hours daydreaming against a train window was far nicer than hurtling down the motorway in her little car. But Cambridge seemed like another planet, not just a city a few hundred miles away. Island life was so far removed from reality, it was hard to remember that elsewhere life was going on as normal. Mind you, thought Kate, for us island life *is* normal. She turned to Morag, surprised at herself.

'How long have I been on the island?'

'Oh, let me think,' Morag frowned. 'It seems like forever to me. September, October, November, December – is it really only four months?'

'And in that time I've sorted out the renovation of two cottages, accidentally kissed my boss, got caught with a half-naked man, drunk about a gallon of whisky and seen two firework displays. Not bad going, really.' Kate looked up. Fiona was entwined around Roderick in a python-like fashion. If she carried on much longer she'd be inside his clothes. 'I think I'll go back inside. I'm freezing.'

Finn was adding logs to the fire in the sitting room. Ted, predictably, was 'resting his eyes' in the big armchair by the fire, legs stretched out on the coffee table. Kate curled up on the sofa, pulling a cushion over her knees and hugging it. She felt suddenly out of place.

Finn sat down on the sofa and looked at her with a rueful smile. 'You're going to sack me as agony uncle, aren't you?'

'Well,' said Kate, 'you did say give it until Christmas and Roderick would be eating out of my hand.'

'Ah. Well, I didn't factor in the return of Fiona.'

'She is beautiful, isn't she?' Kate tried to be magnanimous.

'No, she is not. She has a face like a slapped arse and a personality to match.'

Kate laughed, despite herself. 'You can't say that.'

'I just did. Admit it, she's vile. But she's got her claws

into Roddy again, by the looks of it. I don't know what the attraction is.'

Kate pulled a face. 'I'm not sure, either. He doesn't look like he's happy to be with her, does he?'

'Maybe she's a witch, and she's got a little voodoo doll hidden away somewhere?'

Kate managed a smile. 'She's never tried to ensnare you then?'

'Many a woman has tried and failed. I have no desire to be pinned down.'

'That's not what I've heard,' laughed Kate, throwing the cushion at him.

'Watch it, you. Now come here and give me a hug. I'm starved of affection.'

'One day some woman will come along and whisk you off your feet, and you won't know what's hit you.' Kate allowed Finn to wrap her in a bear hug, closing her eyes.

With excruciating timing, Roderick, Fiona, Susan and Tom walked back into the room. Kate sprang out of Finn's arms, making the situation worse.

'Shall we leave you two lovebirds to it?' joked Tom.

'We weren't doing anything!' said Kate, embarrassed. Finn, infuriatingly, was looking highly amused and was sitting on the arm of the sofa, unabashed. From Ted's corner of the room came a walrus-like snort.

'Right. Well, I tell you what,' said Tom archly. 'We're away to make some coffee. We'll leave you to your – er, nothing.'

Roderick looked across at Kate, his expression unreadable. She felt a dull twist in her stomach. She knew then that what Fiona had whispered to him earlier related to the joke kiss she'd seen in the kitchen, and that being caught in Finn's arms had confirmed Roderick's suspicions. There was no way out of this mess, except on the first train back home.

'Finn, will you walk me home?' The damage was done now. Roderick was in the clutches of Fiona, who'd convinced him that Kate was having a wild fling with Finn.

'Of course I will. Let me get our coats.'

Hating goodbyes, Kate slipped away, hand tucked into Finn's solid arm for balance on the slippery ice.

'You see, despite what you've heard, I can be a gentleman.' He opened the door for her, holding it as she ducked under his arm.

There was a flicker of a moment when she contemplated taking the easy option. He was gorgeous, he made her laugh, he was good company. It would be so easy to . . . No. She batted away the idea. It would be pointless.

'Happy Christmas, Finn,' said Kate, kissing his cheek.

'You have to give it to my mother, she's committed to her charities.'

'She should be committed to something. I can't believe she asked you to come home for Christmas, then forgot to mention she was volunteering at the bloody animal shelter.' Emma rolled her eyes at Kate and they burst out laughing.

'Ah well, at least it gets me out of Christmas lunch with assorted relatives.'

Kate had made the long journey home yesterday, and arrived at Cambridge station tired and full of horrible coffee – desperate for a bath, her childhood bed and some mothering. Unfortunately, her mother had other plans. She'd called Kate as the train rumbled through the damp English countryside.

'Darling, I am sorry. There was a mix-up at the shelter and they need overnight cover on Christmas Eve. I've arranged for Emma and Sam to pick you up – they can't wait to see you, and I'll be with you in time for Christmas dinner.'

'That's fine, Mum,' Kate had said, through gritted teeth.

So rather than being driven the fifteen miles back to the pretty market town of Saffron Walden, she was stuffing her bags into the boot of Emma's car.

'Girls . . .' Emma opened the car door and a blast of high-pitched squealing hit the air. 'Just give Kate a second to get in, before you start.'

But it was too late.

'Santa's coming tomorrow and he's taken our letter, and Katharine isn't going to get any presents because she cut the hair off my Barbie doll and—'

'I did NOT – you did it yourself, and anyway I'm

going to tell Kate you scribbled on the wall with Daddy's special pen . . .'

Kate felt a rush of fondness for Emma's two girls, strapped into the car seats, but straining to escape. 'Darlings, I'm sure you've been so good that Father Christmas will be bringing you *lots* of presents. Just give me a moment to talk to Emma, and then I promise I'll hear all about it.'

Emma, concentrating on the Christmas Eve traffic, shot her a look of relief.

'I can't tell you how much I'm looking forward to a cup of tea and a chance to catch up.'

'Never mind the tea,' Kate patted her shoulder bag. 'I've got a twelve-year-old bottle of Auchenmor's finest here.'

'Whisky? You really have gone native.' Emma pulled a face, drawing the car to a halt. 'I think I'll stick to a cuppa for now.'

'You're getting old, Mrs Lewis.'

Emma's mouth curved in an almost imperceptible smile. She climbed out of the car before Kate could say another word.

In the window of the pretty Edwardian house a Christmas tree twinkled. Smoke curled from the chimney. The girls ran ahead up the path, released from the tether of their car seats, the door opening as Sam greeted them all with a wide smile. Breathing a sigh of relief, Kate allowed herself to be embraced by it all.

*

'So here we are,' said Emma, the following morning. It was Christmas Eve, and she was preparing vegetables while Kate sat at the kitchen table and regaled her with tales from the island. 'Instead of a relaxing Christmas, chez Mum, you're stuck with us. The girls will be in tears by midday, Sam will be force-feeding you his famous brandy-soaked mince pies from breakfast time onwards, and I'll be throwing up every five minutes.'

Behind the kitchen counter Emma slid her hand over her aproned stomach with a tiny, secret smile.

'Are you ill? You should have said.' Kate leapt up from the table to help Emma with the gigantic pile of Brussels sprouts she was peeling.

'I'm not ill.' Emma beamed from ear to ear. 'I've never been better.'

'But I thought you said you were throwing up every five minutes?'

Emma put down the knife, and stood in front of her friend. Speaking very slowly and clearly, she began, 'I'm not sick. I'm *being* sick. I'm being sick all the time.'

Kate's mouth dropped open. She looked at her best friend, not sure whether to hug her or burst into tears. She decided to do both.

'Ohmygodyou'repregnant!'

'Give the girl a coconut. I tell you what, for someone who got a first at university, you're bloody thick sometimes – d'you know that?'

Katharine and Jennifer ran into the room ahead of

their father. Their hair was sparkling with rain, their muddy feet leaving footprints all over the wooden floor.

'Girls, just because the wanderer has returned doesn't mean the rules of the house have changed.'

Sam cornered first Katharine and then Jennifer, removing wellington boots and unzipping them from their raincoats. With only one day left until Christmas, they were reaching new highs of excitement, and Sam maintained that the only way to manage them was to take them out for regular walks, like dogs.

Kate thought of her little Willow, who was spending her first Christmas on the island with Jean and Hector. The prospect of travelling by train with a slightly unpredictable puppy, prone to escaping, chewing everything in sight and weeing in corners, had been too much for Kate to bear. Jean, who had a soft spot for Willow, had leapt at the chance to dogsit for the week Kate was in Cambridge.

Having dealt with the girls, Sam squeezed Kate's shoulder in passing and ducked behind the breakfast bar to fill the kettle. He caught Emma from behind, causing her to drop her knife and shriek with surprise. Kate felt a huge pang of sadness twist within her. Despite the warmth and familiarity of her friends' house, she felt lonely and out of place.

'Would you mind if I popped out?' She stood up. Emma and Sam looked at her, concerned.

'Last-minute shopping?' asked Sam, 'You don't want a cup of tea before you go?'

'Honestly, I'm fine. I've just remembered something I wanted to get for the girls.'

Pulling on her coat and grabbing an umbrella, she set off into the rainy Cambridge street. She didn't quite know where she was going; on autopilot, she marched towards the centre of town, which only a few months ago would have brought immediate comfort in the shape of a friendly Starbucks and a bit of retail therapy. After a few minutes' walk she found herself in the Grafton Centre. It was thronged with last-minute shoppers, songs blaring through the loudspeakers. Shop workers were busy dismantling the displays and Sellotaping huge 'Sale' signs across the windows.

Christmas here seemed tawdry, chaotic and commercial, compared to back on Auchenmor. She looked at her watch. At this time two days ago she'd been sitting on the beach, watching the seals, chatting on the mobile to Mark about Flora, the seal pup. He'd been excited to tell her that Flora had managed to eat her first herring, and that she was swimming happily in the bigger pool. Kate had promised to go back after New Year and visit.

Apologizing for tripping on the wheels of yet another pushchair, she veered left, escaping through a side door and up to Midsummer Common. It was empty in the rain, the willows whipping against the River Cam in the wind. She sat down on a bench, looking down the river at a solitary mallard. Strange to think that she'd sat on this same river bank so many times with Ian, wondering if life was meant to be quite as dull as it was.

The last few months had been anything but dull, she thought, picking at a piece of lichen on the stone end of the bench. Somehow she'd still managed to screw everything up. Roderick was convinced that she was with Finn, thanks to the vile Fiona catching them in a perfectly innocent, if silly, embrace. And now, like the lichen that clung to the stone bench, Fiona was gluing herself to Roderick, and he seemed to be okay with that. Perhaps coming home would be the best thing to do. But – ugh, the prospect of bumping into Ian and his new girlfriend, Jenny the accountant, was gruesome. Emma had told her last night that Jenny had already moved into their old house. They'd spent ages sniggering childishly at the idea of the two of them making spreadsheets for every household activity.

Cambridge no longer felt like home, but life on the island with Roderick back in Fiona's clutches was a depressing prospect. She contemplated the possibility of living in the cottage with Finn as an occasional night-time visitor and a partner for any social events, but, laughing to herself, dismissed it. There had to be some kind of middle ground.

'Are you lost, love?' An elderly man, flat cap pulled down against the wind and rain, bent down to look at her.

'A little bit,' she admitted, confusing him when she said she didn't need directions.

The rain had soaked through her coat by the time she got back to the house. The girls were sitting at the table making elaborate Christmas dinners from Play-Doh.

'Bloody hell, Kate, you're soaking. Where did you walk to – Ely?' Emma looked at Sam, who stood up from the table and disappeared upstairs. 'Hang up your coat, for goodness' sake. You're not on this planet at all, are you? It's all very *Wuthering Heights*, this marching around in the pouring rain, but if your mother arrives tomorrow and you've come down with the flu, I'll be the one getting it in the neck.'

'I've run you a bath,' said Sam, reappearing.

'I'm not six years old,' muttered Kate mutinously.

'No, but you're acting like it,' said Emma, propelling her towards the hall. 'Now go and get yourself warmed up. You've got the Christingle to get through yet.'

Kate groaned in mock-horror, before opening the door of the bathroom and breathing in the lavender-scented steam.

Emma looked at Sam, raising her eyebrows. 'Apparently she's not remotely interested in Roderick.'

'I can see that. Thank God we never have to go there again, eh?' said Sam, folding Emma into his arms as Kate surrendered.

Christmas morning flashed past in a flurry of wrapping paper, excited squealing from the girls, and Emma's visits to the loo. Kate had taken over her share of the cooking and was basting the turkey when Emma reappeared, grey and shaking.

'Urgh! That smells vile. No offence, guys – it's just me.' She had her hand over her mouth, nostrils held closed. 'It's fine as long as I don't breathe in.'

'All this throwing-up is a great sign – it just means the pregnancy hormones are doing their thing,' said Sam comfortably, from the sitting-room floor. He was helping Katharine to build a Playmobil castle, and was surrounded by hundreds of tiny pieces of plastic, all in separate, equally tiny bags.

'So you say,' said Emma, bolting out of the room once again.

'Is she actually being sick?' asked an interested Jennifer. 'What happens if she's sick and the baby comes up out of her tummy and through her mouth and into the loo?'

'I promise you one thing,' said Kate. 'That will definitely not happen.'

Emma returned, sitting down at the kitchen table. She sipped at a mug of cold peppermint tea before looking up at Kate. Her friend looked happier now that she was distracted – perhaps Kate's mother was right, and they ought to try and persuade her to come home.

'So have you heard from anyone on the island today?'

'Morag rang earlier, and Jean sent a text.' Kate laughed to herself, knowing that it would have taken Jean about fifteen minutes, and a lot of cursing under her breath, to achieve the brief message that she'd received on her mobile.

'Nobody else?' Emma raised her eyebrows, then laid

her head down on the cool of the table, waiting for the next wave of nausea to hit.

Half an hour later the doorbell rang, announcing the arrival of Kate's mother, complete with bags of beautifully wrapped presents.

'Just in time for dinner.' She breezed in. 'Darling, can you manage that gravy? Shall I take over?'

'I'm fine,' said Kate weakly, as her mother grabbed the wooden spoon. Really, it was easier not to argue. She picked up the box of crackers, laying the table around the sleeping Emma, who was still sprawled, head down.

'That's not very hygienic, is it?'

'No, Mum, but she's feeling a bit sick. We thought she needed the rest.'

'Sick?' said her mother, turning to Sam. 'She's not . . .'

'She is.'

'Good grief! But you already have two – why on earth would you want another one?'

'Mum!' Kate hissed, horrified.

'Oh, well, I mean, congratulations. It's . . . well, it wouldn't be my choice.'

'That doesn't make it wrong, you know.' Kate turned back to the vegetables, feeling rather pleased with herself. She'd spent years backing down and doing what her mother thought was right, just for an easy life. She stabbed a Brussels sprout with a knife, thinking uncharitable thoughts as she did so. 'These will be ready in about two minutes. Can you wake Emma up, please,

Sam? And, girls, can you two go and wash your hands without flooding the bathroom, please?'

Poor Emma couldn't face any dinner, but sat looking seasick and sniffing at a lemon. 'I'd love to have some, but it just smells like dead bird.'

'That's because it is!' chorused the girls in delight.

'Urgh, Emma, you've put me right off this,' said Kate, pushing her plate away and standing up to clear the dishes.

'I suspect the reason *you* can't eat any more has more to do with the gigantic plateful you've just devoured,' offered Sam helpfully.

'Yes, darling, I think you've had more than enough. I have to say, I think island life is making you a little bit tubby.' Kate's mother patted her bottom as she leaned over the table. 'In fact, I think I'll come up and see what you actually do there. Next week would be convenient?'

Kate caught Emma's eye and breathed out slowly, nostrils flaring. 'Count to ten,' mouthed Emma, help-fully.

'Pudding, anyone?' asked Kate, through gritted teeth. 'I fancy a big slice with extra brandy butter, myself.'

She gathered up the last of the plates and fled to the kitchen, where she emitted a silent scream. I want my dog, and my bonkers orange carpet, and my fire, and my beach, and my seals, and my island, she thought. And I have no idea how long it will last, but anything's got to be better than living with Mum.

11

Hogmanay Ceilidh

Willow galloped joyfully down to the shoreline, chasing her ball. Seagulls wheeled overhead in a cloudless azure sky. It was bright, clear and freezing cold, but it was beautiful, and there wasn't another human being to be seen or heard anywhere. Kate laughed out loud for joy, bending down to scoop up her puppy as she hurtled towards her, soaking wet and covered in sand.

'Willow – yeuch!' she cried, as the puppy tried to lick her face.

They headed back up the hill through the trees and the frost-bleached bracken, towards Bruar Cottage, where the fire was lit and waiting. A figure stood at the top of the path, waving vigorously.

'Morag!' Kate started to run, realizing as she grew closer that her friend wasn't alone. Jean and Susan were standing just over the crest of the hill, peering into the three-wheeled pushchair, talking to Mhairi.

'We've missed you,' grinned Susan. 'You're our fourth Musketeer.'

'It's so lovely to be back.' Kate opened the door, and

the warmth of her little cottage welcomed them in. Five minutes later they were all installed in the sitting room, Mhairi lying on a play-mat, chewing happily on a set of plastic keys. The tea had been made and was brewing in a pot by the fire, covered by one of Helen's hand-sewn tea cosies. Morag had come bearing biscuits and gingerbread.

'We thought you'd like a wee welcome-home party.'

'This is lovely,' said Kate, touched. She'd missed the island desperately, despite having been gone for less than a week. It was nice to know that some small part of it had missed her, too. But, more importantly, she was dying to know all the news. 'So, what's happened?'

'Well,' began Jean, 'I was having a coffee at Bruno's place on Christmas Eve when none other than *herself* came in with her mother, acting like the Queen of Sheba.'

'That's Fiona, in case you hadn't worked it out,' added Susan, unnecessarily.

'I was sitting at the end booth, and they didn't see me. So I just carried on reading my paper, as you do, and you'll never guess what?'

'Will you two fishwives just spit it out?' Morag poured the tea, adding milk and sugar without having to ask who took what. Kate smiled to herself at that little sign of friendship.

Jean rolled her eyes at Morag. 'Will you let me get on?'

'At this rate you'll still be getting to the point by next year,' said Morag, passing her a cup of tea and nudging her, laughing.

'Well,' began Jean again, 'so in come Fiona and her mother, and they sit down at the booth in front of mine, and they don't see me.'

'So you just happened to overhear, and you weren't actually eavesdropping, right?' asked Kate.

'I wouldn't dream of such a thing,' said Jean, primly. 'Anyway, herself is up to something. She told her mother that she's got big plans – plans that involve the island and the Duntarvie estate.'

'Is she planning to ensnare Roderick and steal the estate away from him?' Kate was confused.

'I don't think anyone could persuade Roderick Maxwell to do something he didn't want to do.' Jean looked at Morag, who nodded sagely. 'But that girl is up to something.'

Susan raised her eyebrows at Kate. 'Never a dull moment up here, is there? I bet this is riveting, after an exciting week in the bright lights of Cambridge with all those shops and people and lovely things.'

'Believe it or not, I was dying to get back.' Kate stood up, looking out of the sitting-room window. Through the bare trees she could see the waves breaking on the little shingle beach far below, and in the distance beyond the silver-streaked sea were the snow-topped purple hills of the surrounding islands. 'There's something about this place. It draws you in.'

Jean and Morag exchanged another glance, but said nothing.

*

Hogmanay arrived. Kate had managed to wangle her way out of wearing the hideous yellow tartan. While in Cambridge, she and Emma had spent a lovely girly day shopping (punctuated by loo visits, sniffs of lemon essential oil, and a small impromptu nap for Emma in a corner of Costa Coffee). They had found the most beautiful midnight-blue velvet dress, which clung to Kate's newly enhanced curves. Admiring herself looking glamorous in the mirror, she was tempted to send a photograph to her mother, to show her that she really didn't look tubby at all, thank you very much. Her hair had been curled into shining waves at the new hairdresser in Kilmannan, and her make-up applied with Susan's artistic flair. Her ridiculously high new shoes were safely stored out of reach of Willow this time, and she pulled them on quickly, hearing a firm knock at the door. She grabbed her coat from the hook.

Kate gasped in surprise. Finn was dressed in full Highland regalia, unlike the first time she'd seen him, in a casual kilt with boots and a woollen sweater. He was quite breathtakingly gorgeous. He looked Kate up and down, smiling, and gave a whistle of surprise. 'By God, Kate, I forget you scrub up so well.'

'Always the charmer, Finn.'

'Aye, well, I haven't turned it on yet. Wait till I get to the big house.'

It was only a couple of minutes' walk to Duntarvie House, but Finn had brought his little sports car. 'Just as well, with those shoes – you'll not be doing much ceilidh-dancing in them.'

He pulled the car up on the wide gravelled drive. In the darkness Duntarvie House looked spectacular. Kate had never seen the outdoor lights before. The full fairy-tale splendour of the house could be appreciated, turrets and crenellations highlighted against a velvet-black sky sprinkled with stars.

'It's beautiful, isn't it?' Finn lent her a hand and she climbed out of the low sports car, straightening her dress. 'You've missed a wee bit.' Finn tugged at the hem of her dress, patting her appreciatively on the rump.

'Watch it, you.' She slapped his hand, laughing despite herself. 'You're like something from a seventies sitcom.'

'You can't blame a man for trying.' Finn locked the car, grinning. He was joking, but she sensed that, given the opportunity, he'd be more than happy to oblige.

They crunched across the drive, which was already packed with parked cars. The main door of the house, usually locked shut, was wide open, showing off the marble reception hall. A huge noble fir, decorated with hundreds of sparkling white fairy lights, filled the back of the hall. The staircase was hung with swathes of holly and ivy. Kate recognized Helen's work. Finn turned right, opening the door into the dining room. The huge table, which lay unused most of the year, was covered with discarded coats.

'Let me take that.'

As Kate shrugged off her coat, Finn hung it on one of the ornate wooden chairs.

'Come through.' He held the door open. 'I'll get a drink to warm us up. It's freezing in here.'

Kate hadn't had an excuse to be in the sitting room again since that first night when she'd fallen and hurt herself on the drive. Sitting down on the huge brocade sofa, she smiled to herself, remembering the catalogue of disasters that had led her to the house that day. Waiting for Finn, she pulled out her mobile to look at the most recent seal photographs, sent by Mark yesterday. Flora had shed her white baby fur and was now a beautiful mottled cream and grey. She was settled in the sanctuary, already eating fish and swimming in the big pool with another, older, rescued seal pup. Mark and Melanie had sent her a Christmas card suggesting that she and Roderick go over to visit Flora soon. Kate shuddered at the prospect of a trip to the sanctuary with Fiona in tow.

'You look lovely, Kate.'

She started at the sound of Roderick's voice and stood up, feeling awkward. She thrust the phone at him. 'Look – it's Flora. All her baby fur has gone. Doesn't she look beautiful?'

Roderick took the little screen, glancing at the photograph. 'She is gorgeous, isn't she?' He smiled, handing back the phone and looking at her outfit. 'You know, you look a bit like a seal yourself tonight, in that dress.'

Kate looked down at the velvet dress, which suddenly seemed to be clinging to every lump, bump and wobbling bit. Oh! He thought she looked like a fat, velvety, lumpy, shuffling barrel. Not quite the look she'd been aiming for.

'If that's a line, Roddy, it's a really bad one,' said Finn, returning with a drink for Kate. He handed his own drink to Roderick. 'You have this – I'll be back in a minute with another.'

'How was Cambridge?' asked Roderick stiffly. 'It must be nice for you to get back to Finn?'

Kate paused for a moment. 'Well, it's certainly nice to get back to the island.'

Actually, why should she correct him. Why shouldn't he think she was with Finn? She took a sip of her drink and surveyed him over the top of her glass. Roderick, too, was in Highland dress. She couldn't stop a tiny smile escaping from the corner of her lips as she wondered to herself whether he was a proper Scotsman, or if he'd taken the coward's way out and worn a pair of boxer shorts under his kilt.

Seeing her smile, he frowned.

'So . . . '

'Did you . . .'

'Ladies first.'

'How was Christmas? Did you have a nice time with Fiona?' Kate decided it was easiest to be direct.

'Sweetie,' said the devil, arriving as soon as she was mentioned. 'Oh,' she went on, looking at Kate with un-disguised dislike, 'are you not working tonight?'

Fiona was wearing a dark-green velvet corset top,

with a very short, full tartan mini-kilt. On anyone else it would have looked hideous, but somehow she managed to carry it off.

'No, I'm here as a guest,' said Kate, refusing this time to rise to Fiona's jibes. 'I was just asking Roderick how he enjoyed Christmas.'

'Oh, it was just heaven, wasn't it, Roddy?' Fiona wrapped both her arms around Roderick's waist, looking up at him with adoration. 'Luckily I invited him to the hotel for Christmas dinner, or he'd have had to spend it alone in this draughty old place.'

'I like this draughty old place,' replied Roderick, looking irritated. He removed her hands from his waist and put his empty glass down on the table. 'Now, if you two girls will excuse me, I want to check on Jean. She's supposed to be having fun, not working.'

He disappeared down the side corridor, leaving Kate trapped in the room, stunned into silence by Fiona's basilisk stare. Thankfully Finn reappeared, bearing drinks. Fiona stalked off.

'Thank God you appeared when you did. If looks could kill . . .' laughed Kate.

Finn knocked back his drink, still standing.

'Come and have a look at the ballroom,' he said, taking her arm. 'You'll be needing those dancing shoes tonight.'

Walking along the passage, Kate realized there were whole parts of Duntarvie House that she'd never discovered. The dark-green walls were hung with yet more oil paintings of dogs, deer and kilted men.

'Here we are.'

Seeing the double doors that opened into the ball-room, Kate got her bearings. Behind her was the inner hall, which led to the kitchen and the stairs up to the bedroom she'd slept in.

The ballroom was a revelation. She'd only ever seen it stacked high with old furniture covered with ancient dust sheets, the room freezing cold and echoing. But tonight it had come to life. Tables full of people encir-cled the dance floor, and at one end of the room Murdo was keeping watch over a makeshift bar. A group of youths, presumably back home on the island for the university holidays, were manning it, laughing and shouting to each other over the sound of the music.

The ceilidh band finished tuning their instruments, and the accordion moved from strange, tuneless droning to toe-tapping music, which filled the room. Kate made her way down to the bar, where a delighted Murdo stepped forward, glass in hand, to give her a hug.

'Young Kate,' he shouted over the music. 'Happy Christmas to you.'

She leaned across and kissed his cheek, taking in a blast of whisky fumes and aftershave. 'And to you, Murdo. I hear you had Roderick with you for Christmas?'

'That we did, and we had our little band of helpers working in the hotel over the holiday.' He waved his arm. 'That's Jamie, Stewart, Robbie, Colin and Rosie.'

All five of them gave Kate a thumbs-up and then burst out laughing at one of their own jokes.

'Gin and tonic, please.'

Murdo turned to the optic, pouring her a drink and handing it over.

He looked at her, contemplating. 'So what's the story with you and young Roddy? Don't let Sandra hear me say this, but I'd say you're a far better match for him than our Fiona.'

'There is no story, Murdo,' Kate said, flatly. As he tried to catch her eye, she turned away slightly, spinning the ice in her glass with a finger.

'That's no what Bruno tells me.' A hand on her arm, and a reassuring squeeze.

She took a drink, clattering the glass back down on the bar with unnecessary force. There was a fine line on the island between gentle interfering and meddling. 'Bruno can't keep his mouth shut. There's nothing going on between me and Roderick. And, as far as I can see, Roderick and your Fiona are back together.'

'Well, if they are, he's making a mistake.' He frowned, looking across at Fiona, who was tapping at her phone by the side of the dance floor. 'He's far too nice for her.'

'Murdo!'

'She's my daughter and I love her, but by God, she takes after her mother. I've been married to the woman thirty-odd years. She's the reason I play golf.'

Kate laughed, despite herself. 'You can't say that about your own wife.'

Murdo picked up a keg of beer and winked at Kate. 'Aye, I can. Ever since she was a girl, Fiona's been full of big ideas – this wee island isn't enough for her.'

It's enough for me, thought Kate, looking at the already-familiar faces grouped around the tables. Even after a few months the island seemed more like home than – well, home. A small, sensible voice in her head pointed out that it wasn't feasible to carry on living there with no career and no prospects. The job she'd signed up for was a temporary post, and there was no way the struggling estate could sustain any more employees – unless she could come up with something that would bring in some money. There was half an idea that had been stirring in her mind, but she'd need Roderick onside. And right now every time she looked up he was in close proximity to Fiona. No chance of talking to him tonight. She drowned the voice in her head with another mouthful of gin, and promised herself she'd think about what to do. Only not tonight.

Shaking herself, Kate looked up to find Jean in front of her, beaming with happiness, and with Roderick standing just behind her.

'You look lovely, my dear.' She turned to Roderick. 'Doesn't she?'

Roderick caught Kate's eye for a second. 'Beautiful. Finn is a lucky man.'

The band struck up at the same time as he spoke. Kate was almost certain Jean hadn't heard, or that she had chosen to ignore what Roderick had just said. The floor was full now, the music increasing in pace. People formed themselves into lines for a dance that seemed to consist of people simultaneously whirling around and then galloping up and down. Kate could vaguely remember something like it from her ceilidh days at university.

'You look confused.' Ted appeared, hooking his arm around her waist. 'It's called Strip the Willow. Do you fancy a turn on the floor with an old man?'

'In these shoes?' said Kate, horrified. 'I'll break my ankle.'

'You'll be amazed what you can do if you try.' He smiled, pulling her into the melee.

Kate was being thrown around the floor by an assortment of islanders. After a couple more gin and tonics, it seemed easy enough to keep up with the dances. Either that or she just didn't care that she looked deranged. The air was full of shouts and laughter. Groups of older people stood around, toes tapping, clapping their hands in time to the insistent beat of the ceilidh band.

'Having fun?' Finn twirled Kate under his arm.

'I love it. My feet are falling off, though,' she laughed, as Bruno caught her hand. She kicked off her heels, throwing them under the bar. Suddenly she was skipping around in a circle, the smile on her face so huge that her cheeks were aching. The song ended, the dancers arranged themselves into a line and she looked up.

'Glad you came back for Hogmanay? You've been

smiling every time I've looked at you,' said Roderick, taking her hands.

Oh God, thought Kate, of all the dances to end up with you, it would have to be this one. The prospect of trotting around the room doing the Gay Gordons with Roderick was mortifying. It was the only dance she'd done all night where there was no opportunity to swap partners, and she could already feel Fiona's eyes burning into her from across the room.

'It's been lovely,' said Kate, counting in her head. The twirling-around dances were fine, but this one was slower and more complicated. She'd learned it at university, but it had always got her in a muddle.

'My father used to open up the ballroom for Hogmanay every year. This is the first time I've done it since he died.'

There was something very strange about having a conversation with someone while walking forward for a count of four, backwards for four, then doing four rounds of polka steps.

'Well, it's beautiful. I'm sure he'd love to see the house full of people, instead of covered with dust sheets.'

'He always said this place needed filling up with children and noise and chaos.' Roderick looked at her and laughed. 'Are you counting, Kate?'

'Um, maybe. A little bit. But I am listening, honestly. It's just that if I don't keep count under my breath, I get my legs all tangled up.'

And, thought Kate, if I concentrate on counting and

not on the idea of you and bloody Fiona filling this place with children, I might not throw up.

They danced on in silence. Roderick was a surprisingly good dancer, given his height and long legs. Across the room Fiona was dancing with a grey-bearded man, her nimble feet making the dance look simple. She waved at Roderick with a coy little smile. Still counting, Kate felt quite murderous that bloody Fiona could manage to effortlessly dance, smile and wave, while she was struggling to dance and breathe.

'Mark sent me a message yesterday about taking a drive over to visit Flora.'

'That would be lovely,' lied Kate. Well, she thought, it would be lovely if Fiona wasn't in tow, but there wasn't much chance of that.

'I thought perhaps next Monday? Are you free?'

'I'd love to.'

'It's a date then,' he said, with a smile that made her knees slightly weak. Thankfully the song came to an end, and she disappeared to the loo to splash some cold water carefully on her face, trying not to smudge her make-up, and remind herself very sternly that she had no feelings whatsoever for Roderick Maxwell, thank you very much.

When she returned to the ballroom the band was playing a tune she recognized straight away. The floor was full of people, but they were standing in a circle, looking inwards at something, and clapping. Kate squeezed through to stand beside Susan.

In the middle of the floor, eyes half-closed in concentration, with the first genuine smile Kate had seen on her face, was Fiona. She was dancing a perfect Highland Sword Dance, her feet flying in the air, skipping between two crossed swords, arms held in a graceful arc above her head. She looked beautiful. And that, Kate thought, was obviously what Roderick saw in her.

'She's amazing,' said Kate, leaning across to Susan.

'She's been doing it since she was four. When we all gave it up, in favour of boys and hanging round the shore with a bottle of cider, she was heading off around the country entering competitions.'

'And presumably winning?'

'Of course. This is Fiona we're talking about. She generally gets what she wants.'

The band stopped and Fiona took a bow. Kate hadn't realized that Finn had taken his place amongst them, and was standing with his bagpipes in his arms. He winked at her, and began again – another tune that had the whole place on their feet. Fiona reached out for Roderick, and Kate looked on, feeling sick, as the two of them whirled around the floor.

'She might be a brilliant dancer,' muttered Susan in Kate's ear, 'but she's still an absolute cow-and-a-half. Come on, let's get a drink.'

A couple of hours later, with the prospect of midnight approaching, Kate sneaked off to the kitchen to get a glass of water. The dancing had become increasingly riotous and her feet were killing her. Sitting at the table, she checked her phone:

> Hope your New Year's Eve is more exciting than ours. I'm sending this from the loo. Can't stop being sick. Ugh!

Poor Emma, thought Kate. All those years of wanting to get pregnant, only to be too sick to appreciate it now. She typed a quick reply:

> Have decided to join a nunnery. It's my New Year's resolution.

'What are you doing hiding away in here? It's nearly midnight!' Jean opened the kitchen door, laughing.

'How did you know I was here?'

'Not much gets past me. Now, are you needing a plaster for those feet?'

'I need a bucket of ice and a little sleep, actually, but a plaster would be a start.' Kate was exhausted. Sitting down had probably been a bad idea.

'Right you are. Let's get you sorted out before the bells.'

Jean took some plasters from the first-aid kit and cut them to size for Kate. Her feet felt better instantly, and she stood up, doing a little Highland dance to try them out.

'I'm not quite in Fiona's league, am I?'

'She's in a league of her own, that one,' said Jean,

darkly. 'I'm still wondering what she's up to. I haven't forgotten that conversation I overheard in Bruno's cafe.'

'I think the only plan she had was to get her hands on Roderick, and I think she's achieved that,' said Kate, with a small sigh. The thought of a day-trip to the Seal Sanctuary with a loved-up Roderick and Fiona was a hideous prospect.

'Come on then, let's get you back on the dance floor. After midnight Finn's doing a disco. You can stop worrying about what your feet are doing and just enjoy yourself.'

Kate breathed a huge sigh of relief. It had been wonderful taking part in a proper Highland Hogmanay, but a bit of dancing to Kylie Minogue was exactly what she needed. She might have stopped twirling around, but her head was still spinning.

They left the kitchen, closing the door behind them. A muffled crash was heard from the library. Jean looked at Kate and raised her eyebrows.

'Do you think we should have a wee look and see what's going on?'

Kate pulled a face. 'What if we're interrupting something?'

Jean's natural nosiness won out. 'What if we're not? It could be a burglar.'

'D'you think there are many opportunist book thieves on the island of Auchenmor?' laughed Kate.

'Come on, we'll take a sneaky peep. If they're courting, they'll no notice us popping our head round the door.'

They crept down the dark corridor on tiptoe. The door to the library was slightly ajar. A soft glow indicated that the desk lamp, rather than the main light, had been switched on. Kate screwed her eyes closed as Jean pushed the door open gently.

'Fiona!' Jean exclaimed.

Kate opened her eyes. No half-naked Roderick. Just Fiona, standing with her back to the desk.

'We thought you were a burglar.'

'Me!' Fiona's laugh was shrill. 'Don't be so silly. I was getting a breath of fresh air.'

Kate looked sideways at Jean. The last place anyone would go for fresh air was the library, fuggy with the smell of ancient books and a fire that hadn't been lit in months.

'Anyway,' said Fiona, looking at her watch, 'look at that – it's nearly time for the bells. Come on, girls, or we'll miss our chance for a midnight kiss.'

She hitched her handbag onto her shoulder and swept past, her kilted bottom swishing up the hall.

'I told you, she's up to something,' said Jean.

'She's probably trying to find Roderick's cheque book,' Kate said, as they followed Fiona back to the ballroom.

'Have a glass – it's nearly midnight,' said Tom, thrusting some champagne at Jean and Kate.

Kate stood in a corner, watching as people crowded around the bar.

There was Susan, slipping in behind the bar to join Tom in pouring out champagne for everyone. Jean and

Hector were sitting at a table, smiling at each other, not talking. Across the room Kate could see Sandra holding court, a group of women cackling as she gesticulated wildly. Murdo was in his element behind the bar, teacloth over one arm, well out of Sandra's reach. As she watched, he leaned below the makeshift counter, lifting up a bottle of malt whisky, which he handed to Bruno. They pulled off the lid and sniffed at the bottle appreciatively. Murdo reached down again into a crate, pulling out some whisky glasses, and poured a large measure for himself, one for a laughing Bruno and one extra. Catching Kate's eye, Bruno raised his glass and gave her a grin, beckoning her over.

'What are you up tae, hidin' away in a corner?'

'I was people-watching. And keeping an eye on you two.' She turned to Murdo, who was sipping his whisky with a beatific smile.

'I'm no seeing in the New Year with a glass of champagne,' he said indignantly.

'Aye, well, James widna hae done, either.' Bruno raised his glass in memory of Roderick's father. 'Tae absent friends.'

'Absent friends.'

All three of them clinked glasses, remembering. Mellowed by a mixture of gin, whisky and champagne, Kate thought of her dad, realizing with surprise that she was actually looking forward to her mum's imminent visit. All those years spent alone – perhaps it was time for her mother to move on and meet someone new.

'You lot are looking very sombre.'

Roderick appeared, leaning across the bar and picking up the bottle of whisky.

'You've dug this one out of the vaults, Murdo. Is it a special occasion?'

'Aye, it is,' said Murdo, passing the third glass to Roderick. 'We're celebrating absent friends, and drinking to the future. Your dad would have been pleased to see the house alive like this tonight.'

Kate felt her stomach tighten in sympathy. Roderick winced, almost imperceptibly, and she clenched her fists to stop herself from reaching out to him. That wasn't her place – it was Fiona's.

'He would, wouldn't he?' Roderick smiled, looking up at the oil painting above their heads. A dark-haired man in corduroy trousers, waxed jacket and wellington boots was sitting on a rock, surrounded by a heap of squirming, lolling dogs. He was smiling, but it was a smile that didn't reach his eyes.

'Is that your father?' Kate hadn't stopped to think that the people in the paintings were so closely related to Roderick. It really was another world.

'Yes. That was painted the year after we moved to the island, by Susan's mother. You can see where she gets her talents from, can't you?'

'It's beautiful.' Kate caught his eye. She could feel the heat rising in her cheeks.

'Absent friends, then,' said Roderick, taking a drink, his gaze not wavering.

'Roddy, sweetie, there's a minute to the bells . . . '
Fiona, timing perfect as ever, appeared at his side. 'Come
on, you need to do the countdown.'

She pulled at his arm. He put his glass down slowly,
pulling a rueful face at Kate.

'Duty calls.'

'I can't stand this sort of thing, so I'm going to make it
quick,' said Roderick, holding the microphone and
looking uncomfortable. 'Thank you all so much for
coming. It means a lot to me, and I think it would make
my dad very happy to know that the house was full of
people, which is what he always wanted. And, er – that's
it.' He looked at his watch, checking the time.

'Come on, man, you're going to miss the bells at this
rate!' Laughing, Finn grabbed the microphone out of
Roderick's hands and started the countdown. 'Ten – nine
– eight – seven – six – five – four – three – two – ONE!'

The whole room erupted in shouts of 'Happy New
Year!' and Kate was being grabbed and kissed by Bruno,
Ted, Murdo, Jean, Hector, Morag, Susan and by people
she'd never spoken to in her time on the island. All that
worrying about being the only person with nobody to
kiss at Hogmanay, and she was barely able to take a
breath before another person pounced on her. And then
the whole room was linking hands and singing 'Auld
Lang Syne' at the tops of their voices. Kate looked up
at the painting of Roderick's sad, smiling father, and
thought that he would definitely approve.

12

An Early Start

BLEEP-BLEEP – BLEEP-BLEEP. Kate hit the Snooze button on her alarm for the fifth time and rolled back under her covers. Willow had been up all night barking at the wind and was now fast asleep, curled up at the foot of the bed. Through a drowsy haze, Kate tried yet again to think why she had set an alarm. Unable to come up with an answer, she curled herself under the covers and floated back to sleep.

She was swimming with seals and gliding gracefully in the water.

Seals! She sat up, completely awake now, a cold feeling of horror settling in the pit of her stomach. She remembered the last conversation she'd had with Roderick as the Hogmanay party had come to an end.

'I'll pick you up at 8.15 a.m. We can catch the ferry at quarter to. You will be up, won't you?' Roderick had laughed.

'Of course,' Kate had said indignantly. 'I'll have you know I'm up walking the dog at seven o'clock most mornings.'

All right, she'd done it once, so she wasn't lying alto-gether – but in truth Willow wasn't that keen on getting up early in the morning, either. They'd reached an agree-ment whereby morning walks didn't take place until eight-thirty, after Kate had drunk at least two cups of tea.

Kate staggered out of bed and downstairs into the bathroom. After freezing herself under the shower, she ran upstairs, wrapped in a towel. Oh, help! No clothes. Everything was either stuffed in the overflowing washing basket or soaking wet in the washing machine. Thank goodness Mark and Melanie aren't glamorous, she thought, grabbing yesterday's jeans from the chair.

Hearing the sound of Roderick's car on the gravel outside, she ran downstairs, Willow hurtling in front of her. She shoved on her wellies and grabbed her coat, twisting her hair up with a clip.

'Morning.' She opened the door with a forced smile.

'I was expecting to find you still asleep in bed,' said Roderick.

'Not a bit. Up and ready to go – that's me,' lied Kate. 'Is it all right if we take Willow? She's never been on the ferry, and I thought it would be a good chance for her to get used to it.'

And I've not had a chance to walk her, and if I leave her at home she'll probably have eaten the entire house by the time I get back, she added, silently.

'I'd love that.' Roderick scooped up the puppy, stroking her ears and smiling at her.

'Will Fiona mind?'

'Fiona? Why would she mind?' Roderick's tone of voice was incredulous.

'I assumed she was coming with us,' explained Kate. 'Mind you, I suppose she'd probably still be in bed at this time of day.'

'I can guarantee it.'

Kate pulled the car door closed, feeling slightly sick. He'd obviously left her fast asleep up at Duntarvie House. She could imagine Fiona floating around the kitchen making tea, and probably making plans to turn the house into a luxury hotel. Kate shuddered.

'Are you cold?'

'No, sorry. Just thinking.' Kate looked out of the window, watching the frost-covered rhododendron bushes whizz past as Roderick manoeuvred around the potholes at a ridiculous speed.

They left Willow sleeping in the back of the car, and climbed the metal steps up to the boat's cafe. It was a bank holiday and the ferry was almost empty of passengers.

'Morning, Roddy.' The woman behind the bar leaned over and gave him a kiss. 'Happy New Year to you. I hear the party was a big hit.'

'Happy New Year to you, too, Aileen. It was a shame you couldn't make it.'

'Aye, well, I was looking after Jo's wee ones. She

works hard, so she deserves a night out at Hogmanay. Tea?'

'Yes, please,' said Kate and Roderick in unison. They looked at each other and laughed.

'It's been a long morning. Apparently Kate's been up for hours,' explained Roderick, eyebrows raised. 'Next year, Aileen, bring the little ones up to the house. It's a great place for children.'

'Here you are.' Aileen passed over a tray with a pot of tea and a plate of biscuits. 'It'll maybe no be long till you're filling the house with your own wee ones?'

'Chance would be a fine thing.' He picked up the tray and turned for the table.

Aileen gave Kate the ghost of a wink.

They sat for a while, drinking tea in silence, the drone of the boat's engine lulling Kate into a trance.

'Do you have any brothers or sisters?'

'Me?' Kate was taken aback by Roderick's sudden question. 'None.'

'No, me neither. I think my father would have liked to have had a houseful, but my mother wasn't keen. I think she had her mind on other things.'

Eek, thought Kate, we're treading on dangerous ground here.

'I've always wanted to be part of a big family,' he continued. 'I always wanted to have about five children. I like the idea of them all bundling around together.' Roderick smiled at the thought.

'Yes, me too.'

He looked up at her, a strange expression on his face. 'Really?'

'Yes. I know everyone wants a neat little one or two, but I always envied my friends who grew up with lots of brothers and sisters.'

'Yes, me too.'

'Does . . . is . . . Fiona is an only child, too, isn't she?'

'Fiona?' Roderick sounded genuinely surprised 'She is, yes. But Fiona has no desire whatsoever to have children. It's not part of her grand plan.'

It was clearly a sore subject. Kate had spent long enough with him now to realize when a subject was closed. Roderick turned round, peering out of the window, spotting the houses clustered around the ferry dock, white against the morning gloom. He seemed relieved to change the subject. 'Look, we're nearly here. Let's go and check on Willow.'

Gulping the last of his tea, Roderick stood up. He gathered the cups onto the tray and took it back to Aileen.

'I'm sorry, I don't mean to be so pathetic,' sniffled Kate, blowing her nose again. 'It's just that she looks so lovely.'

Melanie handed her another tissue. They were standing outside, watching Flora. The seal pup had lost all of her white fur coat, and was now pale grey, mottled with darker spots. She had more than doubled in size.

'She's a little barrel with flippers on the side.' Kate

laughed, watching Flora as she and her companion, Reggie, shuffled lumpily around the side of the pool. As if to prove a point, the pups slipped into the water and swam in circles with effortless grace.

'The bigger, the better,' explained Mark. 'She can't be released until she weighs thirty kilos. She's brilliant at catching fish, though – a real natural.'

Mark picked up a bucket and strode across the concrete yard. The Seal Sanctuary was immaculate, even right after the Christmas holidays, the concrete hosed clean and the pools sparkling.

'Watch this,' said Mark, sloshing a bucketful of water into the pool. Kate caught a silvery glimpse of mackerel. Flora and Reggie swooped down, before surfacing, each with a fish in their mouth.

'They're a pair of comedians,' laughed Melanie. 'Looks like they'll both be ready for release at about the same time – I reckon another four weeks will do it.'

'Kate, you'll help with the release, won't you?' Roderick looked at her.

'Of course, but I can't guarantee I won't cry again.'

Mark stacked the bucket neatly by the tap, wiping his hands on his trousers. 'I don't think I've managed a release without a tear sneaking out yet, so you'll be in good company.'

Kate watched the water rippling as the seal pups disappeared under the surface, twisting and turning, their movements graceful. Flora's head popped out of the water and she stared at them, nose twitching, whiskers trembling. Her mouth opened, and she began to sing. The sound was eerie and ear-piercing.

'I think that's our cue to go inside,' laughed Melanie. 'She'll be at it for hours now – I've never heard a pup as noisy as Flora.'

They slipped into the house through the back door, leaving Mark tending to the resident seals. Willow leapt up from the rug, dancing at Kate's feet.

'Leave your boots there,' said Melanie. 'I'll pop the kettle on.'

Kate held onto the door handle, shaking her feet out of her wellingtons. As she did so, something lacy and black shot out of the bottom of her trouser leg. Her hunting instinct on alert, Willow grabbed the thin and trotted round the room, looking proud of herself.

'What's that you've got?' laughed Roderick, bending down to take it from her.

'Stop!'

Kate shoved him out of the way, grabbing the offending article from Willow's mouth and trying to stuff it in her pocket.

'It looks like—'

'Never mind what it looks like,' snapped Kate, carefully pulling off the other boot and checking the contents, before lining it up with its pair by the door.

'A pair of knickers,' finished Roderick, bursting out laughing.

Please, ground, swallow me up now and I will die happy, thought Kate. And I promise I'll never, ever, ever pull my jeans and knickers off together and throw them in a heap on the bedroom floor again.

'It was a sock.'

Roderick looked at her, disbelieving. 'A sock. Right.'

'Coffee, you two? Have you had breakfast?' Melanie appeared at the kitchen door, kettle in hand.

'Perfect.' Roderick nudged Kate, laughing. 'I get the impression that someone might have got up in a bit of a rush.'

Kate and Roderick spent the journey home working on final details for the bunkhouse. The main work on the building was nearly finished, and Kate sketched out her plans for the interior over a cup of tea on the boat.

'Shall we pop in on Bruno on the way back?'

Kate was surprised that Roderick wasn't desperate to get back to Fiona. The idea of a coffee and one of Bruno's gorgeous cakes was heaven, though. They drove off the ferry, turning right along the High Street of Kilmannan and parking the Land Rover opposite the cafe.

'Two nicer faces I couldn't wish to see.'

Bruno greeted Kate with a kiss, and Roderick with a hug. Without asking what they wanted, he busied himself at the coffee maker, while they found a tall stool each by the counter.

Bruno put down three steaming mugs of coffee. The cafe was surprisingly empty for the school holidays. Usually at this time of day it was full of teenagers lingering over fizzy drinks, nagging Bruno to turn up the jukebox, teasing him good-humouredly about the ancient selection of music available. Bruno took a reverential sip, looking at them with an expression of bliss.

'Gorgeous, if I say so masel. So what're ye sayin' tae it today then?'

Kate looked out of the window at the tired benches that overlooked the bay. Even on a grey January, the views were breathtaking. But the High Street was dotted with boarded-up shops, and everyone she spoke to bemoaned the lack of heart on the island, compared to the way it used to be.

'There used to be thousands of tourists here every summer, didn't there?'

'Aye, there did,' said Bruno, 'I used tae be packed wi' them every day afore people started goin' on package holidays.'

Roderick looked up from the paper he was reading. 'It's the same all over the islands. It's hard to persuade people to come this far.'

'Ah,' said Kate, smiling, 'but that's where you come in.' Now was as good a time as any – there was no Fiona, for one thing, and Bruno seemed like he'd back her up. 'I've had an idea for the cottages.'

'Why do I get the feeling I'm not going to like this?' said Roderick. 'You're not going to tell me we should turn the house into a luxury hotel, are you?'

'Yes, that's exactly what I had in mind,' Kate pulled a face at him. 'I thought we'd turf you out, and you could live in a caravan in the garden. In fact, I thought Sandra could run the place.'

Bruno burst out laughing. He handed Kate a piece of carrot cake.

'So tell me, what *have* you got planned?' Roderick speared a piece of Kate's cake with a fork and stole it. She slapped his hand.

'You know the island better than anyone. Why not take advantage of that? You could take people on wildlife-spotting tours. You could rent the cottages out all year round. An ecology centre, maybe even working in conjunction with Mark and the Seal Sanctuary. Boat trips. In fact there are three more derelict cottages. Families would love it here – the beaches are perfect for children.'

'Who's going to come all the way up here?'

'I did.' Kate looked him in the eye, waiting for a flat refusal. The idea of guiding tourists round the island wouldn't appeal to the diffident Roderick, but she knew that his passion for the island and its wildlife would make him the perfect guide. Tourists would love him, and the fact that he was the laird, with a house that looked like a castle, would definitely help pull in visitors.

'You're not like other people.'

Kate raised her eyebrows. 'Is that an insult or a compliment?'

'I'll give you this, boy, ye've got a way wi' words,' laughed Bruno.

'I'll have a look online, do some research, but I don't really fancy dragging a load of tourists around, frightening the animals.'

Kate climbed off the chair and handed her mug back to Bruno. They shared a conspiratorial smile. 'I knew he'd love it,' said Kate, in an undertone.

'I wouldn't go that far,' growled Roderick.

'Your mum's been on the phone, Kate,' said Jean, as they walked into the kitchen.

Willow hurtled up to Roderick's dogs, who were sleeping peacefully in a basket by the Aga. She threw herself on top of them, barking loudly. Stupefied by the heat, neither of them moved. Willow bounced off to investigate the crumbs under the table.

'Why? What's happened?' Kate pulled her mobile out of her bag, realizing as she did so that it had been switched to silent mode all day. Oops!

'She tried your mobile about five times and couldn't get hold of you – I think she assumed you'd be working up here.'

She was due on the island tomorrow afternoon. Kate thought about the mess at Bruar Cottage and decided that she'd leave Roderick to research wildlife holidays by himself.

'I'd better get going. I have a house to tidy.'

Jean turned to Roderick, looking disapproving. 'And Fiona rang twice. She says they're expecting you at the hotel for dinner?'

Roderick, who was sitting at the table with his head over the laptop, already absorbed in research, looked up irritably. 'Oh God, I'd forgotten about that – that's the last thing I want to do this evening.'

Kate caught his eye and raised her eyebrows. 'Don't let her catch you saying that, or you'll be in trouble.'

It was almost easier to bear, now that she'd accepted that Fiona wasn't going anywhere. She and Roderick could be friends, and she'd stick to her 'no men for a year' rule, and then she could leave the island happy. The trouble was that even thinking about leaving the island gave her a lump in her throat. Never mind, she thought, I can worry about that later. She took a deep breath. Jean gave her an odd look. Sometimes it felt as if Jean knew exactly what she was thinking, and it was quite unnerving. Jean reached into the fridge, handing her a Tupperware jug with a lid on, full of soup.

'At least that way you don't have to worry about what she's having for dinner tomorrow night.'

Kate sighed with relief. 'Thanks, Jean. I'll bring Mum over when she gets here. She's dying to look around the house. She's under the impression it's a proper castle.'

Roderick snorted.

'Is she indeed?' said Jean crisply. 'I'd better get the drawbridge polished, in that case.'

13

A Word to the Wise

'Elizabeth Jarvis.' Kate's mother held out her smooth, elegant hand to Morag, who had been walking up the hill from the ponies' field. Kate was fulfilling the dual purpose of walking Willow and showing her mother around the estate in the thin, late-afternoon sunshine.

The two women shook hands, Kate's mother taking in Morag's filthy jodhpurs, wellies and patched, ancient sweater. She, in contrast, was dressed in black trousers, a long floral tunic and a camel-coloured wool coat. It was amazing, Kate thought, how quickly one slipped into the casual way of dressing that was normal on the island. She remembered her own spotless jeans and pale suede boots from her first day, and looked down now at her walking boots, fleece and crumpled, mud-splashed jeans.

'D'you fancy a cup of tea, Morag?'

'That would be lovely. Come to me, though – I have coffee cake, just baked today.'

'Perfect,' said Kate's mother with a grateful smile.

While Morag was washing her hands in the downstairs loo of the cottage and Kate was putting the kettle to boil on the Aga, Elizabeth gazed out of the window and over the countryside. She could see why her daughter had fallen in love with the place. It was so peaceful, and so beautiful. Outside the dusk was sneaking across the valley, the sky streaked red-gold as the sun disappeared beyond the distant hills. And the people seemed so welcoming – she'd had a lovely chat on the ferry with the woman who worked in the cafe bar. She'd hinted that there was more than friendship between Kate and her new boss.

'Big slice or small slice?' Morag appeared from the bathroom, drying her hands on a towel. She lifted the lid of a cake tin, revealing a huge cake smeared with buttercream and studded with walnuts.

'I should say small, but I'm on holiday,' smiled Elizabeth.

'If you're having a big one, Mum, so am I.'

Elizabeth shot an almost imperceptible glance at Kate's thighs. Kate ignored her, and nothing was said.

They sat in the comfortable kitchen, warmed by the Aga, chatting until long after dark had fallen. Kate stood up to turn on the lamps, looking at her mother and Morag chatting animatedly. She'd never thought about Morag's age before, but Kate realized that the two women were of the same generation.

'Oh, I haven't ridden for years,' her mother was saying.

'We'll have to sort that out while you're here. Come up one afternoon and we'll go together – it's the best way to see the island. In fact, come out now – I'll take you to meet Thor,' said Morag, keen to show off her favourite pony.

'Coming, Kate?' Morag held the door open for her, the cold air whistling in, cutting through the warmth of the kitchen. Kate shivered, reluctant to leave the cottage.

'I'll be there in a second – I'll clear the plates away first.'

'I was never happy when she was with that Ian.'

Kate paused on the doorstep, hearing her mother's voice as she stepped out into the chill air of the stable yard. It sounded as if Morag was working her magic again. She had an amazing knack of extracting the truth from people. She thought back, remembering the long chat they'd had when she first arrived on the island. Morag's skill was in listening to the words that weren't spoken, and yet she held her own secrets very closely. Kate stood for a minute, torn between announcing herself and a terrible urge to listen in. The terrible urge won.

'By the sounds of things, he was a bit of a wet blanket – what on earth did Kate see in him?'

'I think she was just happy to settle with the first man who'd have her, and along came Ian. He was nice enough – but he had nothing about him. She's worth so much more.'

Kate smiled to herself. Her mother had always been

so nice about Ian. It was a relief to discover what she really thought of him.

'So you'll not have been sorry to see the back of him?' asked Morag. The two women were standing in Thor's stable, their voices carrying clearly across the silent evening.

'Not at all. I think moving up here has been the best thing for Kate. She seems much happier in herself, don't you think?'

Kate almost gasped, a hand across her mouth in shock. To hear her mother admit that moving away was a good thing was almost unthinkable.

'She's a lot more confident now than when I first met her, that's certain,' agreed Morag. 'And she's met a couple of nice men while she's been up here, although I'm sure I probably shouldn't be telling you that.'

No, you blooming well shouldn't, thought Kate. I'll be getting the third degree tonight over dinner. Mum might have loosened the apron strings, but given half a chance she'll be strangling me with them again.

'Well, that's the best thing that could happen to her, if you ask me. I'd hate for her to end up like me.' Kate's mother sighed.

'In what way?' Morag's voice was gentle.

'I've spent fifteen years on my own.' There was a pause, and when she spoke again her voice was lower, and quiet. 'I didn't feel it was right to replace Kate's father.'

There was a scuffling. Kate could imagine Thor shuffling backwards obediently as Morag opened the stable door, letting Elizabeth out.

'You know,' said Morag reasonably, 'you can't live your life through her.'

'I see that now. It took Kate going away for me to realize that. I was trying to cling onto the life I had before Malcolm died, but that's no way to live, is it?'

'No, Mum, it's not.' Kate had stepped forward out of the shadows and across the stable yard. She stood in front of her mother, tears in her eyes.

'My darling. I felt it was my fault you lost him. If we hadn't argued, he wouldn't have stormed off. And if he hadn't stormed off, he wouldn't have been hit by that car.' Kate's mother reached forward, taking her daughter's hands. 'I had to be mother and father to you. It was the least I could do.'

And she'd given up the last fifteen years of her life to do so, Kate realized. All that time she'd felt smothered, but her mum had been trying to do the job of two parents, drowning in guilt.

'I don't blame you for Dad dying. I never did.' Thinking of the house full of photographs – a life preserved exactly as it had been the day her father died – she felt a wave of sadness. 'And I hate to think of you being on your own because of me.'

'I'm sorry, Kate.' Smiling sadly, Elizabeth looked into Kate's eyes. 'If you've felt suffocated, that was never my intention. You were all I had, and for a long time I felt that if I could just keep you safe, it would make everything else okay.'

Kate let go of her mum's hands, throwing her arms around her instead. 'Don't be sorry,' she said, muffled by the camel coat.

'I just want the best for you. I want you to have the best life you can – to make up for ruining your childhood.' Elizabeth's voice was choked with emotion.

'Look,' Kate pulled away, looking at her mother. 'I love you, Mum, and you *didn't* ruin my childhood, so you have nothing to feel guilty about. I promise. People die. We've only got one life. I want to enjoy this one.'

Her mother fished in her handbag for a tissue, before blowing her nose.

'Let's make a pact,' said Kate. 'You start living your own life now, and I'll live mine. Mistakes and all.'

'Deal.' Elizabeth gave a watery smile.

'Well, I'm glad that's all sorted,' said Morag briskly, closing the stable door. 'Although I'm afraid you've got horse-slobber all down your lovely coat, Elizabeth.'

Kate's mum looked down at her expensive coat. It was smeared with a frothy green slime. Amazingly she started to laugh, and threw her arms around a surprised Thor's neck. Never one to miss an opportunity, he whiffled hopefully in her pockets.

'It's a small price to pay for clearing the air, I think. Now, Kate, shall we get back for some of this famous soup you've been telling me about?'

Elizabeth took her daughter's hand. Morag watched,

smiling to herself, as they set off down the lane to Bruar Cottage.

It was amazing what a difference there was in her mother. Instead of finding fault with everything, and criticizing the muddle in Kate's cottage, Elizabeth curled up on the sofa with Willow, drinking soup out of a mug, watching old DVDs and laughing about Kate's escapades on Auchenmor.

'What's the plan for tomorrow? Are you going to take me to meet the famous Roderick?'

Kate groaned. 'He's a normal person, Mum. He just happens to be the Laird of Duntarvie.'

'And owner of a castle, and five hundred acres of land, and a house in Oxfordshire with more land – and single.' Her mother winked at her.

'Enough!' Kate stood up, collecting the mugs. 'I thought we'd go for breakfast at Bruno's cafe – you'll love it. And then perhaps I'll take you over to see the cottages. One of them is occupied, but I can show you the smaller cottage, and you can see how we're getting on with the bunkhouse.'

'That sounds perfect, darling.'

Bruno placed breakfast in front of Kate's mother. The soft curds of creamy scrambled eggs covered two slices of Italian rye bread. On top lay thin curls of crisply fried pancetta.

'And fresh plum tomatoes as well,' added Bruno.

'You're getting the special treatment, you two. Black pepper?'

'This looks delicious.' Elizabeth smiled up at him. 'I was expecting a greasy spoon and fried everything, not a breakfast that would fit perfectly in a cafe in Rome.'

'Aye, well, we do our best.' Bruno looked rather proud of himself, settling an identical plate in front of Kate with a grin.

'It's gorgeous.'

'It always is,' explained Kate, her mouth full of toast, 'that's why I can't let myself come too often, or I'd end up the size of a house.'

Bruno returned with coffee, slipping into the booth alongside Elizabeth. 'Can I join you two girls for a moment?'

'That would be lovely.' Elizabeth smiled at him, shuffling sideways with a little giggle.

If I didn't know better, thought Kate, I'd say there was a bit of flirting going on here. Her mother and Bruno had hit it off immediately, sharing reminiscences of teenage years spent in cafes that looked identical to this one. The two of them had spent ten minutes flicking through the songs on the Wurlitzer, laughing and remembering tunes from their dancing days. Kate had sat quietly at the table, leafing through the local paper, amused at how well her mother was slotting into island life.

'So where are you girls off to this morning?'

'Kate's taking me over to the cottages she's been

working on. I'm looking forward to seeing what she's done.'

'Aye, she and Roddy have done a grand job over there.' Bruno leaned back on his chair, cradling his coffee in both hands. 'They make a guid team.'

'So I hear.' Her mother smirked slightly. Kate kicked her under the table.

A group of teenagers ambled into the cafe, settling down around the high counter, laughing and joking with each other. Kate recognized some of them as the students who had worked for Murdo at Hogmanay. Standing at the till, rifling through her purse for change, she gave them a shy smile, not sure if they'd be too cool to acknowledge her in public.

'Hiya, Kate – how're you doing? You recovered from New Year?'

Obviously not. 'Yes, it was a lovely night. I felt a bit gruesome the next morning, though.'

The larger teenager laughed in sympathy, turning back to his friends.

'Come on then, Mum. I'll drive round the long way, show you a bit more of the island.'

'I'd like that. Maybe I'll see you again before I go, Bruno?' said her mother, with a coy little wave.

'I'd like *that*.' Bruno leaned forward, kissing Elizabeth on both cheeks. Kate raised her eyebrows. After their conversation of last night, her mother wasn't hanging about. Mind you, Kate supposed, after fifteen years of being on her own, she had a fair bit of catching up to do. She held the door open, winding her scarf up against the biting wind blowing off the sea.

They were at the highest point of the island, looking across the water to the island of Eilean Mòr, which lay forbidding in its emptiness. Snow tipped the hills there, and the wind was even harsher. It was a relief to climb back into the car, even with the temperamental heater blowing out more cold air than hot. Kate's mother wisely kept her gloves on, rubbing her hands together to try and warm them up.

'It's a lot colder up here than it is in England.'

'A lot more beautiful, though, wouldn't you agree?' Kate parked the car up on the verge opposite the track that led up to the cottages. 'Look down there – can you see the grey seals by the water?'

It had been a relief to see the seals returning to the beach, following the scare they'd had. She'd driven over during the following days, checking hopefully, until one day she pulled up to find them back in their rightful places, curving over the stones, statue-like in their peace.

'But there's so many of them! When you said you'd seen seals, I thought you meant one or two – not huge gatherings of them.' The cold forgotten, her mother climbed out of the car. They scrambled across the rocks, Kate stopping to point out a flock of oystercatchers, their long beaks probing the shingle. Seeing her smile as she stood watching the seals, Kate tucked her hand into her mother's arm.

Something in the sky caught Elizabeth's eye. 'What on earth is that? It's huge!'

Kate followed her gaze. Swooping above them, silent and graceful in a sapphire sky, wings outstretched, was a golden eagle. Roderick had told her about them many times, but she had never been lucky enough to spot one. Until now.

'Keep still and don't make a sound,' she whispered to her mother.

They stood together, watching with awe as the enormous bird swooped over their heads and, with two beats of its powerful wings, disappeared out of sight into the pine-covered hills.

'And *that* is why I love it here. I've learned so much about the wildlife on the island,' explained Kate, leading her mother across the rocks and back up the shingle beach to the road, 'and now, with the idea of wildlife tours, there's a real chance that we can start to bring tourists – and money – back to the island.'

The track up to the cottages was still frozen solid. A thin ribbon of smoke curled from the chimney of Fiona's cottage. Her booking had been extended, bringing welcome income to the estate, but in the most unwelcome of forms. Bruno had told Kate that Fiona was using the cottage as somewhere to work during the day, away from the noise of the hotel. And the distractions of Roderick, thought Kate, frowning. As they drew closer it was clear there was nobody in – the curtains were open, no lights were on and there was no sign of her car. She'd probably flounced into the kitchen at Duntarvie House by now, heels clattering on the flagstones, expensive handbag thrown across the table, demanding a drink.

'Looks like we've missed Fiona,' said Kate, 'so I can quickly show you both the cottages as well as the bunkhouse.'

'I'm very impressed with all of this.' Her mother waved a hand, encompassing the whole steading. Billy and his workers had done an amazing job of clearing away all the rubble and the twisted, rusted old pieces of machinery. In their place were old feeding troughs filled with pansies, laced with frost, from Helen's shop. Each cottage now had a beautiful, wide wooden door with an old-fashioned bell attached to the wall.

'Come and look at the bunkhouse. It's not finished yet, but you can imagine it.'

Kate led her mother around the side of the cottages, to the old cow byre. The building, full of straw the first time Kate had seen it, was now floored, the walls lined and plastered. The roof beams had been treated and the old wood was seasoned and full of character.

'There'll be a shower room here,' explained Kate, taking her mother through to an empty space at the end of the building. 'This used to be the room where the cowman washed the milk churns, so we didn't have to build any walls.' She ran her hands along the smooth plasterwork, smiling to herself at Billy's artistry. It was flawless. She could visualize the bunkhouse full of chattering students, talking in the velvety blackness long after lights out.

'Kate?'

'Sorry, I was in a dream. What d'you think?'

'I think you've been hiding your light under a bushel.' Her mother squeezed her hand, looking at her with admiration. 'Morag told me you've run this project pretty much single-handed. I always knew you were capable of so much more than all those temp jobs. You've really worked hard at this, darling. I'm proud of you.'

Kate scratched her head, not quite sure what to do with the compliment. 'I don't think I knew I had it in me. But it hasn't seemed like hard work, and I couldn't have done it on my own – Roderick has been by my side the whole way.'

'Mmm,' her mother said with a small smile, 'has he now?'

'Mum! There is nothing going on between me and Roderick – not least because he's back together with Fiona. Come on, I'll show you round the cottages.'

She locked the door of the bunkhouse, making a note to herself to buy Billy a bottle of his favourite malt whisky by way of thanks for the work he'd done.

'I feel a bit naughty taking you in here.' Kate looked over her shoulder as she unlocked the door to Fiona's cottage. A waft of Fiona's strong, floral scent hit the back of Kate's nose as she pushed the door open. She stopped in her tracks, pulling a face.

273

'Oh, for goodness' sake. If she catches us, we'll say we were inspecting the pipes or something.' Elizabeth pushed her daughter forward into the open-plan room. Kate laughed at her mother's new, rebellious spirit. After fifteen years of doing the right thing, she seemed to be determined to make up for it.

'Come on then, I'll show you round. This is the bathroom – you know I always wanted one of those claw-footed baths,' said Kate, opening a door into a surprisingly spacious room, with a huge window that looked out across the bay. 'I thought it would be nice to have a bath and watch the sunset, and round here you don't have to worry about people peering in at you.'

The bed hadn't been slept in. Kate felt her stomach sink, realizing this was yet another sign that Fiona had been sleeping up at Duntarvie House.

The fire in the wood-burner was nearly out, but the sitting room was blissfully warm after the icy-cold winds of the beach and the chill of the empty shell of the bunkhouse.

'You've made a good job – such a lovely homely feel. I could curl up here by that fire and go to sleep.'

Kate pointed out of the window at the view, which stretched over the bay. 'The sunsets here are unbeliev-able, Mum. I reckon we'll be able to rent these cottages out and make a fortune. I think I've persuaded Roderick to do up the other derelict cottages and rent them out, too.'

'You've got it all planned out, haven't you?' Laughing at Kate's excitement, Elizabeth turned away from the window. 'I love these old reclaimed-wood tables, they have so much—'

She stopped, hand to her mouth. Kate spun round. 'What is it?'

'What did you say Fiona did?'

'She's a journalist – why?'

'Look at these.' Elizabeth pointed down at the coffee table, where Fiona's laptop lay, surrounded by notebooks, pieces of paper and a sheaf of black-and-white photographs.

Kate looked down at the pile of pictures. On top, smiling mischievously, a curtain of blonde hair shining across one shoulder, was Annabel Maxwell. It was the photograph Jean had showed her when she first arrived on the island. And underneath – Kate poked at the pile with a finger, cautiously.

'Oh!' She looked away, hands over her face, which was scarlet with embarrassment.

'For heaven's sake, Kate, don't be such a prude.' Her mother picked up the photographs, fanning them out in her hands. 'Bloody hell. It's Ivar Cornwall. I always suspected he was a lecherous bugger.'

Kate peeked through her fingers, catching a glimpse of naked flesh. She reached out her hand, taking the photographs from her mother.

'That scheming little . . . *bitch*.' The photographs were dynamite. Annabel and Ivar had obviously had a great

275

time with a camera one afternoon. Kate was horrified to think of Roderick coming across them, after his father's death: he must have known about them, surely. Had he shown them to Fiona, or had she found them herself? Kate could just see them all over the Sunday tabloids, lurid headlines screaming out across every news-stand. It would destroy Roderick to see his mother's name dragged through the mud.

'What the hell are we supposed to do now?' She turned to her mother. There was only one thing Kate could think of. She grabbed her phone. 'Jean, it's me – we've got a problem up at the cottages.'

'A problem? Surely you want Roddy or Billy, not me?'

'Shh!' Kate hissed down the telephone. 'Is he there?'

'He's at the fishery, but he'll be back shortly. Shall I get him to give you a ring?'

'No, God – no. Just come here, quickly. I'll explain when you get here.'

'I'll be ten minutes.'

It was the longest ten minutes Kate and her mother had known. They both stood, silent and anxious, staring out the window, willing Jean's little Ford to appear.

'Oh no.' Kate stood, transfixed with horror. A Land Rover with the registration DE 1 was hurtling up the little track that led to the cottages. 'It's Roderick! Quick, think of something. Why are we in here?'

'Smoke . . . a leak – a gas leak?' Elizabeth guessed wildly.

'Smoke! We saw smoke and we thought the chimney was on fire.' Kate exhaled with relief and they both stood by the window, watching as the car door opened.

Jean shot out of the car, slamming the door. Kate and her mother were still recovering from the shock of not seeing Roderick when she clattered into the cottage, dropping the car keys in her rush.

'What a to-do. I've never driven so quickly. Now what on earth can the matter be?'

Kate motioned towards the coffee table.

'I told you that wee madam was up to something, didn't I?' Jean scooped up the pile of photographs, handing them to Kate. 'What else has she got her hands on?'

'I don't think there's anything else,' said Kate, averting her eyes from a particularly graphic photograph of the Right Honourable Member's member.

'Och, I think there is,' said Jean, eyes scanning the table. She seized on a tattered airmail envelope addressed to Annabel Maxwell and held it up, showing the return address to Kate and Elizabeth. Inked at the top was Ivar Cornwall's name. *So that's what she was doing at Roddy's desk on the night of the party!*

'Come on, girls, let's get out of here before we're caught in the act.' Jean picked up her keys and made to leave the cottage.

'But, Jean, you can't just take the photographs. She'll know someone's been here.'

'You just watch me.' She stormed out of the door. 'I'll see you back at the house.'

'That went well,' said Elizabeth, turning to Kate. They both collapsed in giggles as Jean's wheels spun, spraying gravel in her rush to get back to Duntarvie House.

'Come on, we'll have to face the music.' Kate locked the cottage door and they walked down the path back to her little car. 'But it's not going to be pretty.'

Roderick had been relaxing, feet up against the Aga, eating an apple and reading the paper, when they had returned. Jean had placed the photos on the table, face down. Kate and Elizabeth hovered in the hall, just out of his sight.

'Everything all right?' His tone was mildly curious, but he didn't look up.

'Fiona!' Jean's tone was sharp.

'For God's sake, what has she done now?' Knocking the chair over as he pushed it back, he strode across to the table, picking up the sheaf of pictures. He flipped it over. For a split second his face darkened with pain. He threw the photographs down, swearing in a low voice. 'Why I didn't destroy these after Dad's death, I'll never know.' He was talking to himself, and Jean wisely stayed silent.

Long-buried emotions flashed across his face as he muttered to himself, pacing the length of the kitchen. '*Think, think,*' he muttered, steepling his fingers together.

He took a deep breath. 'I suppose it felt like a little piece of Mum, in a strange way. I couldn't bear to lose any more of my past.' He looked at Jean for reassurance, his face suddenly vulnerable.

'I'm sorry, Roddy.' Her voice was gentle.

'I'm so bloody *angry* with her. And with Dad, for putting up with her. And I'm left picking up the pieces.'

'Well,' Jean began, cautiously, 'you'd put it to one side, until now.'

Standing motionless in the hall, still unseen, Kate felt a surge of sympathy for Roderick. Trapped with a house full of tangled memories, and the constant weight of responsibility that came with running an estate, it wasn't surprising that his temperament could be mercurial at times.

'I don't know, Jean. I just . . . ' He ran his fingers through his hair, his jaw tense. 'I thought there was a moment there when Fiona had actually changed and realized she couldn't be concerned only with herself her whole life.'

'That young madam?' Jean bristled, her voice sharp with disdain.

'I'm an idiot. And she's going to bloody ruin us.'

Kate heard the sound of water running. The kettle was going on – Jean's default reaction to stress. There was a clatter of mugs and the banging of cupboard doors. Roderick was sitting at the table now, head in his hands, his back towards them, talking.

'I was so relieved when she buggered off the island to Glasgow. It was the perfect excuse to finish things with her. I should have realized she was up to something at Hogmanay. All that time I thought she was hanging around because she was hoping we'd get back together,' he laughed hollowly, 'and I was trying to work out how I could let her down gently.'

Kate glanced at her mother in surprise. Elizabeth looked back, confused, not familiar with the characters in this drama. They were standing stock-still in the doorway, just feet from Roderick. God, this was awkward – no way of escape, but no way of making their presence known without him realizing they'd heard it all.

Jean cleared her throat. He looked up at her, and she raised her eyebrows in a motion that managed to suggest they weren't alone. Roderick turned in his chair.

Impeccable manners won over embarrassment. He stood up at once, extending his hand graciously. 'You must be Elizabeth. Roderick Maxwell. How do you do?'

Kate's mother stood, mouth open, speechless – *I'm standing in a castle with a real Scottish laird*, Kate knew her mother was thinking. This was exactly the effect that Kate was hoping to harness with Roderick as host of the wildlife tours. After a second Elizabeth remembered her manners and shook his hand.

'I hope you had a good crossing? You've been lucky, the water's been like a mill pond all week.'

'Yes, the ferry was very nice, thank you.' Elizabeth managed a smile.

This was all terribly British, thought Kate. Next we'll be discussing the weather, or cricket. Or both.

'Look, this is terribly awkward. I'm sorry you've been caught up in this.' Roderick addressed her mother, and Kate realized that he hadn't actually acknowledged that she was there at all.

'It's fine. Look, Mum, we can get going back to the cottage now. I'm sure it'll be fine.' Kate was gabbling, filling the silence.

'It might be many things, Kate, but fine isn't one of them.' Roderick turned to her, eyes narrowed in anger. Jean motioned her to sit down, shushing her with a cup of tea and an expression that warned her this wasn't the time for platitudes.

Roderick recommenced pacing up and down the kitchen, the offending photographs now strewn across the kitchen table. Catching a glimpse of them, Kate grimaced and averted her eyes again. Jean caught her eye once more and gave her a reassuring half-smile.

'Conniving little . . .' Grabbing the photographs, Roderick took a deep breath, trying to calm himself. 'I'm sorry. I didn't mean to snap at you, Kate.'

'It's fine.' She ventured a smile. 'I'm on your side, remember?' His shoulders, previously somewhere around his ears, dropped a little as she said this.

Roderick leaned back against the Aga, taking a huge gulp of tea, clutching his mug.

'I might be speaking out of turn.' Elizabeth, who had

been uncharacteristically silent, spoke quietly. 'But all families have their skeletons, Roderick.'

Jean nodded.

'We can't take responsibility for the way our family behaves,' Kate's mother continued. 'All you can do is try *your* best, and let people judge you on that.'

Kate looked at her mother in surprise, reaching out to squeeze her hand affectionately.

'It's not quite that simple. I just can't watch her name being dragged through the mud, no matter what she did,' said Roderick, simply. He sighed.

Everyone jumped as the kitchen door opened.

'Gosh! Are we having a party?' Fiona clipped into the room on dark-purple heels. She dropped her handbag on the table and collapsed dramatically into a chair. 'Oh, Jean – tea. Just what I need. Honestly, shopping on this island is impossible. Thank God I'm going back to Glasgow.'

'I think you have some explaining to do.' Roderick shoved the photographs and letter across the long table. Fiona looked at the black-and-white pictures, then up at Roderick with a little shrug.

'Oh, come on, Roddy, you know how it is.'

Anger flared in his eyes. He gripped the table, his knuckles whitening. 'No, Fiona, I don't.'

'Chip-paper – that's what it'd be by next week. But an exclusive in the Sunday tabloids would make my career.' Fiona laughed, a tinkly, brittle little laugh, which petered out when she saw the expression of fury on Roderick's face. 'Oh, come on, Roddy.' She took one final chance. 'Give me an exclusive? Come on, for old times' sake?'

He leaned across the table, scooping up the letter and photographs. Fiona shrank back slightly as he stared into her eyes.

'Leave! Just leave, Fiona, and we'll pretend this never happened.' He opened the door of the Aga, threw everything in and slammed the door shut. 'Your parents are good people. They don't need to know about this.' Roderick shook his head in disgust.

Kate and Elizabeth sat wordlessly, watching the scene unfold.

'You should be ashamed of yourself, Fiona.' Jean's voice was icily quiet. 'You've been made welcome in this house all your life. Roderick's been a good friend to you – we all have.'

'It's business, Jean.' Fiona spat out the words, her thin lips tight with fury. 'Nothing personal.'

'Young lady, when you start meddling in affairs like this, you *make* it personal.'

Fiona stood up, chair screeching against the floor. 'You're incapable of seeing beyond this pathetic little island, all of you.' Her voice was rising, her mask slipping.

'Plenty of people have left the island without feeling the need to destroy it.' Roderick's anger had now been replaced with a tone of bitter disappointment. 'You don't have to slash and burn your way to the top.'

'Get your head out of the clouds, darling. This place

is falling to pieces.' Fiona turned, as if noticing for the first time that they weren't alone in the room. She stabbed a finger in Kate's direction. 'And bringing in pathetic no-hopers like *her* is why you're going to run this estate into the ground.'

'Kate's worth ten of you,' Roderick roared in fury. 'Out! Just get out. I've defended you one too many times already, Fiona. There really is nothing beneath the surface, is there?'

'On the contrary, I actually want to make something of my life – unlike *some* people, who're happy to act as a glorified skivvy and hide from the real world.'

Fiona spat the words at Kate, who flinched. God, was that what it looked like? She could feel herself flushing scarlet.

'Nothing to say for yourself, have you?' Fiona picked up her expensive bag with a contemptuous sneer.

'Just go, Fiona. We'll pretend this never happened if you just leave.' Roderick's voice was flat now, all fury spent.

'Fine.' Turning on her heel, she couldn't resist one last word to Kate. 'You want my second helpings, darling? You're welcome. Just ask yourself why he's still single.'

She stalked out, leaving a room full of silence. Kate looked at Roderick, but he was staring out of the window, watching as Fiona's car reversed out of the courtyard.

He turned round, his voice ice-cool. 'I'm going to the library, Jean. If anyone calls, I'm not here.'

'More tea?' Jean waved the pot with a hopeful expression.

'I was thinking gin, myself,' said Kate, in a small voice.

'I'm sorry,' explained Jean, as she returned from the sitting room with a familiar green bottle. 'I lost my head for a moment. I knew she was up to something. Roddy's father was a good man – I wasn't going to stand by and let that little minx get away with spreading her poison, simply to further her own career.'

She handed Kate and Elizabeth each a gin and tonic, pouring one for herself.

'Here's to getting Fiona out of our hair at last.' Jean raised her glass and took a large sip. She reached across, opening the oven door of the Aga. The letter and photographs were blackened and melted at the edges, the images unrecognizable. Jean took a pair of tongs and pulled out the remains. 'We'll finish them off,' she explained, leaving the room with them at arm's length. She returned a moment later, carrying the now-empty tongs. 'I put them on the fire in the sitting room. They're gone.'

'Well, she's a nasty piece of work.' Elizabeth took a long drink.

'She is now,' Jean explained. 'She was always spoilt and ambitious, but there's an edge to her since she moved to the newspaper in Glasgow.'

Kate let out an accidental snort. Jean had a habit of

seeing the best in people, but this was taking it a bit far. If there was an edge to Fiona, it was razor-sharp and laced with arsenic.

'Come on, Kate. I know she was nasty to you, but ask yourself what makes someone behave that way?' Her mother was actually bloody empathizing with Fiona.

'Maybe she's just a complete cow?'

'Or perhaps it's dog-eat-dog in the world of journalism and, like a child left with a box of chocolates, the story was too good to resist?'

'Possibly.' Kate was dubious. Leaving her mum with Jean to finish her drink, she slipped off to check on Willow. The car would be fine parked outside Duntarvie House overnight, and the two women seemed to be quite happy mulling over vile Fiona's motivations. She stamped along the path in the rapidly gathering darkness.

They had been gone for hours, and Willow was desperate for a walk. She'd dragged most of her toys in from the garden through the dog flap that Billy had built for her, and the hall floor was covered in mud.

'Come on, you. I think we both need a bit of fresh air to clear our heads.' She picked up Willow's lead.

Pulling the door behind her, she was struck again by the memory of Roderick's face, etched with hurt and sadness. Drawing her mobile out of her pocket, she scrolled for his number. Should she call him and check he was okay? If it was anyone else, she'd do so. No.

Maybe a bit of time would be a better idea. She whistled to Willow and set off up the little path that led to the estate road. The headlights dazzled her. It was Fiona's car, bumping down the track to the cottage. Perhaps she'd taken a wrong turning, thought Kate. A wrong turning down a dead-end road on an island she'd lived on all her life. Perhaps not.

The window wound down, smoothly. Looking unruffled, Fiona popped her head out. 'A word to the wise. I've seen the way you look at him. If you're thinking of moving in on him, you should know this: he's only after a brood mare.'

'What?' Kate looked at Fiona, frowning in confusion.

'Come on, darling.' Her voice dripped sarcasm. 'He does the broken-hearted loner act with every single "Girl Friday" he hires. Did you never wonder why they never last?'

Kate felt a lurch of recognition. He'd been pretty dismissive of the last girl who'd worked here, saying she didn't last long. And the whole haughty Lord of the Manor thing had lasted until he'd had a few whiskies too many at the fireworks night.

Fiona gave a little laugh. 'Penny dropping, Kate?'

'But . . . Susan and Tom? Finn?' She was clutching at straws.

'They're his *employees*. He pays their wages, they live in their picturesque little cottages for a peppercorn rent. They know which side their bread's buttered on.'

Feeling sick, Kate realized she was cornered, and Fiona was going in for the kill.

'Come on, sweetie – get real. Jean was over the moon when you arrived and she realized you were Little Miss Plain Jane. I know he isn't exactly discerning, but clearly he'll have a go at anything, if what I've heard is true.'

So Fiona knew about the night of the kiss. Someone had told her that – one of the islanders who'd pretended to make Kate welcome, and had told her she was one of them. Everything was spinning now, nothing quite making sense. She stood beside Fiona's car, unable to speak.

'Don't you think it's a coincidence that Roderick dumped me as soon as he realized I had no interest in having children?' She laughed. 'He's the last Maxwell. Without someone else to carry on the line, his precious Duntarvie will end up in the hands of some English cousin, who'll sell the house and break up the estate. Everyone knows you've got the hots for him. Let's face it, he's got you jumping through hoops doing all his dirty work, in exchange for this grotty little place.' Fiona looked at Kate's filthy jeans and tangled hair, and pointedly reapplied some lipstick in the rear-view mirror. 'I mean, really, do you honestly think he'd go from me – to you?'

She pressed a button and the window closed. The car reversed perfectly up the drive, leaving Kate standing completely alone.

14

Lost

'Are you quite sure you're going to be okay?'

Standing at the ferry terminal, Kate balled her hands so tightly that her nails cut half-moons in the skin of her palms.

'Fine,' she lied. There was no way that she was grabbing everything she owned, stuffing it in her mother's car and driving home to England. No matter that she felt sick with loneliness, missed her mum before she'd even left and felt completely friendless.

'You know you can always come back – or just let me know when you want me to visit, and I'll be more than happy to come up.' Elizabeth shot an involuntary glance towards Bruno's cafe, which Kate noticed with a small smile. It gave her the tiny shot of courage she needed.

'No. I've spent years doing that. I made a deal with myself, and I'm not going back on it. I said six months.'

'You're as stubborn as your father.' Elizabeth started the engine. The ferry was loading now, and she was holding up the car behind. 'Darling, I'm so proud of you.'

Kate pursed her lips, nodding acknowledgement. She couldn't speak, knowing that if she did, the tears would start. She blew her mum a kiss and stepped back, allowing the car to roll forward and leave her standing alone.

A couple of hours later she lay in the bath, trying not to think. The harder she tried to dismiss Fiona's last words to her, as those of a woman scorned, the louder they rang in her ears.

Hadn't Roderick been the one to raise the subject of children on the ferry? She remembered their conversation with horror. He'd brought it up out of the blue, and she'd thought he was genuinely interested in her. Bloody man! She'd fallen straight into his trap, gaily informing him that she wanted loads of children and a big family, thinking she was sharing confidences with a friend, not being sized up as a potential breeding machine.

Kate lay back in the bubbles, eyes closed, reflecting on her time on the island. She'd arrived, lonely and unsure of herself. But she'd made friends, she'd managed the whole cottages project, and now she was up to her eyes in research for the wildlife tours. She was talking to a tiny start-up company on the island that was creating websites and social-media strategies. The potential for promoting the island online was huge. Social networking pages would draw in tourists from around the world, in love with the idea of being shown around the island by the handsome, self-effacing laird, who had turned out to be simply self-serving and arrogant.

'Huh!'

Kate reared out of the bath, no longer relaxed, but furious. How gullible was she? She'd come up here intending to find herself and escape from reality. The deal was supposed to be a rent-free serviced cottage, in exchange for three days of light work a week. The last few days she'd been researching and planning long into the night. Before that she'd spent months chasing up builders and decorators who worked on island time and had no idea what a deadline was, just to get the cottages and the bunkhouse finished. Much as she hated to admit it, Fiona had a point. That arrogant sod Roderick Maxwell was quite happy to let her do all the work, and then take all the glory as the island's economy improved. Hadn't she stood in the cafe the other day listening to people discussing what a difference he was making?

Fiona had actually done her a favour. Typical upper-class git – her initial judgement of Roderick had obviously been right. Well, he could bugger right off. From now on she was going to work the three days she was expected, and no more. And he could find some other idiot who'd fall for the unkempt black hair, those dark eyes, that three-day stubble that etched his chin . . .

No. She dried herself, rubbing furiously at her legs with a towel. Well, she'd show him. She grabbed her jeans from the radiator, threw on a fleece and shoved on her wellington boots.

'Willow, come!'

The springer spaniel was at the front door before Kate had even finished the sentence. Willow was a gangly adolescent now, huge paws suggesting that she still had quite a bit of growing to do. Her feathery tail was beating with excitement against the boot rack. Kate opened the door and she tore out into the garden, circling madly, tracking the scents from the previous night.

Kate marched up to the top of her little lane and stood, undecided. Left to Duntarvie House, where Jean would comfort her and suggest she was overreacting, that she needed a break? Or right, and down to the warm, messy chaos of Susan's cottage, or Morag's, where a late-afternoon glass of wine would be waiting? None of them appealed. Despite talking over Fiona's tirade with her mother, who'd tried hard to convince her it was nothing more than a last wave of bitterness, Kate felt a little uncomfortable in their company, not ready to let go of the idea completely.

She whistled, and as she scrambled over the stile and into the field that swept down into the little valley, Willow followed.

Ducking under the dripping branches, Kate marched furiously through the little copse. Of all the days for Willow to bugger off, she had to choose today to find a deliciously irresistible scent. An hour of stamping through the fields hadn't done much for Kate's mood. The last few days' rain had left the ground sodden, the heavy soil sucking at her boots with every step. And now she was walking round in circles, she was sure of it.

'Looking for someone?'

Roderick was standing by the stream. Immaculately trained, his two Labradors sat patiently waiting for instructions. A soaking wet, grinning, mud-covered Willow lolled by his feet.

'Thanks.' Her tone was ungracious – she knew that.

'You're welcome.' Roderick indicated the grey sky above the canopy of bare branches. 'Lovely day for a stroll, don't you think?' He grinned at her.

Oh, bugger off, you, thought Kate.

'Come on, I know a shortcut from here,' he said, apparently unconcerned by her scowling silence.

The footpath was narrow, and coated with a thin layer of treacherous liquid mud. Every muscle in Kate's body was tensed in her efforts to stay upright. She followed carefully, treading in Roderick's footsteps, staring at his back. She was fuming that Willow had led her straight to the one person she hadn't wanted to see.

'Give me your hand.' They had reached an ancient stile, which Roderick vaulted over with his long legs. The wood was slimy with rain and covered with moss.

'You're very bossy, aren't you?' said Kate crossly.

'I am?'

'Yes.' She held out her hand with a bad grace. 'You are.'

He helped her over the stile, deftly catching her before

293

she landed in a puddle. Kate dismissed the frisson of excitement she felt as he stood for a second, hands spanning her waist, looking her in the eye, laughing. She needed to talk sternly to her mind and her body, which were definitely not thinking the same thing.

Oh God, maybe she could just . . .

'What's the magic word?'

'Thanks.' Kate said, through gritted teeth. She sidestepped out of his grasp.

He raised one eyebrow, amused. 'You're welcome. Did you get out of bed the wrong side this morning, my bonny Kate?'

'Something like that.' Stop trying to be nice, you arrogant upper-class tosser, she added, silently. With Fiona off the scene, he was obviously on a charm offensive, with one eye on her heir-producing potential.

Whistling the dogs, Roderick set off again, taking a path that led them into a patch of pine woods. The ground was springy underfoot with a thick carpet of needles and the air was rich with the scent of resin. It was a relief to be out of the driving rain – getting lost in the countryside with a coat that wasn't very waterproof, after all, wasn't much fun.

'Here we are.' Roderick opened a gate, onto a familiar-looking track.

'But that's . . . '

'Bruar Cottage. Yes. Didn't you realize we'd end up here?'

Kate was tempted to lie and say she'd known exactly

where they were, thank you very much. But she suspected Roderick would see right through her. He always did. 'I thought we were near the stone gates at the entrance to the estate.'

'That's an easy mistake to make. The paths are similar.' He stepped aside, letting Kate walk down the path to the dark-red front door of the cottage. 'You're soaking wet. You need a hot bath and a fire.'

'I'll be fine.' She was trying to maintain her mantle of frostiness, but he was being so kind, and thoughtful, and . . . well, all the things she'd *thought* he was.

'Look, I'm bone-dry under this.' He indicated his long, waxed huntsman's coat. 'You go in, I'll make you a drink and get the fire going, while you jump in the bath.'

Holding the door handle, Kate hesitated. The trouble with living alone – despite the joys of being able to live in chaos and eat toast in bed – was that there wasn't anyone to be nice to you. 'Okay. Only because I'm freezing, and you offered.'

He looked at her, half-laughing, half-frowning. 'What other reason could there be?'

She opened the door and stumped in, her eyes narrowed, thinking to herself: how about because I thought you were a genuinely nice person and it transpires you're not?

Good as his word, after closing the three soaking-wet dogs in the hall, where they would do least damage, Roderick packed her off to the bathroom with a huge glass of whisky and set to building the fire.

For the second time that day Kate lay neck-deep in bubbles, musing. *The trouble is he's so bloody gorgeous.* He actually took her seriously, which was something Ian had never done. He was clever, sharp and – she closed her eyes, allowing herself a luxurious moment of remembering – if one kiss could have that effect on her, she could only imagine what he'd be like in bed. She smiled to herself. The whisky was going to her head. None of that mattered, if he was on a secret mission to populate the island with lots of miniature Maxwells and perpetuate the family line. She remembered the night he'd rescued her, saying, 'I don't make a habit of scooping up stray girls and bringing them home to my lair.' Huh! Sodding Roderick. Fiona's words echoed in her ears: 'He does the broken-hearted loner act with every single "Girl Friday" he hires.' She climbed out of the bath, wrapping herself in the slightly damp towel from earlier.

She ducked past the sitting-room door – closed, thankfully – ran upstairs to the bedroom, pulled on some pyjamas and found her fluffy dressing gown. She loosened her hair and found herself applying a sneaky coat of lip gloss and mascara. The bath had left a rosy glow on her freckled cheeks. 'Not bad, for a commoner,' she said, sticking her tongue out at herself in the mirror.

'Perfect timing,' said Roderick, emerging from the sitting room as Kate came down the stairs. 'I've got the fire going. D'you want a top-up?'

'Yes, please.'

'I've dried off the dogs – there were a couple of old towels in the kitchen. I assumed they probably belonged to Willow?'

Kate grimaced inwardly. They were her favourite towels, a going-to-university present from her grandmother. Admittedly they were now rather ancient and faded, but still. 'Oh, yes, they're Willow's towels,' she lied in agreement.

Not only had Roderick lit the log fire, but he'd replaced the tea-lights in the little candleholders that were dotted around the room. Kate stood by the fire, hands wrapped round her whisky glass, admiring the sparkly darkness. Everything looked better by candlelight, even arrogant-pig bosses with ulterior motives. He was sitting on the couch, long legs outstretched, T-shirt showing off muscular arms that were tanned all year round from working on the estate. His hair had crinkled in the rain and a dark curl was falling over his forehead. Not that she was looking, obviously.

He patted the space beside him on the couch. 'Come and sit down. I won't bite.'

He's a horrible aristocratic bastard who is using you for his own gains, Kate reminded herself, as she sat down beside him. And you're having a year off men. And you want a normal relationship with someone who loves you for yourself, not your bloody reproductive potential.

Unfortunately she misjudged her landing – two hefty glasses of malt whisky on an empty stomach having gone straight to her head. And now she was sitting beside him, and his hard thigh was right up against hers, and she could smell a hint of sandalwood in his aftershave, and he was turning and looking at her and . . .

'Kate.' A vein was jumping in his cheek. He looked down, into his empty glass. 'I want to ask you something.'

Oh, help. Here it comes. She curled her nails into her palms, closing her eyes.

'You've done so much for Duntarvie. You're like a breath of fresh air.'

Kate opened her eyes and flicked a look sideways. Roderick was looking at her, and a lopsided smile was tugging at the corners of his mouth. Oh, for goodness' sake. He was bloody gorgeous. Perhaps being a brood mare wasn't all that bad. But he'd probably have a bit on the side, called Araminta or something equally posh, and she'd have to live in the scullery and hide when visitors came. Or something. The whisky was really having a terrible effect on her brain. Her muddles were all worded.

'I wanted to offer you—'

'Yes! I know I ought to say no, but sod it!' She felt the room swirling around her. This was a bit like living in one of Susan's abstract paintings. 'I'll live in the kitchen. It's nice in there. And Araminta need never know I exist.' She hiccupped gently.

'Kate?' He put out a hand to steady her. 'Who's Araminta?'

'Your wife. Or girlfriend. I can't remember which.'

'I don't have either.' Even through the whisky haze, Kate could see that he was completely nonplussed. 'I wanted to offer you a job. A proper job, here on the estate.'

'Of course you did.' Kate blinked hard, twice, and sat up.

'A job,' he repeated. 'What else?'

She took a deep breath. 'But I already have a job.'

'You're living in this cottage and supposedly working as a Girl Friday. You should be giving Jean a bit of a hand with some admin and chasing up some of the workmen at the cottages, not managing the entire project and trying to find ways to market the estate and boost the island's economy.'

Kate sat up, feeling a little bit pleased with herself. 'When you put it like that, I sound quite efficient.'

'You are far too hard on yourself, Kate.' He leaned across, pouring another measure of whisky into her glass. 'Do I take it, then, you'd be interested?'

'Yes, please.' She thought for a moment. 'Do I have to wear a suit?'

'No, please don't. Muddy jeans are perfectly acceptable.' Roderick looked at her pyjama-clad legs. 'Maybe not dressing gowns, though. Shall we drink to it?' He clinked his whisky glass against hers and took a sip, not taking his eyes off her. The fire crackled, but the room was silent.

'Cheers.' Kate was horrified that another second and she'd probably have leapt on him. Thank the Lord he'd thrown a metaphorical bucket of water over her, by offering the job. A proper job! Here, on this island, which felt more like home than home had ever done. She slurped the rest of her whisky, which seemed to be going down much faster now that she'd developed a taste for it. And bloody Fiona could bugger off now – she couldn't be accused of hanging on Roderick's coat-tails and living in Bruar Cottage with a part-time job. Now she would be part of the estate, the fabric of the island. God, she was drunk. The room was spinning slightly, and every so often she felt herself hen-pecking as she dozed off for a split second.

'You have very nice arms,' she said, reaching out a finger and running it along, smoothing the hairs on his forearm.

'I think it's bedtime, don't you?' Roderick stood up, changing the subject, extending a hand to Kate. 'Before you do something you might regret in the morning. Or I do.'

It took a few moments for her to register what he'd said, and even then she wasn't quite sure she'd heard right.

He pulled her up from the depths of the sofa. 'Come on, you. Upstairs.' He slipped an arm round her waist to steady her, and then propelled her upstairs to the bedroom. Thankfully she was dressed for bed, so it was a simple case of climbing through the muddle of books

and coffee cups and sliding, blissfully, under the covers.
He leaned over, brushing the hair from her face.

'Watch it, Roderick Maxwell,' she mumbled, half-asleep. 'I've got your measure.'

15

The Release

Kate was walking Willow, who was on a lead this time, and trying to subdue her hangover with fresh air. She'd avoided her island friends since her run-in with Fiona, suspecting their motives, realizing she had nobody to confide in who wasn't close to Roderick.

'You look like death,' said Susan.

'Thanks.'

'I haven't seen you for a few days and you end up looking like something the cat dragged in. Have I missed a night out?' Susan fell into step alongside Kate, walking along the estate road and back towards their houses.

'A night in – and no. Willow ran off yesterday on her walk, and Roderick did his Sir Galahad bit,' she scowled, before continuing, 'and I got soaked, so he fed me the whisky I got as a present from Jean and Hector.'

'I think we need a cup of coffee with this story. You busy?' Susan shifted the huge armful of twigs she was carrying and they walked back to the cottage. They pulled off their boots, leaving them in the back porch, where they joined a mountainous heap of shoes, work boots and wellingtons.

'Is there a reason for the giant pile of twigs?' Kate was trying to keep the conversation topics general. She still felt a bit prickly, even though her logical mind kept telling her that it was Fiona who was not to be trusted.

'I've had an idea for a painting. I knew there was loads of hazel up by the big house, so I left the children with Morag for half an hour, so I could go and collect them.' She opened the kitchen door. Morag was sitting at the table reading the local paper, a sleeping baby Mhairi in her arms. 'Where's Jamie?'

'Here I am!' said a little voice, from the hall. Kate turned round to see a paint-splattered, very pleased-looking Jamie, hand-in-hand with Jean.

'I think someone has his mummy's talent for art – look at these.' Jean helped him to fan the paintings across the floor to dry.

'Sweetheart, they're gorgeous.' Susan leaned down, kissing him on the smudged nose. 'D'you fancy a wee rest while we talk about boring grown-up stuff?'

'*Thomas the Tank Engine*?' Jamie's silence was bought with a kiss, a biscuit and a DVD.

'Right,' said Jean. 'I was only popping in on my way past, to see if Susan needed anything from the super-market. But I'll maybe stay for a wee cup of coffee, if there's one on offer?' She sat down at the table, looking over Morag's shoulder, the two friends poring over the announcements page.

RACHAEL LUCAS

Sensing that Mhairi was about to stir, Susan scooped the baby from Morag, curling her into the crook of her arm. She settled down in the rocking chair to feed her, eyes half-closed, head against the colourful crocheted blanket that covered the cushions.

'I'll make us a drink.' Kate filled the kettle, gathering mugs from the draining board and measuring out spoonfuls of coffee into the cafetiere. The friendly muddle of Susan and Tom's kitchen reminded her of Emma and Sam. She really ought to call and see if Emma was feeling any better. Morning sickness was badly named – poor Emma seemed to feel dreadful the whole time she was awake, but she was so happy to be pregnant that she didn't care. Of course she had Sam: a genuine, straightforward man who loved Emma for what she was. Unlike Roderick, the shit, muttered Kate, under her breath. Mind you, she'd been stupid enough to think that the laird of a Scottish estate would be genuinely interested in someone like her.

'So,' said Susan, one eyebrow raised in amusement, 'apparently Kate spent the evening drinking whisky with Roddy and now she's dying of a hangover. We want details, madam.'

'There's nothing to tell. Willow ran away, Roderick rescued her, I was soaking wet, he lit the fire while I had a bath, we had a glass of whisky, I went to bed.' Kate rubbed her chin. 'At least that's all I can remember. It is a bit hazy.'

'Oh yes?' said Morag.

'You know what it's like, if you have a drink on an empty stomach? Well, I had three. One minute I was having a bath, the next Roderick was putting me to bed.'

Susan's eyes were wide with excitement. 'Ooh, yes?'

'Ooh, nothing.' Kate's tone was resolute. 'There is not, and never will be, anything going on between me and the laird of Duntarvie estate.'

'That's a shame,' said Jean, 'I thought with Fiona well and truly off the scene, there was a chance—'

'Nope.' Kate almost snapped her reply.

'Have I missed something?' said Morag mildly. 'You get on well, you're both single, and we all know what happened in the snug at the firework display . . .'

Susan cackled with delight. 'And we've all seen the way you look at each other. If it's not you sneaking looks at him, it's him sneaking looks at you.'

'Sizing me up, more like.' Kate gave a hollow little laugh. 'After all, he's got to find someone to carry on the family line, hasn't he?'

'What?' said Jean and Morag together.

Kate stood up, gathering the mugs, stalling for time. She was horrified to realize that her vision was blurred with tears.

'Kate?' Morag had joined her by the sink. She put a hand on her arm, her voice concerned. 'What is it?'

'Roderick is the Laird of Duntarvie. He's from a different world. He wouldn't be interested in someone like me, even if . . .'

'We are talking about the same Roderick Maxwell

here?' Morag laughed, despite herself. 'The same man who mucks in and works at the fishery and the wood-yard? The one who spent his overdraft on a Hogmanay party? Roddy's not one for airs and graces.'

'His overdraft?' Kate was dazed. 'You're joking? After I spent ages working out the financing for the cottages? I could murder him.'

'Sorry, but could we get back to the "even if" bit, please?' said Susan.

'Fiona found me the other night before she left. She told me Roderick needed someone to produce an heir for Duntarvie. She had quite a lot to say about his behaviour with women. And . . .' she paused for a second, gathering the nerve to confront them, before the words tumbled out in a rush, 'that you all turn a blind eye, and that he's only interested in finding someone to have his children.'

There was a moment of silence while the three women took in what Kate had said.

'And you believed her?' Jean's face was a picture of shock. She looked at Morag, and then across at Susan, before erupting into peals of laughter.

'Well, I'm not exactly in his league, am I? I come from a semi-detached house in Essex. He lives in a blooming castle.'

'Right,' snorted Susan. 'So you think, because that bloody lunatic Fiona told you, that Roddy wants to have his wicked way with you, produce a son to carry on the Maxwell line and then lock you in the attic?'

'It does sound a bit unlikely,' Kate conceded. She twisted her hair up in a ponytail, biting her lip.

'Unlikely? It's completely bloody insane, Kate.' Susan's voice was loud enough to rouse Mhairi, who stirred in her sleep, letting out a little cry. 'How much did you have to drink last night? I think it's destroyed all your brain cells.'

Kate allowed herself a tiny smile as Morag put her arm round her waist, squeezing her tightly. 'Kate. The man is clearly mad about you. It's just that neither of you can see it. Believe me, I have inside knowledge of the Maxwell men.'

Kate caught her breath.

'I'm very happy with my Ted. But that boy is his father all over again.'

Jean looked thoughtful. 'Ahh, no, Morag. There's a wee difference. James didn't speak up because he didn't have the confidence. If you ask me, Roddy's seen enough to be scared off relationships for life.'

Well, thought Kate, that's positive. Glad we sorted that out.

'I tell you what,' said Jean, looking across at Kate, her face thoughtful, 'I will not stand by and watch that boy make the same mistake his father made.'

'For goodness' sake, Kate.' Morag took her by the shoulders. 'You've got one life. Take what you want from it. Tell him how you feel.'

'Well, I can't think about that right now.' Kate stood up, untangling Willow's lead from the back of the chair.

It was easy for them to say all this, but it was so much to take in that she couldn't get things straight.

Susan opened her mouth to speak, ready to persuade Kate to stay, but Jean laid a warning hand on her arm. 'Let her go. She's had a bit of a week of it.'

'Just promise me you'll consider it, Kate.' Morag shifted aside, making space for her to escape.

'I will.' She needed time. And something for her hangover. She could tell that the three of them were dying to discuss all this in great detail, but right now she needed sleep, not an in-depth analysis of her non-existent love life.

Closing the door, she could imagine the scene within. She called Willow and walked, slowly and carefully, down to Bruar Cottage.

Kate sensed that it had snowed as soon as she woke up. She'd grown into the habit of sleeping with the curtains open, so that she could lie in bed and watch the sky at night as she dozed. Standing up, she peered out of the window. Over the trees, the dawn light stretched pale fingers across the night sky. Her dreams had been a jumble of past and present, faces from her old life mixed with those from the new. Waking was hard this morning. She closed her eyes, last night's dream coming back to her. She'd been in Cambridge visiting Emma and Sam, but she'd been with someone – curled up beside her on the sofa, chatting comfortably, had been Roddy. It had felt quite natural – but it was a dream. The reality was that she hadn't seen him since the other night when he'd put her to bed and, with every day that passed, her resolve to follow Morag's suggestion wavered a little more.

She yawned, jaw cracking as she stretched. Today would be a long day. She'd secured a last-minute booking for both cottages; the two families would be arriving on the ferry late tomorrow afternoon. She hadn't been up to check on the cottage Fiona had been staying in, but thinking about it filled her with dread. She was fairly certain that it wasn't going to be pretty. And then there was Billy, who needed to talk to her about the tiles in the bunkhouse shower room; and then, tomorrow, Flora was coming home. Kate smiled at the thought of the seal pup making her way down the beach and back to the sea.

'Mind yersel and drive carefully on that snow,' warned Bruno.

Kate had popped into the cafe, deciding to treat herself to breakfast to bolster herself for the long day ahead. The windows were steamed up, and the air filled with delicious smells. Outside, Kilmannan High Street looked beautiful, sparkling with an icing-sugar coating of snow. The sea was inky, reflecting a strange, plum-grey-coloured sky.

'That's no the last of it,' said Bruno, following Kate's gaze. 'If I were you, I'd get over tae the cottages and get yer work done, pronto.'

'I'm onto it – look.' Kate indicated two bags full of shopping at her feet. The new arrivals had emailed a request for enough food to tide them over until the next day. The bags were bulging with the ingredients they'd requested, and a couple of bottles of red wine. 'I'll drop this lot off, make sure all the bedding has been sorted and get back. I promise. I've got a load of work to do up at the big house, anyway. Did Roddy tell you about our plans for the wildlife tours?'

'Oh, *Roddy* now, is it?' teased Bruno. 'Aye, he did. You've been a right tonic for him, ye know that?'

Kate ducked her head, blushing. It felt as if everyone on the island was urging them on, but the only person who wasn't interested was Roderick himself. She still wasn't convinced by Morag's theory that he was holding back, from a fear of getting hurt.

'He's a good friend.'

Bruno raised an eyebrow. 'Right enough. He's a good lad. It's nice to see him working alongside you. You make a good pair.'

'He's a good boss to have,' Kate agreed, with a tone of voice that didn't invite further comment. The reality was that if she messed things up, she'd be out of a job, and a home. Lost in thought, she waved goodbye to Bruno and loaded the car with bags. The air was cold and dry, and she turned the heater up as high as possible, shivering as she drove away.

*

Her panic about the state of Fiona's cottage had been unfounded. Susan's aunt had been happy to take on the job of housekeeper for the cottages. Once the bunkhouse was up and running, the job would be full-time; but, keen to make a good impression, for now she'd cleaned the cottages, made up all the beds, left piles of thick, fluffy towels in the bathrooms and stacked logs in baskets by the log-burners. They were ready to go – all they needed were the finishing touches, thought Kate, unpacking the shopping bags. She left the red wine on the worktop, with the corkscrew close by. After a long journey up from England with a car full of children, she was certain the guests would be grateful for a drink.

She was just locking up when her mobile rang.

'Kate, it's me.'

'Roddy . . . Roderick.'

'The weather forecast doesn't look great. I spoke to Mark, and we decided we'd be better doing it today and getting it over with.' The phone crackled as the reception dipped.

'You're bringing Flora home?' Her stomach knotted with excitement. Standing on the doorstep, she looked down to the shoreline. The rocks, as ever, were dotted with seals.

'I am.' The smile in his voice was obvious. 'I've got a crate in the back of the Land Rover and I'll be on the two-thirty ferry. Do you want to meet me at the bay?'

'I'm there already. I'll ring Jean and tell her to keep hold of Willow, and I'll wait at the cottage. I need to run

311

through the spreadsheet of bunkhouse details with Billy in any case.'

'Super-efficient. I'm impressed. And to think when you came here you were allergic to computers.'

'I'm a girl of many talents. I'll see you later.' Kate put her phone in her pocket. That had sounded a bit flirtatious. Maybe Morag was right. But no, as soon as Roderick was back on the island, she'd find it impossible to tell him how she felt – especially when she didn't even know herself. He was her boss. She needed the job. Focus! She took a breath and calmed herself, before heading down to the bunkhouse to check on Billy's progress.

'I reckon we'll be done wi' this by the end of the week,' said Billy. He was standing in what was to be the shower room, tangled wires protruding from the walls, the floor covered with a thick layer of plaster dust and boxes of tiles. Before Kate had seen the cottages being renovated, she'd have struggled to visualize how this chaos could be turned into a sleek, modern-day bunkhouse for visiting students. Now, though, she could see through the dust sheets and the remaining piles of rubble, and the end of her first project on the Duntarvie estate was in sight. The thought that there would be more filled her with a fizz of excitement. She'd forgotten about Roderick's job offer when she first woke up, and the realization when it dawned was so lovely that she'd kept it to herself, not even sharing it with her friends or with Bruno.

'Kate?' Billy nudged her, breaking into her thoughts. 'Are you away with the fairies this afternoon? I've been talking to you for the last five minutes and I swear you haven't heard a word.'

'We'll be finished in a week or so,' she repeated, parrot-fashion.

'Aye, I said that,' Billy rolled his eyes with an expression of exaggerated patience. 'Then I said that Tam has taken the van over to the town, to get some grout because we've run out. He'll be back in half an hour or so. And I said: do you want a cup of tea?'

'I'll make it.' She picked up the chipped mugs. 'Let's have lunch in the cottage – I won't tell, if you don't.'

'Sounds good to me. We normally have it in the van with the radio on.' Billy's eyes crinkled as he smiled at her. 'I tell you what. I'll finish off this wee bit. You get the kettle on.'

Kate flicked on the heating and washed the mugs. A few minutes later, parking his filthy boots outside the front door, and checking the coast was clear before coming into the sitting room, Billy appeared. His weather-beaten face was furtive.

'If Jessie McKay knew we'd been in here after she'd cleaned the place, she'd have a blue fit.'

'We'll keep it to ourselves then,' said Kate, handing him a mug of tea. They sank back into the big leather sofa together, looking out over the bay.

'I just spoke to Roddy. He's on the ferry over. Tam's

had a problem with the van engine, so I'm going to take the Land Rover off him when he gets here. You'll be okay to give him a run home to the big house after you release the seal pups, won't you?'

'Yes, fine,' said Kate. No, she thought, not fine. I feel like a fifteen-year-old, and my hands are actually clammy and I feel sick at the thought. This is ridiculous. 'I might just take a little walk down to the beach, to have a look at the seals. I'll clear up when I get back.'

'Right enough.' Billy flicked open his newspaper, propped it on his stomach and closed his eyes. 'I'll have five minutes and then get on. I'll leave the door on the latch.'

Kate sat on her usual rock, looking out at the sea, hugging her knees, waiting for Flora to come home. The snow was falling again, heavier now, blanketing the sand.

Her mobile buzzed in her pocket, surprising her and breaking the silence. There must be a tiny pocket of mobile reception here on the beach:

Are you still alive?

Emma. Kate breathed a sigh of relief.

Yes. Just. But I seem to have forgotten I'm not Cinderella.

OMG. You've fallen madly in love with Sir Roderick of Posh?

314

Kate smiled to herself as she typed into her phone:

> Slightly. But when he looked into my eyes and told me he had something important to say . . .

> Oh God. You didn't turn him down? Story of your bloody life. You need to realize how lovely you are.

> Shut up! No, worse than that. He offered me a job.

Kate sat for a moment, staring at her phone. Emma clearly didn't have anything to say to that, either. It wasn't exactly an expression of undying love, was it?

> Aha. That's because he wants to keep you on the island.

> Too slow. You had to think about that, didn't you?

Kate grinned at her phone, then looked up, hearing the rumbling diesel engine of the Land Rover.

> Oops. He's here. Text you later. xxx

The Land Rover crept slowly across the verge and down the rutted track to the bay. Roderick pulled to a stop beside Kate's rock, leaning over to open the passenger door. He smiled at her, dark eyes shining with excitement.

'We need to get them as close to the sea as we can. Lucky Billy's here, really – it's a heavy job.' He pulled on a thick waterproof coat. His hair was sprinkled with snowflakes.

Through flurries of snow Kate could see the dark shape of Billy jogging down the little lane from the cottages, woolly hat pulled down low over his forehead. She felt a sudden wave of sadness, suspecting that once Flora was released she'd probably never see her again.

'Let me give you a hand wi' that, Roddy.' Billy opened the back of the Land Rover, revealing a large plastic crate balanced on two long wooden planks. Using a complicated system of ropes and pulleys, they manoeuvred it onto the snowy ground. A plaintive wailing could be heard from within.

'She's been calling all the way here.' Roderick lifted the plastic mesh that covered the crate.

'Oh!' She hadn't expected Flora to be with her rescued mate, Reggie.

It all seemed horribly real now, and Kate dug her fingernails into her palms. Her gloveless hands were freezing, and tears were mingling with the melting snowflakes on her cheeks.

Roderick caught her hand as she swiped at her eyes. He pulled her into an awkward hug, taking her by surprise.

'I know, it's hard.'

She could feel his breath on her hair and her heart was beating wildly. Not trusting herself to speak, she nodded.

'They're wild animals, and we're making up for some

of the damage we do to this planet, by helping them.' He held her out at arm's length, smiling. 'I promise you, it'll be worth it.'

'If you two dinna get a move on, you'll no be able to see a thing,' pointed out Billy prosaically. 'I'll nip back wi' the Land Rover just now – I widna hang around, though. This snow's getting heavier by the minute.'

'I wouldn't bother coming back, Billy. We'll head off as soon as we've released the pups.' Roderick tossed him the keys, and they watched as Billy drove off the snow-covered beach and headed for Kilmannan and an early dinner.

'Right. What we need to do is place these plastic guards here,' said Roderick, balancing the large pieces of plastic on either side of the crate. 'These will stop Flora and Reggie from deciding to disappear *up* the beach towards the road.'

Reggie, realizing he was missing out, had started to wail. The noise was deafening.

'And that's it!' Roderick looked at Kate, and gave her an encouraging smile. 'We can do it together.'

They reached over the top of the crate, each taking a hold of the plastic casing that was keeping the seal pups captive. The side slipped away and the two pups were there, whiskers twitching, eyes bright in the white landscape. Reggie shuffled forward, stopping to nose at the snow. Flora looked up at Kate, liquid eyes shining.

'Go on.' The lump in Kate's throat made it hard for

her to speak. 'Look, Flora, there's a whole sea out there for you.'

Reggie was already nearly at the water's edge, and a group of seals were watching with interest as he approached. He slipped in, and was gone. Kate swallowed a sob.

Flora, ever inquisitive, had stopped to nose at something that was protruding from the snow. The watching seals didn't move, but continued to look on, mildly. One of them might be her mother, thought Kate. Would she recognize her, or was Flora destined to spend the rest of her life without a family?

Unthinkingly Kate reached for Roderick's hand. His fingers were warm and they closed around hers, comfortingly, as they watched Flora shuffle the last few feet to the sea.

'And there she goes.'

Kate couldn't speak, such was her sadness. She stood, holding Roderick's hand, watching as the little grey head bobbed up from the sea, disappeared, then reappeared.

'Look – they've found each other.' Laughing, Roderick pulled her closer to the shore, pointing to the sea. The two seal pups were clowning around in the water, playing just as they had for the last few months together in the outdoor pool at the Seal Sanctuary.

'Hang on, Mr Certified Marine Mammal Medic, are we not breaking all the rules here?' Kate laughed through her tears. 'I thought we weren't allowed within thirty feet of the seals, if they were hauled out on the rocks?'

'Do they look like they care?'

Kate looked around at the rocks, which were dotted with seals of all sizes, all of which appeared completely unconcerned. 'No, but . . . '

'But nothing. I think they approve of us.' He grinned at her, looking boyish all of a sudden, and pulled her by the hand. 'Come on, let's get going. You're freezing.'

A strong wind had blown up, and the snow was so heavy that by the time they reached the cottages they could only see a few feet in front of them.

'Look at my car!' Kate was amazed by how quickly the snow had drifted, whipped into corners by the sea wind.

'Let's get inside. I'll ring Billy, get him to come back over with the Land Rover. There's no way your little car is going to make it over the hills in this.'

They clattered into the cottage in a flurry of snow and foot-stamping. Roderick had the kettle on before Kate had even removed her boots. He was frowning at his phone.

'No signal. Can I see yours?' He reached across, taking Kate's phone out of her hand. 'Bugger! The reception is terrible on this side of the island at the best of times. We'll have to stay put until Billy arrives.'

Was the prospect of being trapped with her so hideous? Kate spun round, looking out at the whiteness, feeling uncomfortable. She'd have to make the best of it and use the time to discuss business plans.

The squeak of the log-burner door opening startled her.

'We may as well be comfortable.' There was a crackle as Roderick lit a match and the firelighters whooshed awake. He glanced up at her. 'I can think of worse places to be stranded than here, can't you?' Behind the glass window of the wood-burner the log fire crackled, instantly bright. 'Coffee or tea?'

'Tea, please. I'm freezing.' Kate curled up on the sofa by the fire. 'Does it normally snow like this in winter?'

She gazed out of the window. It was whirling down in thick flakes now, impossibly beautiful and completely impassable.

Roderick made the tea as she sat in silence.

'Once in a while we get a bad storm, and the roads can become dangerous pretty quickly.' He passed her a steaming mug and sat perched on the coffee table, opposite her. His long legs were taking up so much space that their knees were almost touching. Oh God! Please let me not make a weird gulping noise when I swallow this tea, thought Kate. And please let me think of something to say. The silence as they drank their tea was uncomfortable.

The buzz of Roderick's mobile made them both jump. It was sitting on the table, and they both stared at it with surprise, before starting to laugh.

Roderick picked it up. 'It's a text from Billy. Says the roads are a nightmare, and we'll be better off staying the night.'

'Do you think the guests will mind if we eat their dinner?'

'I think the guests won't be making it here tomorrow in this weather. And I'm sure they wouldn't mind in any case.'

When relaxed like this, he was easy company. Kate curled her legs underneath her, watching the flames as the fire settled. Roderick leaned forward, rifling through the basket of DVDs that Kate had chosen for the cottage. At least if they were to watch something, it might pass the time. The silence was huge, filling the room.

Finishing his tea in moments, he stood up. 'Are you done?'

'Nowhere near.' Her mug was still almost full. He couldn't sit still, either.

He checked his watch. 'Half-past four. I think we can waive the rules in the circumstances, don't you?'

Standing in the kitchen area, pushing his hand through his hair in the gesture she'd come to know well, he gave her a smile. He picked up the bottle of red she'd chosen so carefully and, tucking it under his arm, returned to the sofa with two glasses and a corkscrew.

'We can't drive. We can't work,' he explained, handing her a glass. 'We may as well have fun.'

Kate put down her mug. There was no contest between tea and wine, in the circumstances.

'Cheers!' He clinked his glass against hers, hesitating for a moment, poised beside the sofa. 'Do you mind if I . . . '

'Of course not.' Kate shuffled sideways, making room. She'd designed this, the smaller of the two cottages, to be a cosy, romantic retreat. There was only a two-seater sofa and an old-fashioned, upright reading chair.

Kate took a huge gulp of wine to steady her nerves. There was no television to break the silence, and the evening stretched out ahead of her, never-ending. And there was only one bed. Oh God! What on earth had she been thinking when she planned this cottage?

'Have you heard from Fiona?' she heard herself asking, idiotically, in an unnatural voice.

'No.' A nerve flickered in Roderick's cheek. 'I don't expect to, either.'

'Mmm.'

Well, thought Kate, that was a roaring success. Which awkward conversational gambit shall I go for next? Perhaps I could ask him about his mother's death. Or why he spent his overdraft on a Hogmanay party, when he'd already worked out exactly what the money was going to be spent on. She fiddled with the stem of her glass, spinning it round.

'Roderick?'

'Kate.'

'Why did you spend your overdraft on a Hogmanay party?'

He put his head in his hands and groaned. 'Bloody hell! You can't have any secrets on this island. You've been talking to Morag, haven't you?'

'Um, maybe,' said Kate, pouring more wine into their glasses. 'She didn't mean to say it, it slipped out.'

'Honestly?'

'Honestly. She didn't mean to say anything, it was just we were talking about—' Kate stopped, remembering exactly what the conversation had been.

'I don't mean *you* to be honest – I mean *I* will be.' He picked up his glass, contemplated the contents and downed it in a mouthful, pulling a face. He reared up from the sofa, pacing across to the window and back, before returning to his seat on the coffee table, facing her and looking furious. 'It was for you.'

Everything stopped for a moment while she looked at him. The island, always quiet, was completely silent, muffled by the snow.

'Me?'

'Yes.' There was an expression of resignation on his face. He half-shook his head, hands open in a gesture of defeat. 'I've watched you fall in love with the island. I thought: maybe . . . But no. Finn got there first.'

'Finn?' Kate could hear the laughter in her voice.

Roderick groaned. 'Don't rub it in. I feel like a complete fool. I made a mistake leaving the island without speaking to you, and by the time I got back he'd made a move.'

'Finn?' Kate repeated. She knew she sounded stupid, but she couldn't stop herself.

'I saw you at Christmas and realized it was pointless. I'm as bad as my bloody father. Like I said, I'm going to spend the rest of my life here on my own. A ranting, cantankerous old git.'

'I quite like cantankerous old gits.' Kate reached out and put her hand on his knee.

He looked up at her, laughing. 'Just as well, if you're planning to work for one.'

'I'll drink to that.' Kate took a hefty gulp of her wine, and tipped one-third of the bottle into Roderick's glass. 'More?'

'Are you trying to get me drunk?'

'Come back over here,' Kate stood up, picking up his glass. Emboldened, she held out her hand to him and pulled him up from the coffee table. You've only got one life, she thought to herself. Morag's words bolstered her confidence.

'What are you up to?'

She reached into the cupboard and pulled out the second bottle of wine, then brandished it at Roderick.

'I think we're going to need more wine.' Placing the second bottle on the table for insurance, she motioned to him to sit down again. She tipped some more wine into her glass, catching his eye, suddenly feeling certain.

'What on earth are you looking so pleased with yourself for?'

'Sit down.' She pointed to the sofa.

Roderick raised his eyebrows at her and sat down as instructed. 'I like this new assertive Kate,' he said archly. 'What's next?'

She took a final swig of the wine and sat down on the sofa, curled up again, glass cradled in her hands. Now she was facing him, her knees touching his thigh.

Reaching forward, she placed the glass very carefully on the table in front of them. She looked into his eyes. Now or never, she thought. She reached out, curling a hand behind his neck, feeling him tense suddenly.

'There is . . .' and she leaned forward, hair swinging over one shoulder, a tiny, triumphant smile on her lips, '. . . nothing . . .' she leaned closer, so the words were not more than breath in his ear, and she could hear a catch in his breathing '. . . going on between me and Finn.'

And with that, she ran her other hand through his hair, just as he would have done, and then kissed him, very gently, before pulling away.

'I just thought maybe you needed to know that.' She raised one eyebrow, cheekily. This was the best wine she'd ever drunk, or maybe it was the snow, or letting Flora go, or . . . well, whatever it was, she was in control for once, and it felt amazing.

'You,' he said, running the backs of two fingers down her cheek in a gesture so tender it caught her breath, 'are absolutely bloody impossible.' He twisted a hand in her ponytail, running her hair through his fingers, pulling her closer towards him so that she could feel his heart thumping through his T-shirt.

With a burst of sudden laughter he pulled her into his arms and kissed her thoroughly, and for a very long time. When they came up for air, night was falling. The little sitting room was glowing in the firelight.

'You've driven me mad, you know that, don't you?'

'I have? Well, *you* make absolutely no sense.' She tangled her fingers in his as they spoke. 'If you hadn't marched off the island the night after the fireworks, I wouldn't have had to drive you mad.'

'And if you hadn't spent the next few months making it obvious you'd rather be with Finn, I might have been able to admit I'd fallen in love with you.'

'You have?'

Roddy reached across to the table, picked up both telephones and switched them off. 'I don't think we really want to be rescued tonight. I can't think of anywhere I'd rather be stranded than here with you, beautiful Kate.' He turned back, tipping up her chin, mouth almost on hers, eyes blazing with love and happiness. 'And yes, incidentally. I have.'

'You love me.' She tried the words out. She suspected it was something she'd never tire of hearing.

'Yes, I bloody well do. Have done,' he said, kissing her again, 'since you fell at my feet the first day we met.'

'Excuse me, Roddy Maxwell,' said Kate, laughing, 'that's not quite how it happened.'

'Maybe not,' said Roderick with a grin, 'but it's a good story to tell the grandchildren.'

Epilogue

'She's absolutely adorable, aren't you, darling?' Roddy looked at Kate, then smiled down at the baby girl cradled in his arms. He looked as if he'd been born to it, his face gentle as he bent forward, dropping a kiss on her forehead. The baby let out the tiniest of sighs in her sleep. Kate ran a gentle finger down the perfect cheek, feeling the velvet-soft skin.

It was autumn once again, and they were standing in the long kitchen of Duntarvie House, waiting, as ever, for the kettle to boil. Roddy was sitting in the armchair beside the Aga, with Kate crouched down beside him. It was late afternoon and the shadows stretched long in the courtyard. There was a sound of happy yelling from somewhere outside.

On the table a baby car-seat joined a pile of box files, and the contents of several shopping bags were spilled out, as if someone had been distracted halfway through the job of unpacking.

Pulling out a tin from the larder cupboard, Jean looked pleased with herself. 'I knew we had one of my fruitcakes left. Here, Kate, if you cut this up, we can have it with tea.'

'Pass her back over, Roddy – she's going to need a change in a moment.' Emma reappeared, a muslin cloth still thrown over her shoulder from earlier. Kate jumped up, giving her friend a hug of excitement.

'I can't believe you're all *here*. All of you.'

'You can't? Believe me, this morning at six, when we were trying to get out of the door, I didn't think we were going to ever make it. This one,' said Emma, scooping her third daughter, still milk-drunk and fast asleep, into her arms, 'was sick three times, all over herself and me.'

Kate watched as Emma curled her sleeping daughter into her shoulder with the practised air of early motherhood.

Roderick unfolded himself from the chair, stretching unselfconsciously, his shirt riding up slightly. He caught her glancing at his stomach, with a quick grin. God, he was gorgeous!

'Sweetheart,' his voice was loving, 'I'm going to grab Sam and the twins from the garden and then I'll sort out lunch. I promised them they could help me make the salad.'

He sneaked a kiss as he passed her in the doorway, inviting a tiny wolf whistle from Emma.

'You two are completely gorgeous. And, you have to admit, Lady Roderick of Posh does have a certain ring to it.'

Kate rolled her eyes.

'This place, Kate – it's unbelievable.' Settling herself against the Aga, Emma looked at her oldest friend with huge eyes. 'I still can't believe it's taken you nine months to move into a bloody castle. I mean, I know the cottage is sweet and all, but . . .'

'Look, I wasn't going to rush it. I've told you already.' Kate carefully passed Emma a cup of tea, watching as she shifted the weight of the tiny, sleeping Charlotte.

'Well, I think Kate's done the right thing, myself.' Jean was counting plates, and her voice came from within the larder. 'Those two did everything upside down – they'd been so busy playing cat-and-mouse they hadn't done a bit of courting.'

'That's true, I s'pose.' Emma drank some tea, looking at her friend appraisingly. The old Kate wouldn't have had the self-assurance to make Roderick wait. The island had been good for her.

'Anyway, so now you're giving up the cottage – have you got plans for it?'

'I'll explain over lunch. We've had an idea.' Kate gnawed her thumbnail.

'Oh, come on, give me a clue?' Emma looked eager.

Maybe it wouldn't hurt to have one person onside with the idea, before she and Roderick dropped the bombshell over lunch. She felt another lurch of fear in her stomach.

'Well, you remember that enormous bill for the repairs to the roof lining?'

'The one where you had to talk Roddy out of selling

the house and giving it all up, to live on a yak farm in Peru?'

'Yep.' God, that had been hard work. The trouble with working together was that there was no escape from each other, and the upkeep of a huge estate was an enormous stress. There were times when she'd been very glad to march off to the cottage, which she'd insisted on keeping.

'Well, once we'd had our first major argument, we sat down and talked about the future . . .'

Although she'd resisted moving in for what she considered a respectable amount of time – despite Roddy's constant insistence that nobody on the island would even *notice* what they were up to ('Seriously, Kate, d'you think they've got nothing better to do than keep an eye on what our living arrangements are?') – Kate had already made some changes in the big house. The huge dining room that had lain untouched had been opened up, the permanently closed shutters folded back with a cloud of dust and dead moths. Together with Susan, she'd cleared the whole room, allowing the beautiful carved furniture to speak for itself. But it was so hard to get a sense of scale in a house this size – Kate had come home with the hugest bunch of flowers the afternoon they had finished, certain it was going to look beautiful atop the shining walnut table. They had balanced there, a tiny exclamation mark in the centre of the room, until Roddy had come home to find Kate sitting there, covered in dust, eating a pot-noodle at one of the sixteen chairs. He'd burst out laughing, and dinner that night had been forgotten.

Today, though, the same big table was surrounded by most of the people Kate loved best.

'Kate, look, I've got all the bread – and I've only dropped three pieces.' There was Jennifer, arms outstretched, a wide platter of freshly baked rolls slipping precariously sideways.

'Oops, Jen, let me give you some help with those.' Scooping a balancing hand under the tray, Kate managed to flip it across to the table without any further casualties occurring. 'What happened to the ones you dropped? Have the dogs eaten them?'

'No!' Jennifer looked proud. 'I picked them up and put them back on the tray.'

'Oh-kay.'

Nobody seemed to have noticed, because they were all engrossed in conversation.

'Daddy says there's a five-second rule, and we don't have to tell Emma when I spill my breakfast on the floor when she's feeding the baby. Shall we just make it a secret, Kate?'

Jennifer cast her a sneaky, gap-toothed grin of complicity.

'I won't tell if you don't.' Kate looked at the parquet. 'The floor's sort of clean, isn't it?'

Elizabeth looked at her daughter across the table, her expression suspicious. 'What are you up to, darling?'

'Us? Nothing at all, Mum.' Kate winked at Jennifer, who giggled.

Looking unconvinced, Elizabeth turned back to her conversation with Morag and Ted. They'd become good friends as a result of her regular trips back to the island, ostensibly to visit Kate, although over the summer months they had often seemed to feature 'a little drive' with Bruno, or an evening when they'd take a stroll along the little promenade, before watching the sun set over a drink at the Bayview. Kate watched them with love. After so many years of loneliness and misplaced guilt, it was wonderful to see her mum enjoying herself, and Bruno was completely entranced. He leaned closer as Kate watched, whispering something in her mother's ear, making her laugh.

Sam's arrival was heralded by the now-familiar squeak of Jean's hostess trolley. Both shelves were loaded with big bowls of Roderick's favourite Greek salad, hummus, pitta bread and assorted olives. Discovering his love of cooking had been a genuine surprise, and a real pleasure. And not great for the figure, thought Kate, aware that her jeans were definitely getting a bit tight.

'Ooh, yum.' Katharine reached forward to poke a finger in the dip, but had her finger swiped away just in time.

'Leave that, you.' Her dad handed her a placatory piece of bread.

The room was designed for this, thought Kate. It needs a huge gathering of people to make it make sense. This house is far too big for me and Roddy to rattle around in, occasionally taking off the dust sheets to let visitors come round. She scooped up some dip with her bread, half-thinking, listening to Jean and Susan.

'A "mindfulness centre"?' Jean scoffed. 'Too much money and not enough to do, if you ask me.'

'I don't know,' said Susan, thoughtfully. 'First of all, I quite like a wee bit of yoga myself.'

'You need a nice walk – that's what you need – not tying yourself up in knots. That's not proper exercise,' muttered Jean.

'And anything that brings in a bit of money to the island has to be a good thing, don't you agree, Kate? Have you heard about the plans for the old primary school?' Susan looked over at her friend.

Kate nodded. 'Finn was telling us the other day – we were off to the pub for dinner, and he was all dressed up when we bumped into him.'

'You'll be surprised to hear this, Susan,' said Roderick. 'Apparently he was off out for the night, taking the new owner of this "mindfulness place" out to dinner.'

Susan snorted. 'Aye, that'd be right. I heard she looks like a supermodel. He's got no shame, that one.'

'Anyway, you two said you had something to tell us?' Sam gave Kate a knowing look. He'd been making comments all afternoon about Roderick being broody, and Kate could tell by his expression that he thought he had them figured out.

Kate cleared her throat and took a deep breath. She felt Roderick reach for her hand under the table.

'Um. Well, as you're all in one place, I think now might be the time to talk about this idea we've had.' Emma looked up, giving her friend a nod of encouragement.

There was a scuffle of plates and a clatter of cutlery as everyone, realizing there was An Announcement being made, stopped eating. Kate felt a wave of panic rising, but took a breath. She and Roderick had talked for ages about the way forward for Duntarvie House, and they were both aware that the changes they planned to make would affect everyone in the room.

'Come on then, you two, my salad's getting cold.' Laughing at his own joke, Bruno turned to Elizabeth, who gave him a fond look.

'This isn't the kind of announcement I'm hoping for, is it?' Susan wiggled her wedding finger at Kate and Roddy, a hopeful expression on her face. Sam patted his stomach suggestively.

'Not quite, no.' Roddy turned to Kate with a smile. 'But it does involve a wedding, so you're not that far off.'

'We need to find a way to make Duntarvie pay, and everyone here knows the estate isn't exactly flourishing.' Kate looked at Jean, who was sitting with her hands together, plate pushed slightly to one side. Her expression was unreadable. Morag looked at Ted, who raised a questioning eyebrow. She shook her head. No, Kate could tell she was saying, I have no idea what these two are up to.

Kate realized yet again just why Roddy had seemed so irascible when they first met. The responsibility of owning an estate was huge. He – no, they (she gave his hand a squeeze, feeling it returned immediately) – had to consider the needs of the people who lived there, and balance them against some pretty terrifying financial questions. She'd never considered that Roddy had to worry about money when she first met him; and it had been a long time before she'd realized that it was the rental of Oak House down in Oxfordshire that kept the estate afloat. With Kate by his side, he'd finally felt able to sell the house in England, and the profit had covered the astronomical cost of the roof repairs, as well as paying for the development of the visitor centre they were planning. It had also repaid an overdraft so eye-wateringly huge that Kate had counted the number of zeros on the end three times before she could believe it.

Roderick spoke, his low voice breaking through her thoughts. 'What we realized, when we looked into it, was that this place is the perfect situation for an island wedding. We're lucky to be close enough to the mainland that we can catch a lot of people who might not want to travel right up to the Highlands, or to the Western Isles. We've come up with a plan. We'd like to host weddings here, at Duntarvie.'

There was a long moment of silence. Elizabeth looked at her daughter, a slight frown stating very clearly that she felt she should have been first to know. Kate couldn't help a small smile – old habits die hard, she thought. Or perhaps that's just being a mother. She cast a glance at Emma, who *had* been the first to know, and who, standing in the kitchen earlier, had declared it a brilliant idea. Emma gave her a very discreet thumbs-up sign. Jennifer and Katharine both caught her in the act and echoed their stepmother, delightedly. Kate felt a wave of love for them all.

At last Morag spoke. Glancing at Ted, she said, 'Well, Roddy, I think your father would be very proud to hear of your plans. Estates like this have to move with the times.'

Ted nodded.

Kate felt Roddy relax slightly. One down.

'It's an amazing idea.' Jean smiled at Roddy fondly. 'You know, I've watched you two pull together on the cottages, and if anyone can make it work . . .'

Kate blinked away tears. They'd talked the idea round and round in circles for weeks now, first convinced that everyone would love it, and then – realizing the impact it would have on everyone's lives – worrying themselves sick that their plans for progress would infuriate the people they loved. Even with just one wedding a month, Ted and Morag would have hordes of strangers passing by their quiet stable yard; and Jean – well, she'd been the mistress of Duntarvie really since Roderick's mother had died, and now she was being presented with a huge change.

'Well,' said Jean, having had a moment to reflect, 'there's life in this old girl yet. I've no plans for retiring, and I love a good wedding. Bring it on, as you young people say.'

The whole table erupted in laughter.

'God, what a relief.' Roderick took a long draught of his beer. 'We thought you'd all be horrified. It's going to be a lot easier with you all onside.'

'Aye, well, if you're going to be doing weddings, Roddy, there's maybe something you need to be thinking about yourself.' Bruno gave him a shrewd look.

'Lots of time for that yet, Bruno,' said Kate, quickly. 'We're only just officially moving in together.'

'Lots of time indeed.' Elizabeth raised a glass to her daughter, an expression of pride on her face. 'Here's to Kate and Roddy. And to the future.'

Rachael Lucas's
Secret Escapes

Kate disappeared off to the Island of Auchenmor to escape reality, and I thought I'd share some of my favourite escapes with you.

The Highlands of Scotland are home for me, although I moved away when I was a young girl. When I go back there, it's full of memories. Rainy days in welly boots holding my Nanny's hand as we'd take a trip to the cafe for a bun and a lemonade. Feeding the ducks by the river in Forres, and climbing Cluny Hill. Pan drop mints and white pudding suppers. Splashing in all weathers in the Moray Firth, and taking a trip to visit the clootie well across the water on the Black Isle. Standing in the eerie silence of Culloden, where legend has it the birds have never sung since the great battle of 1746 (and I've never heard one). The magic of Macbeth and standing in Cawdor dreaming of the stories coming to life. The skies are bigger, the air is clearer. And there's a monster to search for in Loch Ness. There's something for everyone there, and I don't think I'd ever get bored.

Cornwall is full of magic. It might sound like an advertising cliché, but when you cross the Tamar I swear there's something in the air. I'm in heaven watching the waves crashing against the huge cliffs as the children rampage across the beach at Polzeath. Coombe Mill in St Breward is our favourite place for a family holiday, where there's something for them all to do – from the smallest child to the teenager. They can run wild and burn off all their energy as well as helping out on the farm, whilst I curl up with a book and a glass of wine by the fire in a fifteenth-century cottage which is full of history. Down in the beautiful village of Boscastle there's the amazing Museum of Witchcraft and my favourite shops full of tarot cards and incense and everything I love ('all that weird stuff' according to the children).

If I can get a snow fix once a year in **Bansko, Bulgaria** I'm happy. I learned to ski there as an adult, and after a bit of a dodgy start (day one: I lay on my side in the snow like a toddler, halfway down a nursery run, and refused to get up for ages, insisting they bring a helicopter to rescue me) I was hooked. The people are amazing, the language is still completely beyond me, and the food is fabulous. When you're skiing down the 'snow road' home, with beautiful mountains ahead of you and surrounded by ice-draped trees, it's hard to remember there's a real world out there of deadlines and paperwork. If you don't fancy skiing, you can just catch the gondola up into the mountain, grab a hot spiced wine and watch the world go by. Bliss.

The Island of Bute is one of my other secret escapes. An hour from Glasgow and a short ferry ride and you're in another world, one which might seem a little bit familiar! Take a drive across the island to Scalpsie Bay, where you can spot ospreys soaring overhead, and the seal population basking on the rocks on the deserted beach. I can't guarantee you'll meet a handsome laird walking his dogs on the shore, but it's a wonderful place to visit . . .

And finally, my other favourite escape is **the bath**. Like Kate, I spend a ridiculous amount of time in there with a gin and tonic or a cup of coffee and a book. More often than not that's when you'll find me chatting on Twitter, hiding from the children and submerged up to my nose in bubbles – my three main vices are bubble bath, scented candles, and Emma Bridgewater mugs. There are worse addictions – or that's what I keep telling everyone . . .

extracts reading groups
competitions books new
discounts extracts extracts discounts
competitions
books new events
reading groups
events books
extracts
new titles reading groups
interviews
events extracts
discounts
new books events
events new
discounts extracts discounts
www.panmacmillan.com
extracts events reading groups
competitions books extracts new